MY REBEL SON

Recent Titles by Joyce Bell

THE GIRL FROM THE BACK STREETS
SILK TOWN
SUMMER OF A THOUSAND ROSES

MY REBEL SON

Joyce Bell

This first world edition published in Great Britain 1997 by
SEVERN HOUSE PUBLISHERS LTD of
9–15 High Street, Sutton, Surrey SM1 1DF.
First published in the USA 1997 by
SEVERN HOUSE PUBLISHERS INC., of
595 Madison Avenue, New York, NY 10022.

Copyright © 1997 by Joyce Bell
All rights reserved. The moral right of the author has been asserted.

British Library Cataloguing in Publication Data
Bell, Joyce
  My Rebel Son
  1.Domestic fiction
  I.Title
  823.9'14[F]

ISBN 0-7278-5219-1

All situations in this publication are fictitious and
any resemblance to living persons is purely coincidental.

Typeset by Hewer Text Composition Services, Edinburgh.
Printed and bound in Great Britain by
Hartnolls Ltd, Bodmin, Cornwall.

Prologue

The Children

1931

The canal shivered under the little humpbacked bridge as a horse-drawn narrow-boat passed slowly, dreamily, its brasses gleaming in the sun. Down where the tangled grasses and flag-irises grew another boat, too heavily weighted with its overload of coal, was stuck fast in the mud, and a boatey's dirty wife struggled with the pole. Any other day the children would have stopped to watch; now they hurried along with the crowd, down to the town to see the carnival.

They wore their best clothes. Marta, tawny-haired in buttercup yellow, swung a small handbag importantly. Ann's dress was pink, with frills; a ribbon rosette glowed like a small sun on her white straw hat. Ken's grey flannel shorts and shirt were as near new as the day they came from the jumble sale. Ken and Marta were cousins, born, as so many babies were, when the men came home from the war. Ann walked sedately between the two, yet felt, as she always did when with them, an infectious excitement that seemed to radiate from some quality in their personalities. Today the feeling was intense, for it was Ken's sixteen-year-old sister, Doreen, who had been chosen for Carnival Queen.

They reached the bottom of the hill and turned into the town. From somewhere came the strains of a brass band, and people crowded the pavement, getting their places. "Where shall we go?" asked Marta, skipping impatiently.

The sound of the band grew nearer, and the children made a dive for the nearest gap in the waiting crowds. The sun shone on hag-ridden faces, and thin stooped shoulders of men, on best clothes, and on those who had no best clothes to put on. Shabby hawkers walked the edge of the pavement as the procession approached, led by Briarford Silver Prize Band, the men marching bravely, sweating in the hot uniforms, each face wearing a look of pride.

And then the motley, spangles, fairies with tinsel wings. "Oh, look, Jenny Naylor," cried Marta. "She's an elf—" knowing her mother had spent weeks on sewing the precious little costume from bits of material gathered who knew where.

"There's our Peggy and Johnny as the Bisto kids," laughed Ken. "And Mrs Deane as Charlie Chaplin – ain't she a caution?"

The procession passed, tots wheeling bicycles covered with myriads of paper roses, decorated prams and pushchairs, a few sad memories of the war.

But at last the moment they had been waiting for. A huge cart pulled by four magnificent shire horses decked out in gay finery, tossing their manes, proud to be bearing the Queen. The cart, filled with flowers, and Doreen, dark and lovely, smiling from a throne high up on the back, six maids of honour surrounding her. Doreen laughed and dimpled, the crowd clapped and cheered, Marta jumped up and down in her excitement.

The royal entourage passed, and the procession went on. More fancy dresses, more comic characters, more laughing and shouting. The jazz bands, resplendent in their uniforms of blue silk or pink cotton, blowing through their bazookas the tunes of the day. 'Happy Days Are Here Again', 'I'm Happy When I'm Hiking', the leader doing fancy work with the mace. A few decorated drays from local firms and it was over, the crowd dispersed, and Marta turned to look for her mam and dad.

William and Liz Phillips weren't far away, and together they went to the open-air market for the shopping. "Cheap tomatoes!" shouted the stallholders. "Ripe bananas, best in the town!" Begging people to buy. On the corner a man stood selling the local paper and his posters fluttered in the breeze. *Nearly three million unemployed. Oswald Mosley forms new party.* The market-place would be a magical place tonight with naphthas flaring and an ox roasted in the centre, but the children fumed impatiently for the carnival field and the fair.

A long walk to the field, William carrying a packet of sandwiches, for it was too far to go home for tea. They could hear the fair outside the gates, its blare mingled with the brass band on a dais near the entrance. William paid the money and they danced inside.

"We don't want any tea, Mam, we want to go round the fair. Don't keep us here."

"You'll be hungry . . . all right, then, take a few sandwiches with you. And when it begins to get dark meet us here by the gates. Mind now, Marta, do you hear?"

"Yes, Mam." And they were away, running towards the kaleidoscope of colour which dazzled the senses. The rich sound of the roundabouts and pied roaring dragons with red seats, the smell of the trampled grass and the sawdust – the many-splendoured fair.

They rode on the horses, Ken and Marta together, Ann alone, flying through space till the gold and blue and red pictures in the roundabout's centre were blurred and the organ's catchy 'You Called Me Baby Doll a Year Ago' dinned louder in their ears. A ride on the roaring dragons and they screamed with fright and excitement . . . a jolty session on the cakewalk, and then, money gone, they stood before the swingboats and the coconut shies, loving the smells and the pushing, the laughter and the noise.

"We've got to see Doreen," said Marta. "We've got to see her go in the hall, there's going to be a dance."

Crowds were already lining up to watch as a car drew up along the road outside. *Fancy our Doreen riding in a car* . . . the crowd pushed and shoved eagerly, and the children, used to such tactics, slid through to the front, like eels.

So she came, the loveliest girl in Briarford in her long satin dress, all white like a bride, and her train edged with fur. Her crown set on her dark curls and her bouquet of flowers. Oh, lovely Doreen.

"Let's go and watch the dancing," said Marta. "Quick, round here, climb up this bank, we'll see through the window."

"I can't see nothing," said Ann, who was last.

Marta moved a little. "There now, they're starting – look."

A different music now, smooth and graceful. The Mayor was taking Doreen on to the floor, and more couples joined them.

Marta was fascinated by the music. "I'd like to dance," she murmured, excitedly.

"Our Doreen goes dancing," Ken said, indifferently. "Then she gets home late and the old man carries on."

They watched while the shadows grew longer round the field and Ann began to worry. "I wonder why they don't learn us dancing at school," said Marta.

"We learn country dancing," said Ann.

"Yes, but that's silly, nobody does country dancing."

"They used to, years ago," Ken told them. "And dancing round the maypole."

"Miss Farrell says dance-halls are common," Ann said, primly.

Marta turned her head from the window. "Is country dancing common?" she asked.

"I don't think so, or we wouldn't do it at school."

"Why?" asked Marta, puzzled. "What's the difference?"

"It's because country dancing's old," said Ken knowingly. "Things aren't common if they're old."

Summer twilight fell over the fairground, long shafts of deep blue covered the sky. "We'll have to go and meet your mam, Marta," Ann worried. "We said we would when it got dark."

"Just a minute." Marta was still entranced.

Ann waited five minutes, then jumped down from the window and walked a few steps, looking hopefully at Ken. But he didn't come, he stood with Marta, and Ann was envious that Ken always did what Marta wanted. Then she felt guilty. Marta was her best friend, and Ken was like her brother really – and wished she had a brother instead of a bossy sister like Sybil. Stuck-up Sybil wouldn't lower herself to be seen at the carnival, of course.

"I'm coming now," Marta called, and jumped down, followed by Ken; together the children ran to the gates. "There's Mam," said Marta.

"Wait a minute," Ann paused. "What's that? That little crowd there? Oh, Ken, it's your dad."

"He's talking politics again," Marta said, relishing the sound of the word, although she didn't know its meaning, had just heard her dad say it. Ken stood still, sullen, hating his father for showing him up in this public place. But he waited with the others while Tom urged the onlookers to join the Labour Party, and a heckler shouted, "The Labour Party's finished!" Ken had his own plan for the future, though his father did not know of it yet.

Briarford Silver Prize Band played 'God Save the King' and the obedient crowd turned away without another word. Away in Germany a few blond Aryan youths were beginning to sing 'The Future Belongs to Us'.

"Come on now, Tom," said Liz. "It's over. We've got to go home. Come on now, there's a good lad." And he followed her without another word. Tom was Liz's youngest brother. She was indulgent to his bolshie ideas, if not quite approving of his way of life.

They all walked home together, but Ken stayed a pace or two behind. Ann hesitated, then slipped back to walk with him. She sympathised deeply, having a father like Tom; she heard all about it from her own mother. "He might work six months on and six months off," said Mrs Cooper with a sniff. "But they get good money when they're working in the Coventry factories; he shouldn't spend it on drink. And he has such a temper. Acting as if he were a common labourer—" She sniffed again, for the car workers were the aristocrats of the labour field, as Ann well knew. "And all those little ones, never enough to eat or to wear. I'll have to sort out some of your clothes for young Chris, Ann. They should never have had all those children—" and she broke off, remembering she was talking to her daughter.

Ann ventured now, "Don't bother about it, Ken," wishing he would confide in her, but he said nothing. Tom walked in front with Liz; Marta was telling her father about the dancing. "You'll let me go when I'm older, won't you?" she coaxed.

"Ah, I suppose so," agreed Mr Phillips, for whom, folks said, the sun shone out of Marta's eyes.

"I used to dance," her mother said, turning round. "Nobody danced more than me. Remember the *Merry Widow* waltz, William, and the time we danced in the street?"

"And your *Merry Widow* hat," smiled William.

Marta put her hand in her father's; tired, it had been a

long day. They walked through the town, full of revellers, and up the long street towards the canal, dark now, a boat's forelight spearing the water. Together they went in their common entry, then parted, Tom and Ken going to the left, Ann and Marta to the two houses on the right. They called goodnight and went to bed.

Marta did not sleep immediately. She gazed into the back field where the council's horses grazed. She had named all the horses, but her especial favourite was Wildfire, a dappled grey, who could be seen galloping round the field under the moon. Wildfire had never settled to pulling the council dustcart as the others had, he was restless, untamed, as though he remembered the time when his ancestors had been free.

Marta loved the back field with its ridges and furrows. She hadn't known why it was like that and not flat till her dad told her it was because men used to plough there. For hundreds and hundreds of years men ploughed, though now the land belonged to Farmer Bates and was used for grazing. But Marta felt the broken chain, the forefathers who had worked the land for a thousand years, long before the hand looms came, or the pits and factories. And the funny thing was, no matter how often the field was flattened, the ridges and furrows always returned.

She turned at last and undressed. Lighting a candle before it was really dark was burning daylight her mam said, but she let her have a night-light for Marta was scared of the dark. Scared of the deep blackness and the sighing shadows from the trees in the garden, the feeling that she was in a pit and might never get out. A night-light was comforting.

Marta slept.

Book One

Marta

The Thirties

The Thirties were the Depression years when the cigarette-smoking, bead-jangling, fast-living females of the Twenties disappeared and fashions became backward-looking and no longer revolutionary. The lower orders were berated by their betters for their addiction to talking pictures, and it was assumed that the young would be corrupted by what they saw on the screen. The wireless broadcast dance bands, and dance-halls became popular.

The poor lived in terraced houses with no hot-water system or indoor lavatory, cooking was done on the kitchen range with an open fire. The rates of infant mortality for the very poor were four times those of the more prosperous.

Food was cheap and good. Chickens and turkeys were corn-fed in farmyards, eggs had a distinctive flavour. Butter tasted of clover and rich grass and buttercups. The passport to success was having been to the right school.

The most popular newspaper was the Daily Express; *the* Daily Mail, *which had raged against socialism,*

Bolshevism, and the League of Nations, fell behind.
   The Thirties were years of waiting for a war which no one expected to happen.

Chapter One

Marta was the only child of William and Elizabeth Phillips, who, having lost three children in infancy, found this baby very precious. William was a craftsman in a brickyard; in a dark and dreary shed he patted clay into two moulds, took them out, drenched them in cold water, joined them on a potter's wheel where they became a chimney pot to be fired in the kiln. He went to this job because his father had apprenticed him to it; he had hated it as long as he could remember, except when he was on short time and had to go in to finish work, then he'd take spare bits of clay and fashion little pots and vases which he brought home. He married Liz Webster in 1913, and after the war, when he'd served as a private, put his gratuity as deposit on the terraced house in Marley Road, and it was here Marta was born.

She was a small, delicate baby with a mop of tawny hair and a sunny smile. Her mother christened her Martha, intending to call her Pat, as was the custom, but in the first years the child gleefully mispronounced it as Marta, and the name stuck. William added her second name, Rose, for she was his Rose of Sharon, his pearl without price.

William was a gardener. Every day when he came home from the brickyard, his fingers stiff with rheumatism caused by working in cold water, he would go either to his allotment, where he grew vegetables, or to his back garden, where he grew flowers. And as soon as

Marta could toddle, she would follow him. He'd show her the first spring flowers, daffodils and primroses and bright yellow forsythia, then the lilac and tulips and pink almond blossom. And all the time he was waiting for his roses.

From June onwards the Phillips's back garden held beauty. The lemon-yellow roses had a look of spring and youth, they bowed like ballerinas before the breeze. The tea-roses massed beside the moss-roses and at the back were the dark red velvety ones, silent and soft, like beautiful women who know the secrets of love. All these things William thought for he was a poet of roses. And all down the street miners, craftsmen, factory workers came from their dark dens and created miracles of beauty in their tiny back gardens. Some of them, loving music, and having fingers too roughened by mining, or bent by water, to play a delicate instrument, invented brass bands. Everywhere there was a triumph of the spirit over the material, as though men were crying for freedom they felt had been taken from them long ago, crying in crippled music played by crippled fingers.

Liz Webster had been a beautiful girl with the tiniest waist in the area and long hair that she could sit on. She had had numbers of admirers yet hadn't particularly wanted to get married, but there was nothing else for a poor girl to do, so she chose William, who could hardly believe his luck. She was a good wife, the house was shining and spotless, the dinner always ready on the table when he came from work. When William was on short time Liz went back to the weaving factory; she didn't like the factory, but she was a good worker, her ancestors had all been silk hand-loom weavers. But the factory hours were long.

Although an only child, Marta was never lonely, loneliness was impossible in a house with a shared yard, and Ann-next-door was a friend from the start. Her Webster cousins were in the next yard, and Ken, being her own age, was always at the Phillips's.

William and Liz managed to buy a second-hand piano, and Marta was sent to lessons with Mr Collins down the road, at the price of one shilling a week. Mr Collins had passed no examinations, he was poor and not very clean, but he loved music and taught her all he knew. Marta learned to play quite well, and William loved to see her sitting in the firelight tinkling away at her little tunes. Then they would go out into the garden, and he would talk about the Golden Rose of China, and how roses were taken to Persia and the Near East by caravans from China. So old they were, roses, as old as peasants.

Marta had the freedom of the streets and the fields. Life was a cycle with the seasons, and William would tell the weather from signs around him. The wind howls for rain; red sky at night; swallows flying high; sky's full of snow. If they were going out for a day trip – they could never afford a week's holiday – they would get up early and run to look if the tiny scarlet pimpernel was open. If it was it would be a fine day for the wise little flower kept tight shut when it promised rain.

Marley Road had once been a country lane crawling into Briarford, that small Midland town which strove bravely to assert its independence from its large neighbour, Coventry. Marley Road's houses were all terraced, some were council-built, some privately owned, with here and there a corner shop.

The children were drawn to the corner shop as by a magnet, fascinated by the fat sweets in glass jars, the more humble assortments filling cardboard boxes at the front of the window: Dolly Mixtures, chocolate drops, Jelly Babies. On flat trays could be seen delicacies for working men: faggots, chitterlings, pikelets and batches; black puddings hung from pot hooks.

The shop was neglected in summer when there were other interesting things to do in the fields, but on cold winter nights the children gathered round its light, playing guessing games and I Spy in the window, or, if they needed warmth, running to the lamppost and back, playing tick.

Tonight Marta and Ann were alone, and as they ran to the lamppost and laughed, they saw that Ken was watching them from the kerb. They stood, a little uncertainly, for although it was all right for him to walk with them sometimes, and climb trees together or play hide and seek, the shop games were for girls, and Ken would only be called a cissy if he joined them.

They stopped the game and he came towards them. "Marta," he began. "Have they asked you about going for a scholarship?"

"Yes. Miss Gainsworthy asked me today."

"And will you?"

Marta shrugged. "Don't know. Don't think so. We might pass the scholarship but then we have to go for the Interview, and nobody passes that from Marley Road."

There was a silence, and Ann felt left out, for only five or six of the fifty children in the class were allowed to enter for the scholarship to the grammar or high school and she hadn't been chosen. She turned to look in the window to show she didn't care.

Ken said, "Old Stret-Westcoat asked me, and I want to go." He put his hands in his pockets and shuffled his feet nervously. "I'm going to ask me dad tomorrow," he went on, casually. "Want to come with me?"

"Me?" asked Marta. "But—" She saw the mute appeal in his eyes and nodded. "Yes, I will, but what for? Your dad'll take more notice of Doreen than me, she's his favourite."

"Doreen's always out with a chap," said Ken. "Besides, I don't want you to *say* anything," and she knew that Ken didn't want her to intercede for him, but her presence might stop his dad from getting in too bad a temper. For Doreen had passed the scholarship easily and Tom had been overjoyed – until she went for the Interview, where she was asked where her father worked, and was turned down. Tom had got into a terrible rage and swore he'd never let another of his kids enter. But they all knew how upset he was that Doreen, his favourite, had been rejected.

"Well, all right." Marta started walking away, Ken beside her, Ann following behind. "I'll come round, then. What time?"

Ken reckoned the best time to catch his dad in a good mood. "He's not at work," he said, glumly. "Come about four when we come from school. Before he goes out."

*

The kitchen was not so clean as her own house. The furniture was shabby and worn, the table was covered with newspaper, and it was reckoned that the young Websters increased their reading power and gained a knowledge of world affairs by silent reading during meals, for when their dad was in a temper nobody dared say very much. But when he was in work his temper was better and the kitchen was a merry place, full of children and clatter. There was a gap between Doreen and Ken, the time Tom had been away in the war. After Ken came Chris, and three younger ones, Johnny, Peggy and baby Rose-Mary. Johnny stood and peed over the yard then ran round and round shouting and screaming.

Mrs Webster sat before the fire, breast-feeding the baby; she gave a faint smile, but said nothing. Meg Webster had never been pretty, but her face had good bone structure, and flanked by its straight black hair held an almost Indian immobility. Meg was passive, but it was never the passivity of despair, and it was to her, and not their mercurial father, that the young Websters turned.

"I'll get your tea in a minute," Meg said at last. "I'm waiting for your dad."

They waited in silence, and Tom came in and dropped into a tattered armchair opposite his wife.

Ken sat biting his nails, studying his father to see if the time was right. Meg stood up to get the tea.

Ken drew a breath, but before he could speak, Chris came in from the yard. A thin, highly strung child of eight, yet with a certain tenacity, Chris crept up to her mother. "Mam, I told Miss Farrell that I'm not going on the school outing."

"And did she give you your half-crown back?" asked Meg.

"No, Mam."

"But—" Meg was agitated. "You paid half a crown, you paid the deposit."

"I know, Mam, but she told me to wait till after school, and I did, and she asked me if you couldn't afford it." The child's head bent in shame. "I had to say no, so she said she'd pay for me to go as a prize for being top of the class."

There was a silence. "But I wanted the half a crown," said Meg hopelessly. "And I'll have to find you pocket-money—"

"What's all this?" thundered Tom. "Teacher paying for our Chris to go to London? Oh no, she's not, I'll pay for the outing, and the pocket-money."

His wife said nothing and Chris went to sit on a chair, white faced. "Go on out to play, Chris," said her mother, kindly. "Or you'll get one of your headaches. Go on, it'll be all right." And the child went, slowly.

"You'd better go as well, Ken," said Meg.

Ken stood up. "No," he said. "I've got to know now. Dad—"

Tom turned to look at his son and Marta trembled, for they all knew that Tom had a down on Ken.

"I want to go in for the scholarship."

"You *what?*"

"The scholarship. I want to enter."

"What for?" asked Tom. "You won't pass. Nobody passes unless their fathers have good jobs."

"You don't know that," said Ken.

"All right, tell me of one miner's kid or one factory worker's kid at the grammar school."

There was a silence.

Ken said, stubbornly. "I want to. I don't want a life like yours."

"Why, you—" Tom jumped to his feet and Marta thought he was going to strike Ken. But Ken didn't flinch, and slowly Tom let his arm drop to his side as if the stuffing had all been knocked out of him. He looked at Ken as if he'd never seen him before. "Aye, you're right," he said, sinking back to his seat. "Right to want sommat better, that's what I'm allis telling people. If only they'd listen to me, but they won't, they're daft, put up wi' anything." He drew a breath. "Enter, then, and we'll see."

*

Ann's mother was annoyed that her daughter hadn't been chosen to try for the scholarship. "After all," she said, "you're as clever as they are."

"I'm not," said Ann.

"Why do the teachers make such a fuss of those Websters? Young Ken won't pass, not with his dad. You stand a better chance, your dad's got a respectable job; engine-driving's good and steady. And my family had the business."

Ann said nothing, and her mother lifted the iron off the fire and smoothed clean shirts over the table. Everything was spotless in the Coopers' house, as befitted one of the most respectable families, one who went on holiday every year, for railway workers had free travel passes.

"Not that he'd have been a driver if I hadn't pushed him into it," her mother went on. "Nor even firing; he'd still have—" She broke off, for she didn't make it known that her husband had been a porter when she married him. "No drive, that's his trouble," she ended. "And you're the same, Ann."

She stood on a chair and hung the ironed shirts on the line hanging across the room. "If only I'd got my rightful share of the business," she bemoaned. "Our Jack was smart there, going up making such a fuss while my dad was ill, and then getting him to leave everything to him. Oh, it's not right. If I'd got my share we could have bought a better house than this, in a better area. I know my dad didn't like me marrying George but he needn't have done that."

Ann, without turning her head, glanced through the window.

"I don't know what I've done to deserve all this," her mother said. "Still, Sybil's got on, even though she didn't pass a scholarship. That's a nice little office job in Bailey's, nice and respectable. I always knew Sybil would get on, not like you, Ann."

Ann sidled to the door where Marta was waiting.

"Oh yes, going out again," her mother called. "You might have stopped in and done my ironing, you're just lazy, that's your trouble. And here I am, having to do everything. You don't deserve to get on . . ." Ann was gone.

Marta asked her mother if she should enter for the scholarship. "Oh, I don't know," Liz replied. "Do you want to?"

"Not worth trying," Marta shrugged.

"It might be a good thing," said William.

"It'd be an awful struggle," said his wife. "Last winter you were only working two days a week. There'd be all the years keeping her at school, all the uniform to buy, then she'd go to college and have to be a teacher, and by that time she'd be getting married and we'd never see a penny return."

"I suppose so," William agreed, and the subject was dropped.

*

It was a bad winter. The canal froze over and the children were able to walk from one side to the other. Christmas came and went and the Phillips had their annual chicken and their annual party where the home-made wine flowed freely. Even Tom seemed in a good mood and said proudly that his son was studying for the scholarship.

But the highlight of winter was going to see the Amateurs. They went every year, taking Ken with them. "I allis used to go to the theatre before it was a picture-house," William told them. "Saw lots of plays. Shakespeare – I liked that – and *East Lynn* – remember *East Lynn*, Liz?"

"Dead and never called me mother," said Liz in sepulchral tones.

"And the *Merry Widow* – and don't start on again about your *Merry Widow* hat."

Liz laughed. "It'll be cold, queueing," she said.

"I wish I could go," Ann murmured, wistfully.

"Well, ask your mother," said Marta. "It don't cost much up the gods."

"She won't hear of it . . . Well, come with me, then, let's see . . ."

The furniture in the Coopers' kitchen was pretty much the same type as that used by all the others in the street.

The table stood in the centre, and was always covered with a cloth, red or green chenille in the afternoons and evenings, spotless white for actual meals, for tablecloths were a mark of respectability. Only the shiftless would eat off a bare table; even Meg's apologies of newspapers were better than the shame of nothing at all. Mrs Cooper's black grate was identical to the neighbours', but hers always *shone* with blackness, her brass ornaments were rubbed and polished till they glittered. On the chest of drawers the two big vases never held papers or spills or other oddments, there was a special rack to keep such things. Nothing was ever out of place at the Coopers' home.

Mrs Cooper was ironing; Sybil sat on the sofa. Marta disliked Sybil, her dark thick hair, her stuck-up ways. Sybil had never mixed with any of the girls in Marley Road, had never even walked home from school with Doreen, even though they were the same age. Now, working in her office, she was very genteel. She looked up as Ann put her request.

"No," said Sybil before her mother could answer. "I want you to help me make a dress."

"But couldn't we do that another day?" ventured Ann.

"No, it's very important. I've been invited out by the Baileys."

"Who?" asked Marta.

"The Baileys. The business firm where I work."

Marta knew Bailey's clothing store with its glassed-in little compartment where Sybil sat dealing with customers' bills. "So why have you got to have a new frock?" she asked.

Sybil's black eyes glittered angrily to think that Marta hadn't grasped the implication of herself and the important people of the town. Mrs Cooper said, "Of course she must dress well to mix with people like the Baileys."

"Why, they say old man Bailey is a real rogue," said

Marta, innocently. "He started off selling cheap junk to the poor then made a lot of money in the war, my dad says, while he was away fighting for him."

"You are a rude little girl," said Mrs Cooper. "Sometimes I think your parents spoil you. Ann will not go and that's final."

Back in her own home Marta raged. "That Sybil's mean. Honestly, I'm sorry for Ann with that mother and sister."

"Aye, she does get put upon, young Ann does," Liz agreed. "And that Sybil won't do a hand's turn."

Marta went upstairs but left the door open as her mother carried on talking about the Coopers. "She didn't want the first, and when she knew that another was coming she nearly went mad. Spited the child ever since."

"Aye," William said.

"As for Sybil going to see the Baileys, well, I'll believe that when I see it. Going out with old man Bailey, more like. You know what they say about him."

"I know there's been a lot of gossip." William lit his pipe.

"There has! About how he always gets young girls in his office and always takes 'em out. And one of 'em had a baby."

"Ah, well—"

"Ah, well. I bet Mrs High and Mighty Cooper don't know that, or she wouldn't be so keen for her precious Sybil to go— All right being too stuck-up to speak to the neighbours, but you get to hear a lot of useful things that way."

Marta closed her bedroom door, thinking what peculiar conversations grown-ups had.

Ann too went to bed, along the passage to the small end bedroom at the back. Sybil had the large back room. Sybil could do no wrong; Ann could do no right. When small,

Ann pretended she had been adopted and that one day she would find her true parents, who would love her. But now she was nearly eleven she knew this to be a pipe-dream, she resembled her father too much for it to be true. Mr Cooper, like Ann, seldom did anything right for his wife, but he had learned long ago not to argue; he sat silent for the most part, as did Ann, while Mrs Cooper talked to Sybil, her darling.

So Ann tried another dream about the future. When she was grown up and went to work she could get married, girls did. Then she would have a home of her own, without bossy Sybil, and a mother who disliked her. And who better to marry than Ken? She loved Ken, he was her friend, as was Marta, but there was a difference with Ken, a difference Ann was not quite old enough to grasp, except that Ken was a boy and so she could marry him, and leave this cold house where there was no love. And if Ken went to the grammar school he'd get a good job, then her mother would not oppose the match. So Ann dreamed in her cold little bedroom.

But although she couldn't go to the Amateurs, the next week the children had a concert in the Websters' back garden. These concerts were popular in Marley Road. Marta wrote the plays, Ann, a good needlewoman, made costumes out of old clothes, Rose and Jenny Naylor from the council-houses up the road would sing, Ken would play his accordion. Other children came to watch; the official price was a ha'penny, but as few had such affluence, they were allowed in just the same.

Ann's mother was disgusted that Tom Webster should waste his money on a piano-accordion when everyone knew he was always on short time and/or the dole. It was disgraceful, she maintained, thinking that if people couldn't afford the necessities of life they shouldn't have any pleasures either. It was a popular sentiment.

Ken never went to music lessons, he played partly by ear and partly from bits Marta taught him. And the children sang and danced and acted and were quite unreasonably happy.

*

And then it was spring again and Ken sat for his scholarship. The news filtered through that he'd passed the Written and now had to go for the Oral, the dreaded Interview.

Marta waited anxiously to hear the result till her mother told her to stop jigging about, and her dad said she was like an ill-sitting hen. But Ken didn't come to their house, he walked round alone. Then the day came when Mr Stretton, the Headmaster, read out the names of the winners in the hall and Ken's wasn't among them. Marta waited for him after school.

"Oh, Ken," she said. "Did you know?"

"Me dad had a letter from Mr Stretton, he's coming round to see us tomorrow."

"Can I come?"

"If you want."

Marta went round after school. The house looked just the same. Meg had started to take the newspapers off the table, then, in a strange moment of pride, put them back again. But when Mr Stretton came she did ask him into the front room, although the Websters' front room looked no more tidy than the kitchen because the children were allowed to play there, unlike in most houses. She asked Mr Stretton to sit down.

He was an elderly man with grey hair who had taught Tom, and he gazed at him for a moment without speaking as he sat in the shabby armchair. Marta sidled in and stood near the door. Ken stood too, his face sullen.

"The reason I've been such a long time coming," said the

Headmaster, "is because I've taken the matter up with the education authorities. I thought there must be a mistake. Ken is one of the cleverest boys I've ever had." He paused. "He passed the written examination, as you know, passed easily, and I asked why he failed at the interview." He paused again. "I was informed that he told lies to the committee."

Tom gave a short bark of laughter. Meg said, "Ken doesn't tell lies."

Mr Stretton said, "Ken told them that his father was a manager."

There was an appalled silence. "Did you, Ken?" asked Tom.

"Yes."

"Oh, lad, why?" asked Mr Stretton. "Don't you see what it's done?"

Ken said, "I thought I wouldn't pass if they knew me dad was on the dole."

"I told them I expected it was something like that," said Mr Stretton. "But you see how it looks to them. They think he's a braggart and a liar."

"It's only an excuse," said Tom. "If it hadn't bin that it'd've been somethin' else. This gave 'em a grand loophole. Anyway, why do they want to know what his father's job is?"

"It's not snobbery, but economics," Mr Stretton told him. "Parents do have to sign that the children will not leave school before they are sixteen at least. And they do like scholarship children to go on to college."

"Ah, cos nobody else'd be clever enough," Tom sneered.

Meg said, "Even if he were a liar, what difference does that make to his cleverness?"

"Well," Mr Stretton said, uncomfortably. "They like children of good character, of course."

Tom barked again. "To mix with the little gentlemen

there, you mean. Billings the butcher's son, shortchanges his customers—"

"*Tom!*" said Meg.

Mr Stretton said, a little coldly, "I have done all I can. I'm sorry, but there seems nothing more we can do. Of course, if you could possibly afford the fees, it would be worth it, Kenneth is so exceptionally clever." His voice faltered before Tom's sardonic gaze.

"We can't afford it," said Meg, flatly.

"Nor we wouldn't," cried Tom. "If he's got too bad a character to go free, then he's too bad to be paid for, ain't he?"

Mr Stretton rose to his feet. "I must go," he said. "But I had to tell you the facts. I feel you are entitled to know. I'm really sorry," he repeated. "Sorry for Ken, just as I was sorry for you, Tom. I remember saying the same thing to your mother when you passed." His face was sad as he remembered all the able children who had passed through his hands and were now, like Tom, on the dole.

"Ah." Tom's rage seemed to have evaporated. "An' me mother would have let me go, cos I was the youngest; the others were working. But it was my own sisters and brothers who were against it. 'We had to go to work at eleven, why should he be different?' they said."

"People don't understand," Mr Stretton sighed.

"No, but I do," said Tom.

Mr Stretton turned to Ken. "Well, maybe your son will pass, though I shan't be here to see."

He left, but Ken stared, blankly. Having a son meant nothing to him. And yet, underneath, there was a very faint glimmer. Not of hope, but determination. Things could be different. *The future belongs to us.*

Marta walked home slowly. She had never heard before that Uncle Tom could have gone to the grammar school but his brothers and sisters wouldn't let him . . . her mother was his sister. Had she been so *mean*?

She saw her mother in a different light. To date she had been perfect, but now . . .

Both Ken and Marta had taken the first painful steps towards growing up.

Chapter Two

Marta spent the last few years at school happily, dreaming away the hours in the pleasant classroom, having little to do as the work was merely a repetition of what she had been doing for the two years she had been in the top class. She helped the Headmaster, ran errands, returned to sit reading books of poems, her favourite subject.

The long summer holidays were spent with Ann in the fields, where the harebells grew, and a few late buttercups. The pollyblobs, those great golden cups of the marsh, were over now, the bluebells too had gone; there was still kek, the local name for cow-parsley, little black chimney sweeps, and red clover. They sat lazily, discussing the latest news, that Sybil was getting friendly with Peter Bailey, her boss's son.

"Do you think Sybil's attractive?" asked Marta. At nearly fourteen sex was beginning to loom large in their lives, and both girls were filled with an overwhelming curiosity as to how people mated, and why.

"No, I think she's horrible," returned Ann.

"She's fat. No, not fat," Marta corrected herself. "But she bulges." And she thought of Sybil's breasts, straining against the white blouses she wore, her skirts, tight over her bottom. "But how does she get all those fellows, Ann? She's been out with several since she worked at Bailey's, and all from the posh end of the town."

"I don't know. Suppose she meets 'em when she goes

out with the Baileys, they take her to the Golf Club, you know."

A half-forgotten memory of her mother's gossip surfaced in Marta's mind. "Do you think—?" She broke off. No, she couldn't put those half-formed bits of scandal to Sybil's sister, even if she did dislike her. "Is she going out with Peter Bailey?" she amended her question.

"Not yet," said Ann.

"Well, then—"

"But she will," said Ann, gloomily. "What Sybil wants, she gets." A remark she was to remember many years later.

"Oh well, let's walk a bit farther," said Marta. "I told my mam I'd get some blackberries, but I forgot the jam jar to put them in."

They walked over the railway line and were suddenly in a drearier world, a piece of waste ground, grey and derelict, full of strange hummocks and holes where men dug for coal during the General Strike of 1926. An air of desolation hung over the moon-crater-like surface, as though men had buried their hopes in the grey holes. Over one side of the waste ground stood a disused railway engine upturned, and besides this a man was watching for the police while his mates played cards below. If the bobbies came he would rattle the engine.

In the next field Chris Webster sat, reading a library book. Peggy and Johnny ran up and down, unheeded. They reached the still figure. "Coming with us, Chris?" Marta asked.

"No," Chris replied, curtly, without looking up.

The girls walked on. "What's the matter with her?" asked Ann, worriedly.

"She don't like having to take the kids out all the time," Marta told her. "An' she wanted to go in for the scholarship" – Chris was reckoned to be the cleverest of all the Websters – "but Uncle Tom wouldn't let her. 'No more,' he said. Chris thinks Ken could try, but not her, and Ken never had to mind the kids—"

"She never speaks to me," said Ann.

"Well, I don't think she likes having to wear your cast-off clothes, Ann, she hates that."

"Oh dear." Ann flushed painfully.

"This is our last holiday." Marta changed the subject. "Where are you going to work?"

Ann brightened. "I'd like to work in a shop. Or office, of course. But if not my Aunt May'll speak for me at Hobson's."

Marta nodded. In their world work, although you had to take what you could get, was carefully graded. Shop was higher than factory, and some shops took only nice girls. Factory work was graded too, Hobson's the hosiery firm paid good wages, and was therefore the most difficult to enter, especially as they allowed married women to work; the only way in was to have a relative there who'd speak for you. Nepotism was as rife among the working classes as had ever been in the aristocracy. There were several other middling types of factory, and lowest of all was Robey's, the artificial silk factory, which, because it employed so many girls, and because the pay and conditions were so low, took anyone indiscriminately. Lower even than that was being a servant, and only the girls who couldn't possibly find a job anywhere else settled for that.

They had reached the estate of Borley Hall, carefully fenced off, and they stopped to look.

"See those blackberries?" said Marta. "Wish we could get them."

"We've got nothing to put them in," said Ann, practically.

"I've got this paper bag we had our sandwiches in. Look, here's a loose railing, bet this is where poachers get in. Come on—" and she wriggled through, followed, hesitatingly, by Ann.

They moved along the hedges, seeing in the distance the land stretching away in rolling grandeur, and at its summit, the Hall, home of Lord Baxchester, and his wife and son. Marta wondered, as she crammed the luscious berries into her paper bag, what such a small family did in so many rooms; it would be like living in a museum.

Suddenly a loud bellow sounded in the clear air, and Ann clutched Marta as a red-faced man came charging towards them. "Is that Lord Baxchester?" she asked.

"No, it's a gamekeeper. Come on, run."

The girls raced for the fence, spilling the blackberries as they ran. "Pig!" shouted Marta from the safety of the other side. "You took my blackberries."

They walked on, giggling. Being chased was one of the hazards of life, you were chased by farmers, park-keepers, caretakers on building sites, you were thumped at home and at school. It was all part of life.

"Wonder what time it is?" Ann worried; her mother liked her to be punctual for tea. "We've been gone an awful long time. Let's hurry."

Marta, whose mother was more casual, hurried for the sake of Ann, and hot and dishevelled they reached the road.

"Oh, look," said Ann, almost crying. "They're coming home from Robey's. That means it's six o'clock gone."

They pushed on to the road and began the difficult walk back to their homes. Difficult because the stream flowing from Robey's in the opposite direction threatened to engulf them. The stream was composed of hundreds of women and girls who were rushing home at great speed, as if they could not get away quickly enough from their factory. All looked hot and tired, some carried their coats, few were talking, but all hurried.

The girls battled through this tide of humanity which meant little to them except as a means of telling the time.

*

On Sundays the girls dressed in their best to go to the church Sunday school in the afternoons, then went walking round the park. The Silver Band played in the small bandstand, boys and girls walked round smiling at each other. If they saw anyone they knew they'd stop and talk for a time, and sooner or later they'd bump into Ken and his friends.

"Do you think he likes you, Marta?" asked Ann, as Ken approached.

"Who, Ken? Don't be daft, he's my cousin."

"Yes," said Ann, relieved. "And cousins can't marry, can they?"

"Marry? You are soft, Ann."

"But he's always stopping talking, and wanting to go walks."

"Perhaps he likes *you*," said Marta, and didn't see Ann's blush. "Come on, see those two lads there, bet they speak to us. Let's give Ken the slip," and laughing she turned away from him.

Ann looked a little dolefully at the two lads. The handsome one would speak to Marta, she knew from experience. She'd be left with the funny one. That's how it always was. Ann turned wistfully to where Ken stood looking after them.

Sunday evening and Marta went down the park again, this time with Rose Naylor, for Ann's mother didn't approve of her going out on Sunday nights. They walked round and round as in the afternoon, speaking to more lads, for Rose, being a year older, had more experience.

"Here's your Ken," exclaimed Rose. "Let's stop and talk to him."

They stopped, and Rose said, archly, "We were just going for a little walk through the fields."

"Can we join you?" asked Ken, politely.

"Well—" Rose hesitated, going through the ritual. Marta looked at Ken, eyes dancing, and he read her thoughts. "Well," Rose said again. "Maybe you can, just a little way."

"Come on, then," and Ken grabbed Marta's arm and hurried her away.

Alone with him, Marta began to laugh. "Rose won't speak to me again," she said. "She fancies you."

"And who do you fancy?" asked Ken.

"Nobody," said Marta primly. "Anyway, Mam won't let me go with lads till I'm fourteen."

"Well, you're nearly fourteen, nearly as old as me." For Ken's birthday had been in June, he left school in August, and so far hadn't found a job.

"Any luck yet, Ken?" Marta asked him.

"No. Me dad's trying to get me in where he works, as an apprentice. But there's a waiting list. So I think I'm going to Jordan's."

"As an apprentice?"

"No. At least, they pretend it is, but there's no proper indentures. But the pay's better to start."

"Can't you wait, Ken?"

"We need the money," he said, baldly.

"Yes."

They walked on, but their gaiety had gone. Ken was moody, thinking of the work he didn't want to do, Marta was silent, knowing that at Christmas she too would leave school and would have the same problem. Not quite so bad for girls, of course, because they married eventually and stayed at home. For the most part they had to, even teachers were not allowed to work once married. Women stayed at home and did the housework and had babies. That was the rule.

She returned to school and dreamed away her last term. A man came to interview the leavers and asked every child where he or she wanted to work. No one knew where this man came from or where he went, they never heard from him again. Marta told him shop or office and he wrote it down and said good afternoon.

William didn't want her to work in a shop, he said she was too delicate to stand all day, and she had a cough every winter when her mam rubbed her chest with goose-grease. Marta tried for several offices but had no luck. She began to feel anxious.

In the end it was Mr Stretton who used his influence to find Marta a job. He'd spoken to the manager of Robey's, and they wanted a girl in the office. Would she like to go for interview?

She knew nothing about the great throbbing factory except that the locals called it the slave-driving place. But she went for the interview and she learned that the work wasn't exactly in the office, she'd have to sit in the factory. But it was office work. She could start on the Monday after the holiday at eight o'clock. So, casually, was her future decided.

She arrived at the factory gates at five to eight, a fourteen-year-old woman and wage earner, to see a great crowd of women and girls milling round the gates, pushing and fighting to get through. Every so often the gate would be opened and a few women struggled in, then the gate was locked again. And when they'd finished setting on there was always a crowd turned away.

Marta pushed with the rest, told the gate-keeper she had

a job, and was allowed in. "Name? Oh, yes. You're on the tables in the winding-shed. Follow me."

When she entered the winding-shed she thought she'd died and gone to hell, such an inferno of noise it was. The winding-shed and the warping-shed adjoined; she sat on a hard stool with no back at a table in between the two, thus getting the worst of both noises. She couldn't hear a word that was said.

Before the morning was out she understood that Joan, who was sixteen, was in charge of her, that Gladys, the other girl, had been on a machine and was being put back now that she had taken her job; that the foreman and forewoman and chargehands were also her bosses. She was given tickets to add up containing each girl's work, the number of bobbins wound, and the amount of silk in pounds and ounces. As the days wore on she learned more about the factory.

The sheds were huge, but there were no windows, just skylights, whitewashed over in summer like greenhouses. Each winder had a row of 'ends', and she started at the first end, taking a skein of silk, putting it on the spindle, wetting the silk with her mouth and throwing it on to the rotating bobbin. On to the next and so to the end of the row. By this time the first was empty, so back to the beginning again. The girls were not allowed to speak while working; they had to ask permission to visit the lavatory, and were allowed to go twice a day. Longer than ten minutes and they were fetched back. There were no tea breaks in each four and a half hour spells of work. Every girl was sacked on marriage which meant they went courting for years and often became pregnant, thus forcing the issue. They all hated the factory.

Tom Webster was on the dole again until the spring, so Ken was pressed into taking the job at Jordan's, he couldn't afford to wait. Doreen was working, she had obtained a job at Hobson's (trust Doreen to fall on her feet, said the family), but she was courting, and saving to get married; Doreen did not take kindly to supporting her family as well.

Ann was happy enough at the hosiery factory, conditions were good there; they had a union to fight for them. Her only problem was her mother's continual sniping. "Why couldn't you get an office job, like Sybil?" she grumbled. "Factory work is so common. But you never were up to much, Ann, you never *try*, that's your trouble."

Now Marta and Ann were grown up they went to the pictures on Saturday nights, and fell in love with Dick Powell, Gary Cooper and Maurice Chevalier, who acted and sang in worlds far removed from their own, worlds where every lady seemed to wear long diaphanous dresses all day long, and all the men were handsome. Marta and Ann thought for many years that everyone in the United States was rich.

When Marta had been at Robey's for a month two things happened. Joan left, and she was put in charge of the work, with Gladys brought back to help her; and the factory went on overtime, and she with them. Now she worked from half-past six in the morning till six at night, plus Saturday mornings, a total of fifty-five hours a week, for which she was paid for fifty-six, fourteen shillings a week, good pay for school leavers, though it dwindled with the years so that the top rate was a mere thirty-three shillings.

Her mother called her just after five in the morning, when she'd jump out of bed in a fright because it was dark and she was scared of the dark. William had already left for his job so she gulped a cup of tea, and ran outside into the dark street. When the sullen dawn broke over the factory she'd been at work for two hours and was able to stop for half an hour for breakfast, though if she wanted to eat anything she had to bring her own sandwiches and take them over the road to the canteen. At half-past twelve she ran home for dinner, gulped it down and ran back to the factory. She finished at six when the surge of women ran out of the gates. She knew now why they ran.

Ann said the hosiery factory wasn't bad at all, and you learned a trade. Some of the women could earn really good money, over two pounds a week; they were on piece work, unlike Robey's. They sat round a table and they could talk and sing if they liked. And the married women were cheeky. "But they're nice," she added. "Nicer than at Robey's."

"I wish I could get in there," Marta said, wistfully.

"They don't want anybody now, and anyway, I couldn't speak for you, I'm only a learner." Jobs at Hobson's were as precious as gold, and as hard to get. Marta pondered the exclusiveness of Hobson's, and Ann felt a vague sense of importance, that she should, for once, be one up on Marta.

Marta had three days' holiday at Easter – unpaid – and on the last day she went round all the factories, and took a bus to the nearby town filled with small hosiery works, some little more than a couple of rooms, where an enterprising worker had 'set up' on his own. She spent the whole day walking round them, up stairs, into dusty offices, seeking out forewomen or bosses. One or two asked if she were experienced, most had large boards outside saying NO VACANCIES. The rest simply said, 'Nothing'.

The girls fought valiantly the harsh world they now inhabited, laughing, talking to lads, singing 'Isle of Capri' and 'Sally'.

"Ann," said Marta. "Let's start dancing."

Everyone danced in the Thirties. Ballroom dancing was to become even more popular as Fred Astaire and Ginger Rogers twinkled across the screens of the world. For Marta, and thousands like her, it provided solace for the grim life they lived during the day.

She and Ann began at local church halls, graduating to the bigger halls, the George, the Co-op. Here the standard was extremely high. The girls wore bright dresses. Colour was needed to balance the drab greyness of the factories; they needed bright colour just as they needed carnival, music and dance. So they went every week and learned the slow and graceful waltz, the easy quickstep and the difficult slow foxtrot with the gradual fluid movement which came easily to the long-legged Midlanders.

She didn't see so much of Ken now; occasionally they'd bump into him in the park, or walking round the town on winter Sunday nights. 'Walking the town' was the popular pastime of Marley Road, and greatly frowned upon by all those who wanted to 'keep young people off the streets'. Well-meaning councillors and churchmen joined the protestors, the police began to grow numerous on Sunday nights, and what had been an innocent pastime was blown up into something sinister when a group of youngsters, talking and laughing, were taken to the police station and charged with loitering.

The same night Ken and his mate bumped into Marta and Ann. They stopped. "'Turned out nice again.'" Ken mimicked the George Formby catch-phrase.

"Daft," said Marta, succinctly.

"'These foolish things remind me of you'," sang Ken, tunefully. "Come and talk to us, girls, we're lonely."

"Who wants to talk to you?" asked Marta, pertly. "We can talk to you any day of the week."

"Talk to me, then," said Ken's mate, John.

Marta had already given John a quick once-over and decided she wasn't interested. Ken stood watching her, hands in pockets, and she wondered how many girls he went out with, he *was* good-looking. She said, "You know what Rose Naylor's saying about you? She says you're the hottest thing in town."

"Marta!" cried Ann, shocked.

Ken laughed. "Maybe she's right. And you know what somebody said about you, Marta?" he said. "'What wouldn't I give to get her alone in the dark.'" Ken looked at Marta intently and she felt uncomfortable, and couldn't meet his eyes.

"Change the subject," she said.

"OK." Ken looked around. "Behind me are some of the old weavers' cottages, joined in a row, with a top storey where he could keep his loom and work when he pleased. Not shut in a bloody factory."

"You are a know-all, Ken Webster. En't he a know-all, Ann?"

"Some of us have brains," said Ken, grandly.

Then the police came.

"Come on," they ordered. "Move on now, quick."

"Why? We're not doing anything," Ken protested.

"Get moving, unless you want to go to the station."

They found themselves being pushed along together, and resentfully they fell in line. The police passed on and Ken said. "We'd better keep out of their way. Let's go in the park."

"The gates'll be locked," Ann pointed out.

"We've gotta go somewhere to get out of the way of the police. Let's go over the field into Aston Road," Ken said.

They walked along and somehow, as they entered the dark field, they were split up, and Marta was alone with Ken. She said, "We don't see much of you at home now."

"Aw, I've been too fed up."

"Don't you like your job?"

"Like it? That's a laugh."

"Why don't you come dancing, Ken?"

"Cos I can't afford it, that's why. I'm supposed to be

an apprentice, and get an apprentice's pay. But I'm not learning a trade, and what money I get I have to turn over at home. Me dad's trying to get me into his place, can't go on like this without money . . . How's your work life?"

"I hate it," she said, intensely. "I really hate it."

"You shouldn't have gone there," he told her. "Not Robey's."

"But I didn't know—"

They stopped and stared at each other in the gloom, two babes in the wood, lost, afraid.

He put his hands on her shoulders and she looked at him uncertainly in the darkness. As his arms locked her she stood passive, still unsure.

He kissed her feverishly and she felt a strange, forbidden delight. "Let's sit down," he murmured, and she allowed him to pull her down. Then he was tugging at her clothes, touching her, and another strange feeling was aroused. She pushed him away.

"Let me," he whispered. "Marta—"

"No." She scrambled to her feet. "No. Ken Webster. It's true what they say about you. Let me go."

He tried to keep her there, but she had fought with him since childhood. She yanked back his hair and said, dangerously, "Let me go or I'll kick you, you know where."

He loosed her and she ran away, panting, dishevelled, afraid, not of him, but the strange delight. She wasn't ready yet for a lover, and especially Ken, who had always been so close to her. It was true, then, he did go with girls . . . and she was afraid of his knowledge, it made him a greater being, and she was annoyed that her childhood playmate should so suddenly change. She refused to speak to him, tossing her head proudly, half hoping he would still pursue her.

He did not, and his absence from the home was noted by the parents but with not much surprise. Ken was working now, he was a man.

Ann wanted to know all about it, but Marta refused to tell.

"Did he try anything?" asked Ann.

"Look, it's nothing to do with that, I'm just fed up with him and that's all."

"You could tell me," sulked Ann.

"There's nothing to tell."

"They say Doreen's got to get married. Is it true?"

"Yes, but you needn't go spreading it around, Ann. She's been courting for years, they were going to get married anyway."

"I know," said Ann, humbly.

"They wanted to save for a house, but now they've got two rooms in Tenley Road. And Jack Walker's a nice chap even if he does work at the pit."

"I know," said Ann.

Marta waited for Ken to come round her house again, after all he practically lived there as a child. She half regretted her hasty dismissal of him, and hardly knew why she'd been so offended. Lads did try it on, all of them. Yes, but *Ken* . . . She wasn't sure why that made a difference, it was just that he was too close. Unsure, afraid of her feelings, she thought, If he speaks again I'll talk to him . . . Won't I? But his pride was as great as her own and he did not speak again or come to the house.

*

King Edward abdicated, and Marley Road shrugged, indifferently. They thought he needn't have given the throne up, kept the other one on the side, that's what most kings did in the past. Liz remarked, "This one said what he was going to do for the working men, but he's done nowt." He'd let them down, why should they care about him?

There was far more talk about Sybil's engagement. "Oh,

her mother's hooked that young Bailey for her then, after all. You can't touch her with a long pole, that Sybil. Now she'll be having a house up Acacia Avenue."

Sybil had been 'friends with' Peter Bailey for some time, the Coopers didn't do anything so common as courting. He had been brought home, sat in the front room, shy and quiet, while Mrs Cooper, who cleaned the house from top to bottom every time he came, talked about her father's business and poured out tea.

The gossip was long and loud, and even Marta's mam had been heard to wonder just how that old Bailey had come to let his son agree to marry a girl from Marley Road. "After all, he's got money now, and young Peter's been educated." The neighbours remembered how old Bailey had taken out his former office girls and how one of 'em had a baby, so who knew how Sybil had persuaded him? So the tongues clacked, suspiciously and a trifle enviously. If somebody had to get on, why should it be that disagreeable Mrs Cooper?

The Munich crisis came and went, Marley Road didn't take much notice. The newspapers told them it was a victory for peace in our time; they shrugged and accepted. The girls at work didn't talk about world affairs, for they weren't allowed to talk, and when dancing Marta was lost in her own world, trying to forget how, at every holiday, she had to make a list of the slowest workers, who were then dismissed, though there was still the crowd of women clamouring outside the gates when they reopened again.

Marta was seventeen now and quite beautiful, her tawny hair was permed into waves, her skin was flawless, perhaps a little too pale, thought some. She still worked twelve hours a day, and if she came home exhausted, she insisted on going out, though her mother protested she was gadding about too much. William noted her feverish gaiety, her white face, and was saddened. Sometimes she would follow him into the garden, as before, and together they'd stand looking at the roses. Then, although his fingers were now bent with rheumatism, he would gently pick some of the glorious blooms, offering them to her as though to apologise for having brought her into such a world.

Chapter Three

Marta took the outbreak of war casually. She felt she had little choice. It had been made plain to her that she didn't matter in the scheme of things, so They who didn't think she was worthy of an education or a good job would hardly ask her views on war. No one she knew rushed to join up, and as the first weeks and months went by and nothing seemed to happen, she shrugged and went on with her life. She was issued with a gas mask and an Anderson shelter was erected in the garden.

Spring came and the main argument in the press seemed to be about unmarried wives – a name the respectable objected to – and the great problem of officers and other ranks being together in the same public house. Or rather, not being together, for other ranks were asked to leave when an officer had his drink.

Spring also brought a spate of weddings to Marley Road, the most important being, in Mrs Cooper's eyes, that of her daughter Sybil, and Peter Bailey. Mrs Cooper was in a quandary. Having refused for so long to consort with the neighbouring hoi polloi, but now wanting desperately to let them know of her triumph, she was obliged to suffer the indignity of running to the corner shop with her information, and being met with a polite silence instead of excited cries. Sybil and Peter wanted to marry before Peter joined the forces, and the parents decided it was only fair to the poor young things to give them a fine reception before Peter went off to his patriotic duty. *She wants to have a good do while she still has the chance*, translated the corner shop behind her back. They were great friends of the Baileys, being business people like themselves, said Mrs Cooper, and so had decided to hold the reception on the Baileys' lawns. *That way no doubt the Baileys would be paying for it*, the tongues clacked.

No one from Marley Road was invited to the wedding, they read about it in the local newspaper. "A hundred guests," marvelled Meg to Liz. "Wonder who was there. She wouldn't want any of the Coopers, the only one she speaks to is May."

"And he wouldn't want any of the Baileys."

"And look at this, six bridesmaids, and not young Ann," said Meg. "Oh, I reckon that's a shame, and Sybil got so much. Tain't fair to make fish o' one and fowl o' the other."

"She don't care tuppence for Ann," said Liz. "And she's a nice child. Like her dad."

"He should stick up for himself sometimes," Meg criticised. "Letting that old crosspatch ride rough-shod over him. Aye, she's a funny woman."

"But she gets her own way," said Liz.

Sybil and Peter went to Cornwall for their honeymoon, then moved to a house in Acacia Avenue. Ann confided to Marta that she was glad that Sybil no longer lived with them. Mrs Cooper returned from her glories with her nose half an inch higher, and insisted that Ann start shorthand and typing classes; there might be a chance to get on in the war.

Several dance-halls were closed down, only the George remained open. Some local lads went away, and strangers took their places, soldiers from a camp at Borley Common, airmen from an aerodrome the locals hadn't known existed.

Marta prepared for the dance, as always. "Going out again?" her mother fussed.

"Oh, don't keep on, Mother," Marta said, impatiently. "I shan't be late."

"Our Ken never comes round now," Liz went on. "I miss him, he was like a son to me. Ah well, young people these days—" She sighed. "Meg says he's in a reserved occupation. Course, they make aircraft parts now."

"Is he?" Marta asked, offhandedly.

"Well, they're growing up now." William answered his wife. "Got their own lives to lead. Maybe it's for the best."

Ann knocked at the door. "I'm surprised Mrs Cooper lets young Ann go dancing," Liz commented. "Well, don't be late, Marta."

The girls entered the George. Into the cloakroom to leave their coats, then into the hall, with thick blackout curtains over the windows, and the band, drums, trumpet, sax and piano, was playing 'South of the Border'.

"Oh, look," Ann said. "Ken's here."

Marta shrugged. "Is he?" Why was everybody talking about Ken?

The evening wore on, Marta danced, and Ken watched her broodingly. But he didn't come to her. Then he went home with a girl who was known to be easy, and she said to Ann, "Our Ken does go with some common girls."

Ann wished he had asked her to dance. After all, if he didn't speak to Marta, it didn't mean he couldn't dance with her. She had hoped she'd have a chance now Marta was out of the running. Still, there was time . . .

Marta was restless. She had no lack of boyfriends; she'd arrange to meet a prospective swain, thinking, Maybe this is the one, then after a few meetings she'd wonder whatever she'd seen in him. What was this love they talked about? Was Doreen happy with her husband? Was that plain girl down the road contented with her mild swain? What was it all about?

"I don't believe in love," she said to Ann.

"That's because you've not met the right one," Ann told her.

"The right one! Don't make me laugh."

Then suddenly, it seemed, the war began in earnest. Hitler lost his figure of fun image as he swept through Europe. France fell, and the Germans approached the Channel. Britain stood alone.

Invasion was expected, and Marley Road braced itself. Forgotten now were the class wars, the poverty, as Churchill boomed: "We shall fight on the beaches . . . We shall never surrender."

And now the real war began, the sirens sounded practically every night as the bombers came over to Birmingham and Coventry. As these cities were protected to some extent by guns and barrage balloons, the bombers could not, at first, get in to drop their loads and would leave them casually with Briarford on the way back. The Phillips's slept in the Anderson shelter which was cold and damp, being sunk low in the ground. William made a sort of paving over the floor, but still the damp rose from the earth and moisture dropped down the corrugated iron sides.

Marta said to Ann, "I'm thinking of joining the forces."

But the next day the pain began.

It was a sharp, stabbing pain in her right side, almost as though someone was sticking a knife into her, and making her catch her breath. After several days of pain she told her mother, who insisted on taking her to her insurance 'panel' doctor. "You don't look well," Liz worried. "You ought to be in a warm bed, not in that damp shelter."

They sat in the dark green, dimly lit surgery, waiting their turn.

"Nice fire they've got here, Bill," said a miner opposite, nodding at the tiny paraffin heater.

"Ah," grunted Bill. "Is it alight?"

"Don't want to mek you too comfortable, Bill, else you'd be here all night."

Bill grunted again.

At eight o'clock Marta's turn came and she entered the surgery with her mother. The doctor examined her and told her it was indigestion.

But the pain continued, grew sharper, and two days later Marta collapsed at work. She was sent home, and again they visited the doctor.

Again she was examined. "Pleurisy," said Dr Green.

Now she had to stay in bed, bombs or no bombs. It was September 1940. She lay in her back bedroom, the bed pushed to the window so she could look over the field, and the doctor visited every day, a sure sign it was serious.

Ann came regularly to see her, so did Aunt Meg. And one day her mother came in to say, "Ken's downstairs, Marta. He wants to see you."

"No," Marta answered. "Not now, I look such a mess. Look at me, my hair all over the place—"

"Well, goodness me, he won't bother about that."

"No. Wait till I'm better."

But he didn't come again.

Marta lay supine, almost apathetic. Nothing seemed to matter any more. When the sirens went, William came and sat with her, but she no longer cared.

After three weeks she was sent to Birmingham for X-rays.

"I think," the doctor told her, "you should go to a convalescent home for a month or so. Down south, where it's warmer."

They went out, but Liz slipped back. "Will she be all right, then?" she asked. "It's nothing serious, is it?"

"There was a tiny shadow on one lung, but it seems to have healed," he told her. "But it won't be wise to sleep in shelters, and not get her rest. A few weeks in Moorfield Home should put her right. It's near Torquay."

"Will we have to pay?"

"Not for this, no." And Liz understood. Not for threatened tuberculosis, the white plague which killed so many people and was reckoned to be contagious.

*

The home stood on the top of a hill, and was quite small. Even so, Marta had to share a room with two others, one a pallid woman of about forty, the other elderly, neither of whom ever left their beds. Marta was allowed up, and could go for walks. And after two weeks her lethargy left her.

"I'm fine now," she wrote to Ann. "It's nice here, but I suppose it will get a little boring with no work to do. I'll be glad to come home."

Ann received the letter on November 13th, the day before the Coventry blitz. She and her mother spent the night in the air-raid shelter, listening to the monstrous din of the screaming bombs, hearing some of them drop perilously close. Wave after wave of bombers came over without a break, all the dreadful night long. And when, at four in the morning, they finally left the shelter, it was to stand at their bedroom window and see Coventry burning.

Marley Road had four bombs, the Coopers' and Phillips's windows were broken, farther along a pile of rubble was all that was left of the Naylors' house. Ten people were killed.

Ken's factory was in Coventry, and he'd been working nights. Ann waited for him to come home in a shiver of terror. Suppose he didn't come back. Suppose he was one of the thousands dead . . . Ann admitted to herself that she loved Ken.

She cleaned the dirt from the damaged house, but when the morning was well advanced, and her mother was resting, she ran round to the Websters', knocked on the door.

"I wondered—" she began. "I know Ken was working. Is he safe?"

He came in then, dirty, ragged, weary.

But safe.

*

Marta came home in early spring. Her mother met her at the station, then they caught the bus to Marley Road, Marta staring in shocked horror at the piles of rubble in the streets, the bomb craters, houses standing drunkenly, their fronts blown away. "I'm glad you're all safe," she murmured.

They walked in home. It was five o'clock on a Monday, and William had left work early. He greeted his beloved daughter with tears in his eyes. "Oh, my little wench," he muttered.

"Come on, now, let's get a cup of tea," said Liz, briskly, moving to the kettle, singing on the hob. "Sit down, Marta, do. Eh, it's good to see you home again."

And after tea Meg came round, with Chris, now a tall nineteen, with fair hair worn in a long bob à la Veronica Lake. Chris was still the same prickly girl she had always been, Marta was a little surprised to see her. Later still Doreen popped in, and then the younger ones. Ann, of course, was there the minute she came home from work.

Marta sat silent as they all talked together, till Meg said, "Look, we'll have to go, we're tiring you."

"No, no," Marta replied, listlessly.

"You'll have to go to bed early tonight," Liz fussed.

"And take care of yourself," Meg cautioned. "You're looking well now."

They left and still Marta sat.

"Is Ken still reserved?" she asked.

"Oh yes," her mother replied.

"I expect he's courting," Marta pursued, trying to appear casual.

Her mother grunted. "A girl a night according to your Aunt Meg. Anyway, that's nothing to do with us."

"Well, he is my cousin," Marta protested.

"Exactly," said her mother.

At nine o'clock her mother again brought up the subject of bed.

"In a minute," Marta said. "I'll just go for a breath of fresh air first."

"Shall I come with you?" asked Liz.

"No, I'm only going as far as the corner shop. Don't fuss, Mother."

"All right," said her mother, aggrieved. "I only wanted to help—"

Marta put on her coat, and walked across the yard to the entry. The nights were drawing out now, but the narrow entry was always dark. She stood for a moment at the top, then saw a figure entering the other end. It was too dark to see clearly who it was, but her heart began to pound.

He came close and stopped. "Ken," she breathed.

"Marta."

For ten seconds he stood quite still, then, without a word he drew her into his arms. He did not attempt to kiss her, just stood holding her, so tight she could feel the beating of his heart. His cheek was pressed close to hers and she whispered. "I thought you weren't coming to see me."

"I couldn't – not with all the others there. Oh, Marta, are you better?"

"I'm fine. Really."

"I've missed you so."

"Me too."

"Have you? Really?"

"Really, truly and not pretendingly." She used one of their childhood phrases and he chuckled, tension relieved. "When can I see you?" he asked.

"Come round tomorrow," she invited.

He came in, again pretending to be casual, making no mention that he'd seen her the night before. Ann was there, they chatted together.

"Going to the dance?" Marta asked Ken.

"Probably." He hesitated. "How about you?"

"Not tonight," her mother said, sharply.

"I'll go next week," Marta promised. "Tuesday."

And when he'd gone she ran upstairs and studied herself in the mirror. Her tawny hair was shining, her face was smooth, her lips curving into a smile. "I've put on weight," she told herself, and looked into her meagre wardrobe. "I need new clothes, and for that I need money."

"I'm going to find a job," she told her mother when she went back to the kitchen. "I shan't go back to Robey's," she continued.

"You can't," Liz said, shortly. "They sent your cards weeks ago."

"Anyway, I expect they've been taken over for war work." William smoothed over the awkward pause. "Just as mine has. I've had to move to the Bilton Aero Engines."

Marta had no trouble finding a job, there was plenty of work around now. She applied to the Heavy Aircraft, where the foreman, thinking she did not look very strong, gave her a light job on Inspection.

Now she was in another big shed, with more wheels and machines. This shed, called a shop, was dirty and greasy and oily, so she wore an overall and a turban round her hair. Still there were no windows, she could not look with eyes, wistful or otherwise, at the tent of blue called the sky. For a good part of the year she didn't see daylight at all. Yet she was far happier than at Robey's, her wages were much higher, and she found the work and conditions easier. She could talk and even sing, in fact singing was encouraged, for a new climate for workers was emerging, they were so necessary to the scheme of things. Without workers the war would grind to a halt. They were given lunch-time concerts, music while you work, higher wages. And as the German blitzes continued, it was agreed that this time we were in it together. As the bombs continued to rain down on the Midlands the workers agreed on that last point, at least.

Marta went to the dance on Tuesday, with Ann, and Ken came in. He crossed to her immediately. "Dance?" he asked.

She went into his arms, acknowledging now that she had wanted to dance with him for a long time. They swept on to the floor, dipped and spun and wheeled slowly, and she felt a sense of coming home, of finding at last what she had been seeking.

As the last waltz ended, Ken said, "I'll wait for you," and she nodded. She got her coat and remembered Ann. The three walked home together, saying little. Marta said into the silence, "I didn't know you could dance like that."

Ken said, "We'll go tomorrow."

"Yes."

They had reached the entry, and Ken stopped. Ann took one look at him standing next to Marta, then went in home. Ken said, "I've been called up."

"But I thought you were reserved."

"Not any longer." He looked down at her, then bent and kissed her goodnight. "Tomorrow," he said. Marta ran in home.

The next evening he called for her, and together they

went to the dance. But when she came home her mother was waiting.

"Did you enjoy yourself?" Liz asked, casually.

"Oh yes, it was great."

Her mother hesitated. "Why did you go with Ken?"

"Why not?"

"Because he's your cousin, you're too closely related to go out together."

Marta laughed. "Oh, for goodness' sake, I'm not—"

Her mother sighed. "Well, you know your dad don't approve of cousins marrying." *Especially when there's consumption in the family.* But her mother did not tell her of the shadow on her lung.

Marta went out early, and called for Ann. Together they waited in the entry for Ken. "Don't tell anyone I'm going out with him," she said to Ann. "My dad would go mad."

"Well, cousins can't marry," said Ann.

There was a pause. "Who's talking about marrying?" Marta asked.

"Why are you going out with him, then?"

"Cos he's a good dancer," and Ann was silent.

Marta was exultant, and afraid. Wasn't he part of her? The same flesh? The very closeness of the relationship seemed to make it all the more exciting and she shivered with fear. But she knew the attraction had been there for a long time, she'd known it subconsciously when she refused to speak to him. Now she couldn't resist.

Ken kissed her and she trembled with ecstasy. He took her over the fields and they lay on a bed of wild thyme, she could hear a horse cropping the grass in the stillness. He said, "You know I've always loved you, don't you?"

"I suppose so."

"Why did you keep away from me so long?"

She let her hand run through his hair. Why had she run away . . .?

"I love you," he whispered. "That's why I tried it on before, I wanted you . . . I still do. Oh, lovey." He kissed her and she wound her arms round his neck. The trees rustled above and somewhere she was lost in a world of terror and beauty and desire, and then there was nothing but love in the silence of the night and the sound of the horse cropping the grass. And she marvelled at the sudden flared passion, for nothing in her reading or education had prepared her for this. She stroked his hair, so much like her own, and kissed his cheek.

The summer passed, and led to winter, and they loved in Bates's barn, with the warm smell of cattle and hay. He was in the army now, but managed to get weekend passes pretty often; still they loved and danced, and Marta felt, with the egotism of youth, that the whole world had been created for her benefit, maybe even her drab factory life had its merits for it made this sudden blossoming all the sweeter. And her one escape, her dancing, now fused into her love, giving her a double joy.

Then there was embarkation leave, he was sent abroad, and all the colour went out of life.

*

Ken wrote from Gibraltar.

> 'Haven't got much to do here, I'd quite like it if I didn't miss you so much. We all talk a lot about the future, and we're determined not to go back to the old ways. Have you read the Beveridge Report? Free health service, education for all? That's what we're fighting for, no more unemployment, more equality.
>
> The future, Marta, you and me married, perhaps

even a son. Do you remember when Mr Stretton told me that maybe things would be better for my son? Well, he was right. My son will have everything I was denied. Everything. Education, a good job. Have you told your parents about us yet? You know I love you, I always have, I only ran around with those other girls while I was waiting for you, you wilful little madam, leading me such a dance. I can't tell you the joy I feel when I think of the future, the marvellous new world we'll build.

Take care of yourself, my love. If there's an air-raid go into the shelter, I couldn't bear it if I lost you. You're the one who reads poetry, not me, or I'd send you some. All I can think of is a song my dad sings, 'My Love is Like a Red, Red Rose', and I think that fits, as your name is Rose, and your dad grows them so well.

'All my love, Ken.'

*

'My darling Ken,

Thank you for your letter, I'm so glad to hear you're all right. No, I haven't told my mam and dad yet, you know me dad's funny about cousins marrying, doesn't believe in it, and you know, Ken, if I tell him now, it'll be me has the bother of it all, with him and mam and Aunt Meg and Uncle Tom. Oh, I don't suppose they'll mind really, but they will go on a bit. They're old, Ken, they don't understand. Anyway, it's nice to keep it to myself, I can't explain how I feel, I suppose I've always loved you too, though I didn't realise it, and now . . . the whole world's just you and me, and I don't want to share it with anybody. I told Ann, but not that we're serious, or that we made love. Oh, Ken, when I remember . . . I go to the dance sometimes so

Mam won't suspect, but it's all so boring, all the other chaps are like cardboard dolls after you.

Don't worry about me being bombed, no bomb has got my name on, I know. But you take care of yourself, because without you I wouldn't want to live. There just wouldn't be anything left.

Yours till the stars lose their glory,
    All my love,
        Marta.'

Chapter Four

Ken came home in February, 1944 and was sent to the south of England, now a vast armed camp. He had a weekend leave in April, and at first Marta thought they'd never get a minute alone. But on Sunday night he told his parents he had to see a friend, and he and Marta slipped away to Bates's barn. It was warm in the hayloft and he drew her close to him. "Oh my love," he murmured. "My love."

"I wish you didn't have to go," she breathed.

"I'll try and get another leave before—" He broke off and took her in his arms again.

They parted at last, and Marta crept in home, tears running down her face. She did not go to the station with Ken, his family would be doing that, and she dare not let the family see her grief.

"Come soon, my love," she whispered.

On June 6th D-Day was announced on the radio, and Marta trembled. She went to work in a dream, and the foreman, seeing her white face and guessing the reason, said nothing about her faulty work. She went home to bed, and her mother watched her, asking if she wasn't well. Marta shrugged off her solicitude impatiently. She was waiting, with dread, with hope, with fear . . .

Two weeks later Ken was reported missing, believed killed.

*

Marta was dazed, she could not even talk to Ann. She went to the dance, had one waltz with a former partner, then refused every other boy. After Ken, everything seemed second-rate, and she was frightened that life could be so empty without him. Soon she went home.

Her mother nagged her, asking what was the matter, worry making her anxious. William saw the intense, almost feverish look in his daughter's eyes and thought of his roses, how, when the soil wasn't just right, they bloomed rapidly at the touch of the sun, but frailly, because their roots had never received much nourishment.

Her mother fretted, but Marta was listless. She had no feeling for her dancing now, and this too frightened her, for she had nothing to put in its place. Her days were hours of deadness, and she peered into the future uncertainly, seeing rows of factories, rows of wheels, rows of little dolls dancing till their wires snapped . . .

William hovered in the background, clumsily offering her his roses. "Isn't this a beauty?" he'd say. "It's a Hugh Dickson," and he would look hopefully for her approval. But she was apathetic.

After two months she said to her mother, "Mam, I reckon I'm having a baby."

"Oh, damn all men to hell," said Liz. "Who is it? You'll have to get married."

"I can't marry him, he's gone."

William said: "Never mind if he's gone away, I'll fetch him back."

Marta hesitated.

"I'll break his neck," said William.

"It wasn't his fault any more than mine," said Marta. "I love him, we were happy." And the old man's heart was wrenched that some young rogue could give his daughter so much while he, who worshipped her, could offer only roses.

She went with her mother to the doctor. "Missed periods?" he asked. "Have you had sexual intercourse?"

"Yes," whispered Marta and the doctor gave her a little lecture on morals. Marta was shamed that her love should be so dragged through the mire.

"Old fool," said her mother when they were safely outside. "Everybody knows he drinks like a fish. Don't tell your dad."

But when they got home Marta said: "I suppose you'll have to know. It's Ken."

"Ken?" asked William, amazed. "Our Ken?"

"I'm not surprised," her mother said.

"Not surprised?" asked William. "But you never said anything to me."

"I don't tell you everything," said Liz, shortly. "I don't know what Tom will say."

"What's it matter what they say?" asked William. "It's our girl who's in trouble." There were tears in his eyes.

"We were going to get married," said Marta. "You can tell them that. It wasn't just an affair, it's been going on a long time. But I knew you wouldn't like it."

And again William was saddened that she hadn't told them.

Meg and Tom, whatever they said in the privacy of their bedroom, had nothing to say outside. Wrapped in the grief of losing their son, they could hardly grasp that anyone else had troubles. The fact that they would have a grandchild did not dawn on them yet.

The days passed, and Marta went to work, came home and sat. Her winter cough lingered on, and her mother rubbed her chest with goose-grease. Liz wanted her to go to the doctor again but Marta, remembering the former shame, refused. She booked in the nearby hospital for the birth, and waited.

*

London was enduring the V-bombs, and Marley Road sympathised with the battered southerners. In the Midlands there was still the odd raid, none of the venomous fury of the first onslaught, just the occasional bomb. The war was a weariness now, queues and dried eggs, waiting for the end, listening to ITMA and Vera Lynn. Ann's father came home white and drawn from driving a train in the blackout, even his wife was moved to pity, and ministered far more to him than ever before, getting nearer to the working-class idea of protecting the breadwinner, realising perhaps its common sense. Without her husband's pay-packet what would she do? Ann ate in the canteen, but coal and tea were scarce. Everyone was on the fiddle for the first time in their lives, old William the upright, moved from his brickyard to a factory, brought home a lump of coal every night for his wife and daughter. Sybil's husband was in the Stores, from where he kept his family supplied with food, and a little found its way to the Coopers. Ann's boss registered her as a shorthand-typist, a reserved occupation, though she was still only a clerk-typist.

The Websters' became more crowded than ever. Doreen had another baby and was turned out of her lodgings so that her landlady could take in single men. She and her family all came to her parents' and crammed in the back bedroom. Life went on.

*

On a cold night in January 1945, Marta walked to the hospital, a rug round her shoulders, supported by her mother and Meg. It was past midnight, frozen snow lay on the ground, a siren sounded in the distance. Battles raged, the Red Army entered Germany; Marta cared nought for these events, she walked in a vast primitive world where nothing existed but birth, her energies turned inward for protection and survival. The hospital loomed grim and dark, and Marta asked through chattering teeth how long she'd be in. Ten days for good behaviour, said the nurse, no temperature rises, no infectious illnesses. Come along to the Labour Ward. And they walked through clanging corridors and shut doors to a cell where she was bathed and then told to lie on a high hard bed. They left her alone and she heard them talking in the next room, and their voices were callousness personified that they should leave her alone like this. The pain was sharp and she could not lie flat on the hard bed, her body urged her to crouch so she rolled on to the floor. The sister came in and heaved her back on the bed and left. Marta moaned and rolled off the bed again, crouched and climbed back. The little window, high up, was blacked out, but shadows of trees outside waved grotesquely over it. She wanted someone with her, she wanted her mother, Aunt Meg. Something gushed from between her legs. "Sister!" she screamed, and they came running.

The next morning Liz walked to the hospital, it was no farther than going to a phone box.

"Yes," said the sister. "Your daughter had a beautiful healthy son."

Liz's face relaxed into a smile.

"But I'm afraid your daughter is rather ill," said the sister. "Didn't you know she was ill?"

"No," said Liz, frightened.

"Hasn't she been to the doctor at all?"

"No," breathed Liz.

"Then she should have," said the sister, sternly. "She had a haemorrhage. I'm afraid she has TB."

Liz stood wide-eyed, lost, feeling she was being blamed. "C—Can I see her?" she asked.

"She was taken to the sanatorium this morning. We'll keep the baby for a week or two, but he seems fine . . ." And the sister went on her starched way.

"What a thing," said the neighbours, shaking their heads wisely. "Comes of too much gadding about, I always said that would happen." William thought again of one of his roses, how, if the soil was not just right, it wilted, but what could you do for wilting humans? He didn't know.

Every Sunday William and Liz visited the sanatorium. They walked to the bus station, waited for the special bus, for it was a long journey; they saw their daughter for an hour or two, then trekked home again, cold and hungry. "She's as well as can be expected," said the nurse, brightly.

Marta was in a world of white ghosts and feverish eyes, people in little beds, coughing their lives away.

*

When the Red Army entered Germany, they were to link up with the Allies in a prearranged plan that had been made at Yalta, with the British under General Montgomery taking Berlin. But General Eisenhower changed his mind, and allowed the Russians into Berlin first, to the dismay of Montgomery and Churchill.

Montgomery crossed the Aller en route for Bremen and entered the concentration camp at Belsen, where 40,000 men, women and children were in an advanced state of exhaustion, having been starved for a long period.

*

The war meant little to Marta now. At first she had been on the veranda, then she was moved inside, to a small ward whose occupants were dying, and they all knew it. In Ward 10 no one came out alive. Marta stared at the occupants in horror, emaciated creatures whose bones stood out from their bodies as if they were already skeletons. They coughed and spat into little pots all day long and all night through. In between they lay back, exhausted, and waited.

Marta knew she would not get better, it was impossible not to know it in a hospital where places were awarded in terms of recovery, progress, better, not good, hopeless, doomed. She thought over her life, and it seemed to stretch for a long, long time, years and years of childhood, years and years in the factory, years and years of dancing. Only her time with Ken was too short. She thought of his words, "Why did you keep away from me so long?"' and wondered at her foolishness, the foolishness of a young girl who thinks life goes on forever. She wondered if there was an after-life as the Church said, and if so, if she'd ever see Ken again. But she didn't worry too much about it, she was too tired. Looking back it seemed she'd been tired for as long as she could remember, when she came home from the twelve hours at Robey's, when she danced feverishly through the blackout . . . now her exhausted body had given out.

In March she said to her father, "Dad, I want to come home."

William shook his head. "You'll be better in hospital."

"They won't let you," Liz fretted, anxiously, fearfully.

William said, "I'll see the doctor."

"Well." The doctor cleared his throat. "I'll be honest with you, Mr Phillips. Your daughter is very ill."

"I know." Did he think people didn't understand the significance of ward grading in hospitals?

"In fact – we fear there is little more we can do. It's like that sometimes, especially with young people. When it gets a hold it spreads like wildfire."

William bowed his head.

"But coming home – well, to be frank, we'd be glad of

the bed. But we couldn't let her stay in the house with the baby."

"My relations would take care of the baby," William said. But his heart sank. They were sending her home to die.

The doctor pondered. "As long as the baby is kept away ... she doesn't ask about him very much, but of course she is so ill. Then again, your wife isn't a young woman, how would you manage?"

"We'll manage," said William, doggedly. "Our relations live nearby."

"She doesn't seem to have the will to live," said the doctor fretfully.

So Marta came home.

She lay in the bed by the window looking over the back field where the horses used to run. She didn't seem interested in the baby, now with Meg and Tom. "You must get better, Marta," William tried to rally his daughter.

"What for, Dad? After the war I wouldn't want to go back to Robey's again."

William looked at her sorrowfully. He didn't tell her that Robey's wouldn't want her now with her damaged lungs. Factories, like armies, want only the flower of youth.

He said, anguished, "Oh, my little wench," and she whispered, "Don't be upset, Dad, you were always good to me."

Ann came round every night to help. She washed the drenched sheets, taking more on her shoulders, said her mother, than she could manage. Ann said, "I don't understand it, Marta seemed so full of life, so – vivid. Now she's collapsed to nothing."

"It happens," said her mother. "They just burn themselves out, it seems. I feel sorry for her parents, they've aged ten years."

Marta died as the sun set over the dance-hall, and the world went on fighting for the New Jerusalem.

William and Liz went to the funeral, two old bowed people who crept along, hand in hand, bewildered, lost. Tom and Meg walked behind them, grieving, more relations, then Ann. Somewhere in the distance an all clear sounded.

Every Sunday William took a bunch of gorgeous roses to the cemetery. He would sit a long time at the grave, his perplexed face looking at his crippled hands. He was an old man and had seen many things; he had been a law-abiding citizen, believing in God and honouring King and country. He'd fought in the first war and worked hard all his life. He'd been good and true, honest and brave. And now he wondered why.

Book Two

Ann and Ken

1945 and the war in Europe was over. In London crowds flocked to Piccadilly on VE day, and 12,000 still slept in shelters as they had no homes to go to. In August the atom bomb was dropped on Japan.

The Labour Party's manifesto ended the political truce that had existed between the three parties. Battle lines were drawn up. Labour offered the Welfare State as in the Beveridge Report of 1942, which had been an instant bestseller. Beveridge regarded full employment, a free health service and family allowances as merely the basis for further reforms. The Conservatives offered individual freedom and national greatness.

Marley Road painted great signs on houses, 'Welcome Home', George or Jim or Fred. There was no sign on the Websters' house and in No. 32, Ann sat alone.

Chapter One

I've felt so alone since Marta died, for she was my friend. Not that she was perfect in any way, not like her parents thought, she wasn't shy, like me. But she didn't have a continual barrage from a mother always saying don't do this or that. She was good fun, and would say the most outrageous things, like, "What's the difference between selling your body as a prostitute and selling it to a rotten job?" And she would always take my part against bossy Sybil. Still, Sybil's push paid off. She married the boss's son . . . And was I glad to see the back of her!

My mother was the daughter of a businessman who had married beneath her, or so she told us every day. Father was an insipid shadowy figure who seemed hardly to exist in his own right, but once he flared back in anger. "Business my foot. Just a little corner shop, and if he scratted some money together he never lived to enjoy it. Neither did your mother, cos he worked her to death." And my mother replied, "At least he was more respectable than your father, always drunk."

I was shocked at this, a drunk was the lowest of the low. My mother never let me meet the Coopers except for Aunt May . . . I felt I had no family life, so I loved to be part of the family life of the Websters, to feel I belonged. There was little love in my own home, what love Mother had was given to Sybil, the successful one.

Mother wouldn't allow me to mix with the Websters,

though Marta was accepted as Mr and Mrs Phillips were wholly respectable. Some nights I used to slip round to the Websters' house with Marta, when Meg and Tom went out leaving Doreen in charge. Doreen would slip out too, to meet a chap, and we kids had a high old time. I remember the laughter, the fish and chip supper, playing the gramophone with the broken handle, Ken's accordion . . . that was belonging . . .

I'd always loved Ken, but I knew I never had a chance with him, not while Marta was there. But when I saw them dancing together it was so beautiful, I couldn't envy her. It seemed such a waste that the whole world couldn't see them.

I can't bear to think of Ken. I can think of Marta, but not Ken. I go into next door with Meg and Chris to help with the baby, Liz sits old and wan, and William grieves in the background – they've both aged ten years. Liz looks after David now, as they've named the child, but it's obvious she feels no love for it, even some resentment, and it's William who gets up in the night when he cries. He has to be looked after well, the doctor says, because of the TB, but he seems strong enough. It must be true what Liz says, he took all Marta's strength and that's why she resents him.

I go to work in the daytime. With Sybil's elevation to a high-class family, Mother redoubled her efforts to push me into a similar life style. The war brought crying needs for workers of all grades, so Mother saw her chance, and got me to enrol at a secretarial school – I paid the fees, naturally. I suppose I could have refused, but I give in for a quiet life, anybody would who lives with my mother.

When I'd got a fair speed I presented myself at the Moonlight Aircraft Limited, where I was given a job as a typist without, it seemed, much consideration.

The Moonlight's general office was a long dismal room with no windows, and hundreds of men and women sitting round tables pretty much the same as the factory. I was given a typewriter and some schedules to type out. I wasn't very fast, but I persevered, and no one seemed to be hurrying much anyway. The office was overstaffed and some of the men did far less work than Marta had at fourteen. It was the war, they said, plenty of money around now.

We worked a five-day week plus Saturday or Sunday, for which we were paid overtime. The atmosphere was far gentler than the factory's, no one shouted, "Here, you," it was always "Miss, do you mind . . ." People were even sacked politely, though perhaps more deviously, like Mr Staines who tried to start a union for the staff and was dismissed, though sacking was forbidden in wartime. They said he was a bad worker and so got away with it.

But people had a different attitude, they were more demanding, wouldn't be pushed around, and some of this rubbed off on to me, and changed me I think.

The factory workers eat dinner in a dark canteen with bare tables and self-service; we of the staff walk right through this none too clean room into a special separate one where we eat lunch with tablecloths and waitresses and are charged an extra tuppence. High life indeed.

The other girls are friendly enough, so I've settled in comfortably. And that's been my life for the past few years, going to the office, coming back to a dreary home, with occasional visits from Sybil, who told us she wished she were single, she'd have joined the forces, some girls she knew did this and met and married such nice *men. Thought she could have done better for herself. Of course, she wouldn't have gone into a factory to help the war effort, not Sybil. Come to think I don't know how she got out of the call up, expect her father-in-law fiddled it in some way.*

Mother keeps nagging me to find a 'nice young man'. It might be worth getting married if only to get away from her, but I don't know any young man, and don't go dancing now. I'm twenty-four and just sit in home, looking after Marta's baby. For years my office companions have been getting engaged, proudly showing their flashing rings, talking of John or Peter or Roger in the forces, about weekend leaves and singing 'We'll Meet Again'. The war's over now, but there was no rejoicing for us.

Some days I feel I am getting over it, I don't think of either of them for hours. Then the next morning I wake and it's in my mind more than ever, the sense of loss, the feeling that life isn't worth living, the terrible finality of death.

I don't dance now, I don't want to, I eat, sleep, work, and inside me a great vacuum, an emptiness that will never be filled.

I sometimes wonder if I will be an old maid.

*

Ann sat in the kitchen making some alterations to a dress she had had for two years. The trouble with working in an office was that you had to appear well-dressed, she had heard of a girl who had been 'spoken to' because she looked untidy. Ann gave her mother half of her wages, which didn't leave enough to buy coupons. This method of 'paying your board' was usual after the giving all and receiving pocket-money of pre-eighteen days. The spring winds blew chill and Ann shivered.

She heard rather than saw the commotion in the yard, the flying figure of Chris Webster running into the Phillips's, talking in a high voice. Out again, and knocking at their door.

"It's Ken," said Chris, breathlessly on the doorstep. "He's alive. We've heard. He was a prisoner. Now he's coming home . . ." She flew off again, and Ann followed.

The Websters were in uproar. "He was a prisoner, sent to Germany with a working party . . . escaped when there was an air-raid . . . got to the American troops . . . they flew him home. Yes, he's here now, he posted this letter in England . . . he's coming *home* . . ." Tom was shouting, Meg was silent, peaceful.

Ann didn't sleep that night, nor did she finish her dress.

She came home from work and her mother said, offhandedly, "He's home, then." She had tea, and sat where she could look through the window, one wary eye on her mother. "Does he know about Marta?" she asked, and her mother shrugged.

He walked round the yard, slowly, and she thought: '*He knows.*' There was a blankness on his face, in his eyes. He went into the Phillips's and stayed a long time. Ann tried to sit still, wondering if he'd come to see her, and what she'd do if he didn't. She heard the door close and he stood outside, thinking, then knocked at their door.

"Come in," said Mrs Cooper, a little distantly, for he might be a returning hero, but he was still a Webster.

"Ken—" Ann said. "It's good to see you . . ."

He didn't smile. Mrs Cooper said, "Sit down."

"No," he said. "I won't stop. I wondered if you, Ann, would come to the cemetery with me, show me her grave."

"Of course." Ann put on her coat, and they went out together.

"I'm glad you're back, Ken, that you're all right. Was it bad out there?"

"What? Oh, nothing much."

"You – didn't know about Marta." It was a statement, of course he didn't know.

"No."

Ann made one or two stammered remarks, but he didn't answer. She led him to the grave and they stood in silence. It was getting dark, a few rooks flew across the ragged sky, crossed with bare branches. Ken said, "Did she suffer?"

"Not really."

"She thought I was dead."

"Yes."

"Oh, God." He turned and began to walk away, Ann following. They stumbled along the cemetery and it was dark now. Ken stopped by one of the gravestones as though he couldn't go any farther. Ann, troubled, put her arms on his shoulders, and then he was holding her. "Don't leave me, Ann," he said, and she was moved to her depths that he should so need her. She wanted to comfort him and drew him towards her. She felt his body shake, and then he was pushing her away.

She said: "I don't mind, Ken, honestly . . . I've . . . always liked you, you know." He unbuttoned her coat and pulled up her skirt. He entered her and she felt nothing but a sense of astonishment that seemed to envelop the world. Was *she* doing this? Was this Ann Cooper? The branches waved across the sky and seemed closer than Ken; she felt no pleasure nor even shame, just wonder.

They moved apart. "Did you mean that?" he asked. "That you've always liked me?"

"I love you," she said, and was amazed at her words.

"Would you marry me?"

"Why? Because of this?"

"No—" impatiently. "Not because of this. We've always been together, maybe we could make a go of it."

She stared around at the waving trees. "Yes," she said. "Let's get married."

"As soon as possible," said Ken.

*

She told the girls in the office with a shy pride. Now she

was one of the elect, she too had a fiancé, and could talk about returning heroes, take a proprietary part in the war. They welcomed her into the secret society of initiated girls.

In the evening she made up her face, put on her coat, and saw her mother eyeing her.

"Going out?"

"Yes."

Her mother looked suspicious. "You're not going with that Ken, I hope?"

"And what if I am?"

"If you'd got any sense you'd keep away from him."

"As a matter of fact," Ann faced her mother, "I'm going to marry him."

"You're *what*? Not if I have anything to do with it."

"But you won't have anything to do with it. I'm over twenty-one." Ann was quiet but firm.

"You won't do much good with somebody who works in a factory, on the dole most of the time like his dad."

Ann didn't reply. Already those days of dole queues seemed far away, and she didn't look too closely into the future. Life was the present, the war was over, but the atmosphere lingered on, eat drink and be merry for tomorrow you might be bombed. The old days of long courtships and careful planning, of saving and 'bottom drawers', were far behind, girls married in haste and had babies in haste, crowding a lifetime's living in the short time they had together. It might be an unreal world but it was the only one they had. Ann worked in Coventry, her life had been at risk for years, and her mother advised caution . . .

She said in a low voice, "I'm in love with him."

"Love." Her mother almost spat. "Where does love get you? You want to marry a good quiet man who works regularly and brings home the money, like your father."

"I don't understand you. You're always grumbling about my father, now you're saying he's a good husband."

"So he is, in that way."

"In what way?"

"He doesn't go with other women, like Tom Webster."

"Well, Tom Webster's a handsome man, I expect women like him, I can't see why you're so down on him."

"I think it's disgusting, that's why. You don't know what marriage is. At least your father's very respectful in that way."

"What do you mean?"

"I mean—" Her mother swallowed. "He doesn't care for that side of it very much."

"And Tom Webster does?"

"Well, look at his family ... he seems to think of nothing else."

"I don't see why it should worry you, you're really obsessed with Tom Webster."

"Like father, like son," said her mother. "One minute he's getting Marta into trouble, then he wants to marry you. Doesn't say much for you, does it?"

Ann said, trembling. "I'm satisfied."

"Why, you little fool," her mother said, shrilly, "he only wants you to look after the baby." She sat down, virtuously.

Ann went to the door.

"I'm only telling you for your own good." Her mother's voice followed her. "I don't want you to have a life like Meg's." Ann thought fleetingly of Ken and Marta making love, Ken and she ... how had it been with Tom and Meg? Rapture? She turned to look again at her mother a little pityingly.

"One thing I'll tell you, you won't come to live here ..."

Ann closed the door.

She knocked timidly at the Websters', and they welcomed her warmly. Tom and Meg, Doreen, Jack and the children, Chris, Peggy and Rose-Mary, now sixteen. Yet she sensed their surprise beneath their congratulations. Meg was holding the baby, and Ken was staring at it in wonder. "It's just like her," he said.

"Just like you, you mean," his mother said a little sharply. "Spitting image of you. And Ann's been very good helping look after him."

"I know." Ken came to her then, put his arm around her, and his face was kind. Ann was filled with gratitude that he had rescued her from her mother and given her the family she'd so long desired.

"There'll be a lot to think about, with the baby and all," Meg said, hesitantly.

"We've been talking about it today," Ken said. "I'll have to adopt him, and you too, Ann, if you want to."

"Yes, of course."

"I've got forty-two days' leave. I want us to be married before I go back."

"Do you think we should go and see the Phillips?" Ann asked. "I mean, will they agree?"

"He's my baby," said Ken. "But I went in today and told them. They didn't mind at all. I think Aunt Liz was relieved."

"Well, they won't live forever," said Tom, practically. "Then he'd only have to come to us."

"Here." Meg pushed the baby into Ken's arms. "I want to have a word with Ann. Come into the front a minute."

She closed the door behind them. "Are you sure, Ann? Taking the baby and everything."

"I'm sure, Mrs Webster. I've always liked Ken, you know."

"Yes, I thought you did. He's a good lad – but he will go his own way."

She did too. "We'll be all right," said Ann.

When they went back Ken was staring wonderingly into the baby's face. "My son," he said.

The next few days were hectic. They went to see the Phillips, they talked about the wedding. Ann didn't have enough coupons for a dress, so Doreen offered to lend her hers. No reception, said Ken, everything quiet.

"I'll have to give up my job," Ann said. "And where are we going to live, Ken? My mother won't have us with her."

"You'll have to come to Mam's. Tell you what. You serve your notice, then we'll be married, and when you leave work we'll take the baby. How's that?"

The girls in the office collected for her, and gave her the money as presents were unobtainable. And they were married in an almost empty church, early in the morning.

Ken was demobbed, the family hung a 'Welcome Home' sign on the door. Ann, waiting with the baby, was tremulous with joy. Now her dreams would come true. But first they had to fit in the small house. Meg and Tom had the front bedroom, Doreen and Jack and their three boys had the back room. The girls slept in the boxroom, and Johnny, when on leave from the army, slept on a couch in the kitchen. Ken and Ann had the downstairs front room. Peggy, now eighteen, eased the situation by getting married and going to live with her husband's family.

Ann found that the sense of belonging took a few knocks. She felt suffocated at times, and couldn't help contrasting the Websters' shabbiness with her mother's spotless cleanliness. Yet there was an atmosphere of happiness in the house. No one mentioned the word love, or kissed or touched – excepting the children who were readily hugged – but the feeling was there. Doreen and her miner were in love, Tom had sent Meg a valentine, causing much mirth in the family, and if he'd ever been out with other women there was no sign of them now. He had a regular job, didn't drink, and was no longer poor. But the house was too crowded for it to ever look nice, it wasn't even possible to clean in rooms so full of furniture, mostly beds. Baths were a problem, each having to carry hot water, and the bath, into his own bedroom. Ann began to understand why Meg had let the housework slide, but she herself persisted, listening to peals of laughter from the kitchen.

She felt she had been thrown into motherhood at the deep end, for although she had helped with David when he was with Liz, she had never bathed or even dressed this slippery piece of quicksilver that was a baby; she felt a novice, both as wife and mother. If David woke in the night, she'd hush him gently, trying not to disturb Ken. She'd wake tired in the mornings, stumble into the kitchen to make David's feed at six o'clock, where Jack had already departed for the day shift, and Doreen was clearing up. Ann would get their breakfast, and now Meg and Tom were down, and the other children; there'd be no peace or quiet for the rest of the day.

She'd take David for long walks in the afternoon, when he'd sleep. By bedtime she was weary again and though she tried hard to respond to Ken's love-making she could never really let herself go, there were so many interruptions: David waking, one of Doreen's children crying upstairs, a late home-comer entering the kitchen, or one of the men visiting the outside lavatory, and she'd tense and freeze lest the wanderer would hear. Ken, who could have taught her so much, desisted, either because he thought she was not interested, or because he too put David first. He never mentioned love and Ann was disappointed.

Yet she was thankful to be with them, for all the drawbacks. She worried about David, she was terrified he'd be ill. She took him weekly to the clinic, and regularly for the TB checkups. She was grateful to Meg, just for being there, standing among her own children and grandchildren, the mother, the wise, knowing all things.

Ken returned to the factory, and the first thing he did, when he came home, was to go to David. If he were awake, he'd pick him up, cuddle him till the baby shouted with glee. Ann watched, smiling at first, but as time went on, a little enviously. She wanted a baby too. But Ken always took care she did not become pregnant.

One night, as he settled David in his cot and came to her she said, "I'd like a baby, Ken."

"We've got a baby," he replied.

"Yes, but, I mean one of my own." He didn't answer, and she went on, "Don't you want any more at all?"

"I don't want a houseful of kids like my mam had. No money to spare for any of 'em. Anyway, we can't have one here, can we? There's hardly room to breathe as it is."

"Will we ever get a house of our own?"

"We're in line for a council-house, you know that."

"Yes, and then, my parents won't live forever, and their house will come to me and Sybil."

"That could be a long time ahead, Ann."

"I know. But when we do have a house, Ken, I'd like a baby then."

He hesitated. "Well, perhaps later. Hush now, David's stirring."

*

Ken was home when the election results were announced. Everywhere people were listening to the wireless, more excited than on VE day. In the Websters' kitchen the family was gathered, and when the news of the Labour victory came over they shouted and cheered and Johnny ran to the pub for some beer to celebrate.

"Our kids'll have a better deal now," Ken said. He held David high in his arms and the baby laughed with glee.

"Last war they promised us a land fit for heroes to live in," roared Tom. "And this war we're going to get it."

"No more unemployment," said Ken.

"Drink your beer, Dad," shouted Johnny. "You never expected this, did you? Thought you'd be on the dole forever. Well, we did this for you, and don't you forget it."

Tom lunged at his son, Johnny ducked, and the beer dropped over the floor. Meg fetched a cloth; the family laughed.

And when the celebrations were finally over Ann and Ken went to bed, where David had been sleeping for some hours.

"Do you know?" Ken said, drowsily. "There's a little poem, I don't remember much of it, except the last line. *'I saw the morning break.'* That's how I feel."

Ann stared. "I didn't know you were interested in poetry, Ken."

"I'm not really."

"Where did you hear that, then?"

"She showed it to me."

"She?"

"Marta. She liked poetry, you know."

"Yes."

He went to the cot where David slept. "You'll have

everything she didn't," he said to the sleeping baby. "And me. Your mother and me."

Ann lay staring into the darkness. And when he got in beside her and put his arm around her she turned away.

Chapter Two

When Ken returned to the factory he was determined to help start the new world. He was one of those instrumental in starting a union and became a shop-steward. At home, Doreen had been allotted one of the new council-houses, a steel semi-detached with garden, and inside, hot and cold water, a bathroom and a cooker. All the Websters trooped up once weekly to use the bath. With Doreen and her family gone, Ken and Ann moved into their bedroom, with Chris and Rose-Mary in the boxroom. Johnny was still in the army.

David's first birthday had passed, he was a forward, healthy child, with Marta's tawny hair and infectious smile. Every Saturday Ann and Ken would walk into the town to the market, Ann pushing the utility pram, and every Saturday Ken would buy David some little toy. At eighteen months he possessed a number of picture books, and at bedtime Ken would read to him; every Sunday morning he'd carry him into the garden or the field. Ann never told anyone he wasn't her own, but she herself could never forget that he was Marta's child.

*

Ann's father had collapsed, luckily before he went out to drive his train. The doctor was hastily summoned and talked to Mrs Cooper downstairs. "He's had bronchitis for years," he told her. "Now his heart is affected."

"He won't be able to go to work for a time?"

"He won't be able to go to work ever again," said the doctor drily. "And certainly not driving a train, a lot of people's lives happen to depend on him. In fact, he never should have been driving a train in the first place. Didn't he have to pass a medical?"

"I suppose so."

"Well, it's been too much for him. He seems to have been driving himself as well as the train for years. Naturally he collapsed."

"Won't he ever get better?"

The doctor glanced at the hard-faced woman before him. "Frankly, I doubt it," he said.

He left, and Mrs Cooper sent for Ann.

Ann went every day to help her mother, leaving David with Meg, and with Ken when he came home. Emma Cooper's voice grew more shrill, more querulous, more complaining. "He never was any good to me," she said.

The new world progressed. William, who had worn glasses bought in Woolworths, obtained a new, free pair, as did the man next door, who said he'd never realised, in all his thirty-five years, eleven of which had been spent down the pit, that he would ever be able to see across the road, he hadn't known anybody *could*. Mr Cooper received free treatment, but for him it was too late, he was dying and they all knew it. Next door Liz began to ail, the doctor was overworked in Marley Road. So were Ann, Meg and Chris.

The pattern changed. Mr Cooper and Liz died within three weeks; Ann went to both funerals, Ken was at work. It rained on both occasions.

"Deaths go in threes," said Meg. "I wonder who'll be the next?"

"That's an old wives' tale," said Ann to Ken. "How can deaths go in threes?"

But they did, and the third was Ann's mother.

"Took bad quite sudden," the neighbours said. "Rushed off to hospital, seems she had cancer, been there a long time, eating away at her. Then she went sudden-like at the end."

Ann could feel no grief for the loss of her parents, though she tried; she thought with pleasure that she'd get half the proceeds from the sale of the house. They'd be able to buy a house of their own.

She didn't. Her mother had made a will, everything to go to Sybil.

"Oh, it's not fair," said Ann. "She never came near. I looked after her and my dad all the time."

"Perhaps she'll give you some of it."

"Not her," said Ann. "Not Sybil." She thought bitterly that her mother had done it because she'd married Ken.

Sybil came to see them, to explain why she could not share out the money. She sat in the front room and placed her expensive handbag on a chair.

"You see," she said, "the business isn't doing too well, we need money desperately."

"I'm sure you do," said Ann. "It takes a lot to keep up that house in Acacia Avenue, I expect."

"There's no need to be unkind, Ann. I've already explained—" She turned to Ken. "You understand, don't you?"

Her bold eyes flashed and Ann thought, *I've always considered Sybil to be ugly – I still do. She's not thin, she bulges. But I never noticed her eyes before.*

Ken shrugged. "By rights, Ann should have had something for all the work she'd done, I'd have thought. But it's all one to me."

"I tell you what I'll do," Sybil said. "I'll give you

fifty pounds, Ann, to show there's no ill-will. As a gift."

"Don't bother," said Ken. "Keep your money."

She's got a moustache, Ann thought. *And I read in a book the other day that women with hair are sexy.* She said: "We'll take it. It'll go towards your boat, Ken."

"Boat?" asked Sybil.

"Ken's heard of an old canal-boat for sale. He wants to do it up and go on the canal for holidays."

"Go on the smelly canal for holidays? With those dirty boaties?" Sybil was disgusted.

"Not many boaties left now," said Ken. "That's why the boat's for sale."

"Well, it's your affair, of course." Sybil flashed her eyes again. "I'll let you have the money, but I would have thought—"

"We could have put it to better use?" asked Ann.

She took her sister to the door, and once away from Ken's hearing, Sybil said: "Really, Ann, buying a *boat*. And you living here in one room. Just like his father, the money wasted on that piano-accordion, do you remember? I bet Ken doesn't save, either."

"No, he spends royally. Just as if he lived in Acacia Avenue." Ann was over-defensive.

"My dear girl, we don't spend much."

"Ken has the funny idea that money is for spending."

"I'm sorry for you, Ann, really. To think you might be buying a house." Sybil's eyes were looking restlessly around.

"There aren't many houses—"

"You can get a licence to build. We're going to—"

With my share of the money, thought Ann. And aloud: "You don't have to be sorry for me, Sybil. We might get a council-house."

"Oh, Ann. To think a sister of mine will live in a council-house—"

"Well, you won't have to visit us, will you?"

Sybil gave her an odd look. "I feel I should visit you from time to time," she said. "To keep an eye on you, perhaps advise you about money and so on."

She walked away and Ann slammed the door.

*

William said to them, "Look, I'm on my own, I know you two want a home, why don't you come and live with me? Maybe I won't be here long, and when I'm gone you'd have the house. Talk it over, I'm fond of both of you, I think we'd get on well enough."

There was little to talk over. A furnished place of their own, while at Meg's the best they could hope for was a council-house and paying rent for life. And council-house tenants were still regarded as the lowest stratum of society. Ann knew she didn't really want that, her mother's influence was too strong. She still loved Ken's family, but life in such overcrowded conditions was not much fun, and Webster tempers were short. She said, tentatively: "I suppose it would take years to save a deposit for a new house."

"Years and years."

"Perhaps we should have saved the boat money."

He turned to look at her. "Oh no," he said. "I've had no money all my life, I'm not scratting every penny now. And I'm not keeping David short, either."

His voice was sharp, but Ann persisted. "I don't think you want to leave Marley Road, Ken."

"I don't. I like it here. Anyway, I'd like to help Uncle William, he was always good to me."

But what about me? Ann asked soundlessly. She said, "I'll be able to have a baby now."

They moved in. William asked them if they'd like him to give them the front bedroom, but Ken said no, it was time David had a room of his own, he and Ann could have the back, Marta's old room. Downstairs, the kitchen was the same as it had always been, black cooking grate with kettle on the hob, plain table with its cloth, horsehair sofa, chiming clock on the wall. Marta, a lovely sixteen, smiled down perpetually from the mantelpiece.

Ken lifted David to look at the photograph. "Your mamma," he said.

"No," contradicted William. "Ann's his mother now, it's no use confusing the child. Let him call her Aunt." But David never did, he called her Marta.

"If you agree, Uncle Will," Ken said, "I'll have some alterations done as soon as I can."

"What were you thinking of?" William asked, cautiously.

"Well." Ken looked round. "There's the bomb damage to be repaired to start with. But what I'd like to do is get new grates put in, have electric fires."

Electric fires. Ann was amazed.

"And an electric cooker. You'd like that, Ann."

"Wouldn't I!"

"And in time an electric washing-machine." Ann did have a washing-machine now, it had been her mother's, kindly donated by Sybil; hand-operated, it was still easier than the old dolly and tub days. But electric . . .

She thought of her childhood, always dominated by housework. Her mother fighting a lifelong battle against dirt, Monday, washing-day, come rain or shine the washing must be out on the line at six o'clock or you were a slut, the rising before five, lighting the fire under the copper, humping in the dolly-tub, dollying, boiling whites in the copper, the great iron mangle. And the sheer misery if it rained . . . Tuesday, ironing with the flatirons on the fire, the difficulty in not getting coal-dust on those starched whites; Wednesday, cleaning the front room with brush and shovel, sweeping the pavement and yard, and washing it; Thursday, all rugs taken downstairs and out on the line; Friday, black-leading the grates; Saturday, shopping; Sunday, cooking for the week. And every day scrubbing the red-tiled floors, lighting fires, emptying slops . . . for the first time Ann wondered if her mother had really liked doing all that work, or hated it underneath but been afraid to say so, for no woman ever admitted to not liking housework then, now attitudes were changing, but would their home have been happier without the sheer backbreaking burden of *keeping clean*? She marvelled at the changes Ken would bring about, and thought he must love her. "It'll be like a palace," she whispered.

"Perhaps in time we'll get a refrigerator," Ken said. "Then you won't have to keep running to the shops every day in hot weather, or have to mess about standing the milk in cold water, and covering meat to keep flies away."

He picked David up and went into the garden. "I'll do a bit of weeding," he called.

"He's a good lad," said William.

"You don't – hold it against him because of Marta?"

The old man sighed. "No. What's done is done. But I think Liz did."

"They would have got married, you know, Marta didn't tell you because she thought you didn't agree with cousins marrying."

"No more I do. And I never thought of them two being together, Ken had always been with us. But it seems hard that such a lovely gel had to die. It don't do to have only one child, when you lose that you've got nothing. You want to have some of your own, Ann."

"I do want to," Ann murmured.

"Well, there's plenty of time," William said, comfortably.

They settled in. Ken helped William in the garden, making a small lawn where the Anderson shelter had been, but the roses still stayed in pride of place. He bought his boat, and worked on it in the evenings, then painted it, naming it *The Rose of Sharon*. Sometimes Ann and David went with him and he'd talk to Ann about work and unions, but not much. "You women don't understand," he said. "All you're interested in is knitting patterns and the rubbish in those soppy magazines you read."

"I worked in a factory when I first left school, and we had a union there," Ann retorted. "The first sign of trouble all the women would march down to the boss's office and get it put right. How do you think the hosiery factories got such good pay? We were nearly all women, and we got our union while you men were still dreaming about it."

And he laughed then, and tickled David, child of his love. Back at the house his face went sombre as he glanced at the laughing picture hanging over the mantelpiece. Why hadn't his family been notified that he was a prisoner? She'd have lived then, knowing he'd come back. If only he hadn't escaped, maybe that was the reason, the bloody Jerries would think he was dead, or not care, anyway. He remembered that last weekend, with Marta in Bates's barn . . . He hadn't been so careful then, had gone a little mad, knowing he'd soon be away. Guilt gnawed at him, and because the guilt was unacceptable he switched his thoughts to David, who was to be living proof that Marta had not died in vain. David, who was to inherit the earth. So Ken turned to the new world, born with David, for David, for consolation and justification. Both must succeed.

And the new world was coming along. Grammar schools for the academic types, technical schools for the engineers, secondary moderns for the rest. Equal opportunity. A wonderful health service, free. No slump, people getting good wages; overnight it seemed dirt disappeared from Marley

Road and children became clean, with shining faces and fancy clothes. There were still shortages, clothes, furniture, food, people still queued, shopkeepers stood with a take it or leave it air . . . but it was all grand.

The new world really came home to him when they asked for a rise. Ken went with the other stewards to confab with the management, still expecting them to say, "Get out, no work here, we don't want you." But the firm had orders and needed workers desperately, and the workers were, for the first time in their lives, in a position of power. So as Ken looked at the men before him the power surged within him and he asked for more than he'd intended. This for the poverty I knew, this for the humiliation, and this above all, this for Marta, and because of Marta, for David.

The newspapers hoped that, after the comradeship of the war, the workers were not going to get too greedy.

*

In the summer of 1948 Chris married Joe O'Brien. The family were against the marriage, they felt an Irish labourer was not good enough for their daughter, nor did Ken find anything odd in this sentiment, Marley Road had always been subdivided into factions far more rigid than anything in Acacia Avenue. To clannish Marley Road the Irish were forever the ones who came over in the nineteenth century and blacklegged their jobs. The bridegroom's family remained in Ireland, with no wish to meet an English Protestant family. To them the Websters were the rich English who had ground them down centuries ago.

Chris was four months pregnant and although Meg told her she could stay at home, Chris refused, to her mother's surprise, for if anyone believed in attacking conformity it was Chris. Meg could only conclude she was 'fond of' her lover, and stared in some amazement at the hefty talkative man, a drinker, and quarrelsome with it, already known to the police for brawling. Joe's voice, when talking to women, might hold a caressing note, but Meg was too old a bird to be taken in by Joe's soft words, she'd had her share of those in her time. As he was a Catholic, and Chris refused to be converted, the mixed-marriage ceremony was short, the Websters giving them a reception in their home, for much as the family might disapprove of the marriage this was no excuse for not having a good 'do'. Ken and Ann were naturally invited, so, with William and David, they crossed the yard.

The house was full of Websters, so the family ate in the kitchen, in relays, and Ann helped Doreen and Meg wash the dishes. She took David to bed soon afterwards, William went too, saying he'd baby-sit, and the family went into the front room, bringing chairs from the kitchen, overflowing on to the floor. Ann drank more than she normally did, and when they started a singsong she joined in, sleepy with the warmth and the wine. 'Roll Out the Barrel' . . . 'Bless 'em All.'

Someone said, "Ken, have you still got that piano-accordion," and he answered, "Yes, where is it, Mam?"

"In the glory-hole—", the cupboard under the stairs, and after some search he found it, put the strap round his shoulder, and began to play. The light was turned off and couples sat, arms linked, in the firelight. First one then another would ask for a popular sentimental tune of the past, each bringing some poignant memory. "Play 'South of the Border'," said Doreen. "That reminds me of my wedding night." "Which one?" asked a wag.

There was silence as Tom stood up to sing alone, and his fine tenor voice rang out. "'I have loved you for your beauty, but not for that alone'" . . . and Ann was moved. The requests died away, they all sat half asleep in the firelight, the muted sound of a late bus dwindled into a memory. Ken began to play softly the love songs of the war and the room faded away, it was the dance-hall again, he and Marta dancing. 'All the loveliness I have longed for . . .' Where was that loveliness now? . . . Beads of sweat stood on his forehead, slivers of pain seared through him . . . 'only you . . .'

A knock came at the door and Johnny answered it. "Someone for you, Ken," he said.

Ken put the accordion down, went to the door, the songs went on behind him. He blinked in the dark, and said: "Sybil? Do you want Ann?"

"No. I went to your house, William was in bed. I've brought the fifty pounds."

"Well, come in."

"I don't want to go in there. Let's take it to your house."

He followed her, and in the kitchen she handed him the money silently. He took it just as silently, but she still stood.

"I wanted to see you," she said. "Just you. Alone."

He didn't ask what for.

She moved towards him, pressing her body to his, parting her legs, unbuttoning her blouse, pulling him to the sofa. "I've wanted you for a long time," she said.

He took her carelessly, without pleasure. And when he had finished he left her and went back to the party.

*

It was the following afternoon that Ann found Sybil's handbag. "Whatever is this doing here?" she asked.

"Oh, she came round last night," Ken said.

"Sybil – came round here?"

"Yes. Seems Uncle Will was in bed and she sat waiting for us. When we didn't come she called at Mam's."

"So that's where you went. I thought it was some union man. What did she want?"

"She brought the fifty pounds."

"But why didn't you call me?"

"What for? You were enjoying yourself."

Ann picked up the bag. "Well, I'm not taking her bag back. She's never once asked me to visit her. I'll drop her a line. Ken—"

"Yes?"

"I reckon she fancies you."

He laughed. "Don't worry. If I'm going to run off with another woman, it won't be Sybil."

"It hadn't better be," Ann said. "I'd never forgive you for that."

*

Christmas preparations were marred by the news that Chris's baby had been born with a twisted foot. Doctors talked about operations, but were dubious when asked if the child's leg would ever be normal.

"Nothing goes right for our Chris," said Ken.

"But they can do marvellous things now. Why, they're talking about curing TB. This penicillin they've discovered from a mould." Ann tried to be optimistic, for her own sake as much as anyone's. If things went right for Chris, then maybe they'd go right for her too, she'd get the baby she wanted, and Ken might say 'I love you', as they did in all the magazines.

"My mother used to cure us with mouldy bread," said William. "Allis put it on cuts till the doctors stopped it. Said it was an old wives' tale."

"Penicillin won't help Chris's baby," said Ken.

Ann stood up to clear the table, glancing at Marta's photograph as she did so. Just a few more years and she might have been cured. The unspoken thought hung heavy in the air.

"Was that a knock at the front door?" asked William.

"It's Sybil," said Ann, peeping through the window. "It would be, at the front door, everybody else comes to the back. Wonder what she wants, she hasn't been for months. Not since Chris's wedding. Oh, I know, she's come for her bag."

"I'm going in the garden," said Ken.

"No, it's raining, and you know David always follows you. Anyway, what can you do in the garden this time of the year?" Ann opened the front door and Sybil sailed in.

"Hallo, all of you. I thought I'd call for my bag, Ann. I wondered if you might bring it back."

"Not me," said Ann, shortly. "I've never been asked to your house and I'm not one to go where I'm not invited."

"Well, I'm inviting you now, both of you, to a christening party." There was veiled triumph in Sybil's voice.

"Whose christening?" asked Ann, startled.

"Well, whose do you think? I'm four months pregnant, so the event should be about April. Don't look so surprised, Ann." Sybil addressed herself to her sister, but she was looking at Ken.

Ann muttered something that sounded like a congratulation.

"It will be rather nice," Sybil said complacently, "We do need an heir, after all. But how about you, Ann? When are you going to start a family?"

"I don't know."

"Perhaps there's something wrong. I mean, it can't be Ken, can it?"

There was a heavy silence. Ann flushed. William looked disapproving. "It is," Ken said, sharply, "our own business, Sybil."

97

"Oh, yes—" airily. "Far be it for me to rush in where angels fear to tread. I just wondered if you wanted my advice, Ann. I was talking to Mrs Grantham this morning at the Bring and Buy sale at church – we go to St Margaret's now, of course. Mrs Grantham is the wife of one of the medical officers and she was saying how much can be done these days—"

Ann gave her sister a black look. Sybil had, at one bound, jumped from being the Girl who was Too Good for Marley Road to the Woman of Importance, the Lady Bountiful who descended to the lower regions bearing gifts – except, Ann thought sourly, Sybil doesn't give anything away but advice. She wondered if her sister was really on such intimate terms with the doctor's wife as her words implied. It was possible. Sybil had been ambitious, had determined to get on in the world, and what use was getting on if no one noticed? That was why she came to see her, Ann decided, to show off, and glanced up to see Sybil throwing a challenging look at Ken, who sat with David on his knee.

"Such a lovely child, and a real daddy's boy," Sybil said, smoothly. "I hope my baby turns out just like him."

"Maybe he'll take after your father-in-law," said Ken. "Driving around in his grand car, the old rogue."

"I know people are envious of his owning a Daimler—"

"In Briarford, only mayors and corpses ride round in Daimlers. Not that there's much difference between the two." Ken looked angry and Ann couldn't understand why.

"Those of us who are better off feel we have a responsibility towards the less fortunate," said Sybil, loftily.

"Funny bloody way of showing it," said Ken, red-faced.

Ann was bewildered. There were undercurrents in the room, Ken and Sybil were saying something entirely different from their spoken words and Ann was uneasy. Sybil intercepted her look. "I'm proud of my position, proud of going to St Margaret's. If you went to church more often—"

"You've got more need to go than me."

Sybil stood up. "I didn't come here to be insulted."

"You didn't have to come here at all. At any time."

"Ken," said Ann in some alarm, for the two were staring at each other with hostility. Sybil was breathing hard. She turned. "I must dash. We're going to the theatre tonight, in Birmingham."

"I used to like plays," said William, peace-making. "Saw 'em all when they came to Briarford."

"I'm talking about culture," said Sybil distantly.

"Is that what they call it now?" asked William.

Ann saw Sybil to the door. "I shall still send you the christening invitation," she said, forgivingly. "I expect Ken's angry because I'm having a baby and you're not, Ann."

Ann returned to the kitchen with heightened colour. "What was all that about?" She turned on her husband.

"All what?"

"You were so nasty to her, really insulting."

"She gets my goat," muttered Ken.

"She puts years on me," agreed William. "But you shouldn't talk like that about religion, Ken."

"Sorry, Uncle Will," Ken said. "Sybil just riles me."

"But why—?" asked Ann. "You've never been like that before."

The atmosphere was tense. Ken swallowed. "She ought to have been a sergeant in the army," he said.

"In charge of you," Ann laughed, good humour restored. "What was the army like? You never talk about the war."

"I enjoyed it."

"What? Being a prisoner?"

"Wasn't bad. Anyway, I wasn't there all that long."

"You escaped, I know."

"Oh, I didn't dig a tunnel or climb over barbed-wire fences. I was sent out in working parties, so when there was a bad air-raid two of us got away in the commotion. We hid in an old building till some Yanks found us."

"You are funny."

"I know. The only thing I regret is that I couldn't take one of those courses."

"What courses?"

"Educational. To go and be a teacher or something. There's a shortage of teachers."

"You never told me." Ann was hurt.

"No." But it had been there once, the hope and the promise. Coming home from bloody Germany, on the train from London, he'd been excited. Teacher training course. It wasn't quite university, but it was *learning*. And then they'd be together for always, he and Marta, maybe move away if she wanted . . . perhaps she could come and live with him on the course . . . And then the home-coming, the asking about her . . . and suddenly there was a nothingness, a blackness that enveloped him and choked him and which he'd never lost. Some of the blackness still remained somewhere in his head . . . The news of the baby, her baby, his son, so much like her, and he knew that something was salvaged after all. And his son would have to be cared for . . . And Ann offered herself, and he took her in the cemetery, in the *cemetery* for God's sake . . . but he saw it was the only way. Aunt Liz was too old, and she didn't want David, the only alternative was to have him brought up in his own crowded home, straggling after the other kids, and Doreen's kids . . . He'd always been a bit ashamed of his shabby home, had always been glad to get to Aunt Liz's, clean, with tablecloths on the table . . . there'd been so much shame in his childhood, shame that his dad drank, that he was on the dole, that he talked too much and too loudly . . . the girls were shamed too, for other reasons, Chris, for wearing cast-off clothes, for telling the teacher they hadn't enough money to go on the school outing . . . the time Mam found nits in her hair and scrubbed it and covered it with vinegar . . . Johnny wearing his, Ken's, cast-offs, going to school in pants too big . . . the kids shouting 'Johnny long-britches', and this from ragged-arsed kids no better . . . Johnny fighting his way out of it . . . Oh no, there'd be none of that for David. So he accepted Ann's offer, as he saw it, gratefully, he'd always be grateful to Ann. He didn't really want any more kids – she was so set on it, but one more would be enough . . .

Ann was looking at him, and he said, "Well, how could I? I couldn't get married and then say, 'Well, I'm off for a year or two, leaving you with the baby', could I?"

"I don't know. If it was what you wanted." *You might have asked what I wanted . . .*

"Ann, talk sense. There was no way."

"But it's a bit off, isn't it? If it hadn't been for David you might have been a teacher now."

"If it hadn't been for Ken," said William, "there wouldn't have been any David."

Ken laughed and lifted the child high in the air. "That's true," he said. "Come to bed, Daddy's boy."

The Fifties

Since the ending of the war little of the outer world troubled Marley Road. Throughout the Fifties a few events came to their knowledge: the war in Korea, Suez; for the rest they were as inward-looking a society as they had been a hundred years ago. Coventry rebuilt its city, with a new modern cathedral.

The Tories came back in 1951 'to set the people free', and were fortunate to reap in the improvement of external balance of payments, what the socialists had sown. They built smaller council-houses called People's Houses, and the April budget revealed that price rises would not be compensated by higher wages, while the social services would be cut to help pay for rearmament. Supermarkets began to come to the High Streets. King George died and was sincerely mourned. Teddy Boys and rock'n'roll arrived and the younger generation was bitterly attacked by bishops and others. There was still plenty of work, only half a million were jobless in 1959. Japan's industry boomed and they kept on investing. Britain was spending proportionally less on education than in 1939, while other countries, even the less prosperous ones, spent more, thus making her one of the worst educated nations in Europe.

Chapter Three

Ann put on David's new cap and blazer, took his hand, waved goodbye to William and left the house. It was his first day at school; Ken had made such a fuss you'd never believe, going round telling the authorities that he intended to send his boy where he, Ken, wanted, no matter what they said. And after all he needn't have bothered, his old school – the nearest – had satisfied him. Ann was surprised he hadn't taken a day off work to accompany David himself.

He trotted beside her, without any trace of shyness or fear. And as she left him at the school gate and made her way to the doctor's surgery she told herself she must have a baby of her own. A little girl, perhaps, Ken would love a daughter, surely, all men did . . .

What happened to dreams? she wondered. Get married, live happily ever after. And you never thought about the after. You had your man now, but he wasn't quite the same as the one who'd whispered, "Don't leave me, Ann." Now he was back to normal, work in the week, home and David, playing with David on Saturdays, in the boat on Sundays . . .

Oh, there was nothing wrong, Ken was kind and considerate, generous with money. But if only she could have a child of her own, his child. Children. Boys and girls. A picture of Meg came to her, surrounded by her family, and she saw herself with sons and daughters, the matriarch, belonging. And she knew the longing came from some deep need within her, a longing to love and be loved.

But Chris's baby's foot hadn't been put right, she recollected as she joined the queue outside the doctor's waiting-room. There had been an operation and the foot had been straightened, but he would still have a limp for life. Poor little Tommy. Sybil's baby had been a healthy little girl, why did Sybil always get what she wanted? Perhaps because she had a convenient gift for looking after Sybil. It had been murder getting Ken to go to the christening party, but Ann had wanted to see the new house. Detached, plain, modern flat windows, stark and bare among the fussy bays and imitation Tudor relics of the Thirties. And the furniture wasn't utility.

The queue shuffled in and she sat on a hard chair in the dark waiting-room. Talk swirled around her. "Which doctor is it today, the old 'un or the young 'un?"

"If it's the old 'un you won't be long. Starts writing the prescription as soon as you open the door—"

Ann's turn came and she went in the surgery. It was the young doctor and he asked her to sit down, quite polite.

"We've had the results of the tests," he told her. "And I'm sorry, it isn't good news. You see, the tubes are blocked ... you had appendicitis once, I believe, maybe that had something to do with it ... I don't really feel there is anything that can be done."

"You mean I can't ever have a baby?"

"It seems very unlikely." The doctor thought fleetingly of the patients who had too many, the girls who got in trouble, and sighed. He was very young.

Ann left the surgery in a daze. Shoppers thronged round her, the sun shone, birds sang, she walked alone, apart. *This can't be true. Why me? Why . . . ?* She went home. Prepared dinner for William, down to school to fetch David. Did you like school? Yes, Mam. Come on, then, time for dinner.

Back to school. *It seems very unlikely* . . . Doctors can be wrong, can't they? But the pain inside her knew . . . Home again, washing up, William in his chair, asleep. Round to Meg's. Meg was alone.

"Rose-Mary's leaving home," said Meg. "Going to live with her chap's family. Doesn't say much about the wedding, I don't think she wanted to invite us all . . ."

Belonging. Why do I even care?

"I've been to the doctor's," she said. "He told me I can't have any children."

Meg left the table and sat in her rocking-chair. "Are you upset?"

"Yes. I wanted a baby."

Meg rocked to and fro.

"You see, David isn't mine. I love him as if he were but—" Again the memory of the past, Ken and Marta, now Ken and Marta's boy. Herself in the background, as always. Starkly Ann unravelled from her tangled thoughts the knowledge that Ken had loved Marta, always loved her, and still did. And David was Marta's child. She was still there.

Why was life like this? They loved and she died. Ann's tidy soul yearned for life in neat packages where everyone met the right mate and there were happy endings as in the romances.

"I think I'm jealous," she said.

"Oh, Ann, you always seemed so level-headed. You mean you're jealous that Ken thinks so much of David? It's natural, you know."

But they both knew that Ken's love for David amounted almost to an obsession.

Ann rose abruptly, and Meg watched her, troubled.

She fetched David home for tea. "Did you like school?"

"Yes. Can I go tomorrow?"

She smiled. "You can. What did you do?"

"We played with toys. And the teacher read us a story. I told her I could read."

"Show-off."

"Hey, Uncle William, I've been to school—"

She gave William his meal, ate her own, prepared Ken's dinner, for he seldom ate in the canteen. Wasn't so good as home cooking, he said.

He came in, and again David talked about school, Ken ate his dinner, then there was an hour of revelry.

"At least," Ken said to Ann, when David's bedtime came, "he's accepted school quite normally."

Yes, it's just me that's not normal. And you forgot to ask about it, Ken.

"Do you want a bath?" she asked. "I'll put the copper on."

She poured water in the copper, ten bucketsful, lit the fire underneath, took up the rugs, hauled in the bath from outside. Waited. Sybil wanted to move, she said, she fancied one of those new chalet-type bungalows now. Imagine being able to move whenever you wanted.

The water began to steam and Ann ladled it into the bath, poured in buckets of cold, fetched David and bathed him. Then she took him, rosy and chubby, to bed, while Ken took his turn in the bath.

Goodnight, David, sleep well. Sybil's father-in-law was dead now, Peter owned the business; Sybil had had her baby in a private nursing home. Goodnight, David. Ann emptied the bath, raked out the fire under the copper, took the ashes to the dustbin, hung out the bath, cleaned the floor, started to prepare supper. Ken was reading to David.

He came down. "Well, I'm glad he's settled in school all right," he said. "He didn't cry or anything?"

"No."

"Well, he wouldn't. He's a real lad." He looked at her. "You're quiet. Anything up?"

"I went to the doctor today. He says I can't have any children."

"Oh. Oh, I'm sorry. I forgot in the excitement . . . You don't feel bad about it, do you?"

"Well, you know I did want . . ."

"Yes, I know. Never mind. We'll go for a nice holiday on the boat in August, shall we?"

She smiled tremulously, and went to David's room. She straightened the covers, brushed back his hair from his face tenderly. "It looks," she said to his sleeping form, as if you're the only baby I'm ever going to have. So love me, David. Don't ever leave me."

*

"Hallo, my little sprig o' mint," said Ken, coming in from work. "Been to school?"

"Yes, Dad. O' course."

"You're a big lad now, right enough."

"Are we going out tonight, Dad?"

"Hey, wait a minute, I don't know yet." Ken sat at the table, and as Ann put the meal before him, he let David clamber on to his knee.

"Let your Dad have his dinner first, David," said Ann, a little sharply.

"He's OK," said Ken, easily. "Oh, all right, do as your mam says, run in the yard till I've finished."

He ran, and Ken watched him, smiling.

Since David's birth his life had changed; he lived for and through his son. He did not fully realise this; he went to the factory by day, worked in the garden evenings, sailed his boat. But his life now held another dimension. It was as if he had life over again where all wrongs could be righted.

David was a popular child. He was a 'real rogue', a 'proper lad'. William loved him, as did his Webster grandparents. Strong, fearless and unafraid, a child of love, David was to inherit the earth.

A knock came at the front door and Ken left his meal unfinished and made a dive for the back. "Come on, David," he said. "We're going on the boat."

"Are we?"

Ken took his hand and pulled him through the entry, chuckling to himself as he looked down. He was proud to walk with this fine sturdy son, it was good to see his mates and explain: "This is my lad," and listen to: "Oh, ah? Chip off the old block, all right", "You couldn't deny him if you tried", and other pleasantries.

They entered the field. "Dad. There's Aunt Sybil's car. She's come to see us."

"Why, so she has."

"Don't you like Aunt Sybil, Dad? You always go out when she comes."

"I suddenly remembered I've got to see your Uncle Johnny, see their new council-house, 'People's House's they call 'em."

"And Carolyn—"

"Carolyn's just a little girl."

"But you're her uncle, Dad. Don't you like her, either?"

"I don't know much about her."

They jumped aboard. "Friday today," he told David. "You needn't go to bed quite so early tonight." David must be brought up right, no sitting up half the night as he had done when his parents were out and Doreen had been left in charge and had slipped off, gallivanting.

Ken didn't altogether go along with the new cult of the experts who were saying that children should never be smacked. The new world seemed to have pushed up a lot of new ideas and Ken didn't approve of the half of them. Liberalism had never been his creed. His son could have everything he asked for, but the final word must be from him, Ken.

He sat idly for a moment, lighting a cigarette, watching the green light filter through the trees to the water, seeing the occasional plop of a fish, swallows skimming the surface. "Flying low," he said. "It's going to rain."

David peered over the side. "Look, Dad, a water-rat."

"Yes, keep still, we might see that kingfisher." So they would sit for hours in dreamlike peace.

"Tell me about when you were a lad, when you used to play here with Marta."

"I should think you know that off by heart."

"Tell me."

"You know," Ken said, carefully, "Marta was your mother."

"Yes, you told me before. But my mother's here."

"I know, but— Oh never mind."

"We haven't told her we're going, Dad. Shall I run and tell her?"

"Yes, I suppose so. Mind how you cross the road."

David ran and Ken, brooding, looked into the canal. Those nights in the fields, and in Bates's barn, those nights when Marta had flung herself to him in abandon, meeting and matching his love. Well, he'd always known she would, hadn't he? He'd always loved her, always, since she was a skinny little kid.

"Why did you keep away from me so long?" he'd asked.

"I dunno. I think girls always feel like that at first, you know, Ken, when they meet someone they really want, they run away."

"Yes, but for such a long time . . ."

She laughed. "I thought you'd come after me. You couldn't expect *me* to come to you."

"I thought you didn't want me."

"Ah, you always had it too easy, didn't you, Ken? Listen, I want to tell you this now. I don't know how much this love-making means to a fellow, I mean, whether one girl's different from another. But I want you to know that you – you changed everything for me, you know? The whole world. You read all this stuff about love and you laugh, and then, with you, it was as though I'd been travelling through the universe for centuries you know, just for this."

He'd wanted to kneel before her then.

He couldn't believe she was dead. He never went to the cemetery after that first time. She wasn't there, she was here, all around him, running in the fields, dancing, loving. And in David.

David trotted back. "I told her," he said.

"All right. Come aboard, then. Off we go." Ken loosed the mooring-rope, started the engine and chugged away in a swirl of waters.

"Tell me about the fairs, Dad, when you were little."

"Oh, they were big and grand, steam engines and organs playing. Aunt Liz used to take Marta and me round all the big fairs when they came, it was the only holiday we had. Nottingham Goose Fair, Stratford Mop, Lichfield Bower. And our own, held every May, always had a fair here since the fifteenth century. Not any longer. We saw the end of it."

"Why didn't you have any money when you were little, Dad?"

"Cos there was no work, and nobody had any money. Not round here, anyway. And I couldn't go to the grammar school, but you will. To King Alfred."

"Will I?"

"If you work hard, you're a clever lad. Then you'll go to the university and do some wonderful job and never be out of work."

"Will you be out of work, Dad?"

"I don't think so. Not now. They promised us. Look at that blackbird, David. Chasing all the other blackbirds away from that piece of bread. And while he's doing that the starlings come in a group and eat his bread."

"Silly old blackbird."

"We're here now. Come on, help me moor her. That's it. Now off we go, up the slope to the road. This way. By God, what a lot of houses. They look like barracks," and he began to whistle 'Lili Marlene'. "'By the barrack gate . . .'"

They walked along the road. The new council-houses were not semi-detached as the first ones had been, but in blocks of eight or ten, with cramped backs and tiny gardens encircled by two strings of wire. Ken looked for No. 17, where the door stood in a tiny porch with the dustbin inside. He knocked, and Johnny's wife, Doris, invited him in. They walked into the front room where Johnny and Chris sat. A baby cried in a pram.

"Hi, John. Chris."

"Anybody else coming?" asked Johnny. "If so, open the other door and let 'em walk straight out again. Only room for six in here."

"Well, it's a house," said Doris. "Maybe in time we'll be able to save enough to buy one."

"Not if you keep having kids you won't," Chris retorted. "They're talking about building high-rise flats now. Spreading up in the air. I wouldn't like that."

"Well, you won't be asked your opinion," said Johnny.

"Hallo, David," Chris smiled. "Come and sit by me."

"Is Tommy here?" asked David.

"No, he's in home with his dad." Chris had also been allotted one of the new council-houses.

"Has he started school yet?" Ken wanted to know.

"No." A frown furrowed Chris's brow. "When I married Joe I had to sign a paper saying I'd bring the children up

Catholics. But their school's too far away, not quite three miles, so he couldn't go free, and I can't afford the bus fares. And he can't walk very well. They say it's not such a good school, either."

"I wouldn't send David to a poor school," Ken put in. "He's bright, he's going to King Alfred."

"If it's still there," Johnny put in. "They're changing education, the technical school's gone, and nobody wants to go to secondary moderns."

"Things are changing, Ken," Chris said. "Prescription charges put on, paying for teeth and glasses."

"Oh, well, we all know enough free teeth have been given away," Johnny replied. "And people have been sitting in doctors' crummy surgeries for hours just for fun to get bits of cotton-wool. Nice way to pass the time. They're thinking of putting a dart-board in and a bar."

"America insisted we pay 'em for the war," Chris said. "Either the last war or the next, or both. Wars have to be paid for. That's what you men forget when you go gaily marching off."

"I didn't go gaily," Johnny said. "I were called up. Press-ganged."

"Our Peggy's emigrating to Australia, did you know?" asked Chris. "And Rose-Mary's thinking about it. Their husbands are both skilled men, they'll be welcomed there."

"You ought to go, Ken," Johnny advised. "They're more democratic out there, so I've heard." He looked down at David, listening wide-eyed. "Hey, little 'un, what do you make of all this, eh? Wondering what sort of world you're going to grow up in?"

"David'll be all right," said Ken.

He walked to the window, looking at the sunset. It was impossible to see the sun from the Marley Road window. *If I went abroad what about David? They say education is good out there, but David is marked for King Alfred and Oxford. Making an entirely new life, could I do that ... forget everything here?* He looked at the sun, a great ball, pinky-red, hanging in the sky like a big lantern, and knew a sudden delight. *She'd* have loved to see that. She had taught him to see the wonders of the world. She had given him so much. With her he'd been stronger, more confident, he had felt capable of discovering the secrets of the universe. And her presence was here. He knew he could not leave or something would be taken from him.

Chris moved to the door. "I'll have to go, I've left Tommy. And Joe'll want his dinner."

She departed. "Her husband don't treat her right," said Johnny. "He don't like her going to the Labour Party meetings, there's a row every time she goes out. I'd go round and punch his nose if she gave the word, but she won't have it."

"You're a bloodthirsty young devil, our kid," said Ken.

He took David and they went back to the boat. Boys ran along the towpath, a dog barked, a light shone in the black water. Ken stared at the shimmering reflection, lights moving and dancing to a pattern, all separate, yet all interdependent, a little vision of perfection. A boy carelessly threw a stone at its centre and the vision died.

Chapter Four

"It's like a palace," said Meg, entering Ann's home. "A carpet in the kitchen, no more floors to scrub, suppose you'll call it the living-room now. New tiled grate, no more black-leading, and a dining-table, why, you won't even have to scrub this... And the front room..." They stood in awe before the carpeted floor, the three-piece suite. "Have you got carpets in the *bedrooms*?" Meg asked in disbelief.

"Yes, Mam," said Chris. "Just run over them with a vacuum cleaner, no lino to wash."

"See the bathroom," said Ann.

The shiny white bath stood with glistening taps in the partitioned bedroom. To the side was a wash-basin, opposite a lavatory. "I'm thirty-four," said Ann. "And for the first time in my life I can enjoy having a bath." She turned on the tap. "Hot water," she marvelled. "It's like a miracle."

"And an upstairs lav," said Chris. "No more slops to empty."

"But come and see the kitchen," Ann cried, shaken out of her usual calm. "That's the – the—"

"*Pièce de resistance*?" asked Chris.

They stared. A new sink in place of the old yellow one, the copper taken out, an electric cooker. "But look," and they touched the shining square box in the centre, half reverently, half in fear, as primitive peoples gazed on magic.

"Lord God of Washerwomen," said Chris.

"My goodness," said Meg. "I wish I'd had one of these when I had my family at home. I could've taken in everybody's washing then."

"Labour saving," said Chris, thoughtfully. "I bet if this was an invention in a factory, like the steam engine, they'd be calling it a revolutionary wonder. But because it only saves women's labour nobody'll bother, I suppose."

"And the refrigerator. My, my, Ann, you won't have any work to do at all," said Meg.

"Now, don't take that tone, Mam," said Chris. "It's time something was done for women. I know you were brought up to the idea that all your life consisted of getting meals and scrubbing and washing and keeping the men happy, and you lapped it all up, your generation. Women not only kept themselves in chains, they polished them up as well. Things are changing now."

"They certainly are," and they went back to the living-room and sat down with William. "We were just saying how different things are today," repeated Meg, for William was getting deaf.

"Aye, and it was worse in my mother's day. Women had it rough in them days."

"And were dead at forty," said Chris, caustically.

"Well, there weren't much to live for before you had the pension," said William. "Mind you, I think sometimes, here I've been scratting all my life to keep this house on, for my old age, and nowadays they can spend it all and have money given 'em."

"Now, Uncle William—" began Chris, but her mother nudged her to silence.

"Are Peggy and Rose-Mary really going to Australia?" Ann asked Meg.

"Yes, they're determined. Think they'll do better there." Meg sighed. "I wish it wasn't so far away."

"Cheer up, Mam, you'll be able to go there for your holidays," said Chris.

"What? To Australia? I've never been farther than Blackpool."

Ann went into the kitchen to make a cup of tea, and Chris followed her. "I must hand it to our Ken, he's done a lot for you," she said. "Must have cost a fortune, all this."

"Well, we've no rent to pay, and it adds to the value of the property."

"You might as well have bought another house."

Ann busied herself with the teapot. "I don't think Ken wants to move."

"Hm." Chris wandered round the kitchen restlessly. "At least he seems to have settled down. Doesn't he want to go dancing now?"

"No." Briefly the shadow of Marta was with them. Ann knew Ken would never want to dance with anyone else.

"You should get him to take you out."

"Oh, he does." Ann was silent, thinking of the day in Birmingham. It had been Ken's idea, and they went, for once, without David. He'd done whatever she wanted, walked round the shops, not the little cheap emporiums, but the big swanky stores, where your feet sank into the deep-piled carpets, so you felt you were in another, luxurious world. They had looked at all the lovely things, fabrics, glass, porcelain, and in the cosmetics department he'd bought her a small, but expensive, bottle of scent. Then they'd gone to the kitchen-ware, and he'd inspected the washing machines and said: "Would you like one?" And he'd ordered one then and there, and a fridge, and carpets, with the salesman talking to them as if they were important, even when they said they wanted instalments, so that she felt like a queen. It had been a lovely day. And when the house had all been modernised, and everything installed, she'd crept down in the night and walked around, touching each shining fitment with awe and delight. And then she'd turned and Ken was there, watching her, and his face held a look she'd never seen before, a sort of wry tenderness.

She saw Chris gazing at her quizzically and said, apologetically, "I expect I just like simple things." Washing blowing on the line on a fine day, the wind billowing the sheets against the blue sky; David's face, soaped and shining when he was ready for bed; sitting by the fire with Ken, the curtains drawn to shut out the world. "I'm not clever like you," she ended.

"No," said Chris, harshly. "Nor so damned complicated as the Websters are. Do you know I go to Labour Party meetings just to upset Joe?"

"Why does that upset him?" asked Ann, astonished.

"He'd like me to stay in home and have lots of kids. Church, kitchen, children, that's Joe. And I won't."

"Oh, Chris," said Ann, troubled.

"Oh, Ann," Chris mocked. "You think I should accept my lord and master's way of life? No birth control? Your politics shall be my politics? Down with the proletariat? We're the proletariat."

"I'm not—" Ann began, piqued. She never saw herself as a member of the proletariat.

"You are, you know. While you're married to Ken and live in Marley Road. Anyway, I don't think birth control's a sin. I don't want to have a life like my mam, too many kids and not enough money, just because the men were too selfish—" She stopped, horrified. "Ann, I forgot . . . that you can't—"

"It's all right," said Ann, her momentary hostility vanishing in a wave of pity. She wanted to say she wished Chris was happier in her marriage, for it was common knowledge now that Joe drank a lot, came home and beat her up. But she dared not express her sympathy, there was a touch-me-not quality about Chris that forbade intimacy. But Chris seemed in an expansive mood. She said, "Joe doesn't like it because I'm cleverer than he is."

"Well, that's natural, I suppose."

"Why? Where is there any law saying that a man must be superior to his wife?" And Ann could not answer, except to think that it was a sort of pretence that had to be kept up. So why couldn't Chris do it the accepted way?

Chris said. "So as Joe can't beat me into submission he has to bring the big guns of other man-made laws into play."

"You mean the Church?" asked Ann, shocked again.

"Of course. You think the priests have a hot line to God?"

Ann did think that Church laws were somehow inspired by God and said so.

"How can that be when all religions are different?" Chris asked, reasonably. "Though most of 'em keep women submissive. I think I'll go in for witchcraft."

"Witchcraft?" asked Ann, faintly.

"They have a goddess in charge. No wonder they were persecuted," Chris laughed.

Ann blinked, out of her depth, and Chris said, thoughtfully, "I suppose you can't blame our men altogether. They're kept down too. Headmasters, bosses, the whole system. Then they take it out on us, or just carry it on."

Ann put the teapot and cups on a tray. Chris said, "Ann," hesitantly, and as she looked up, "You don't go to the club with Ken, do you?"

"No."

"You ought to, you know."

"Why?" Ann was astonished; working men always went to the club on their own, or at least they used to. She didn't like the club, and preferred staying in home with David.

Chris closed the door. "My mam did, you know, that's why she started going out with my dad. Said that if he was going to spend money he might as well spend it on her."

"You mean," Ann began, as the full meaning hit her, "instead of other women?"

"Look," Chris said, "hate me if you like for an interfering busybody. But better me than—"

"Has there been any talk?" Ann asked, expressionlessly.

"Just a bit. Only that he was talking to Nancy Bell. You know—"

"Yes." She knew Nancy Bell, who went to the club on her own, who was married, but one man wasn't enough for her, Marley Road said, though her husband seemed to think the world of her.

"Don't worry about it," said Chris. "But don't forget, either. Men like our Ken don't change. It don't mean anything to 'em, you know." She laughed. "I wish my old man'd find himself another woman and run away." She opened the door to the living-room.

*

The canal glittered with tiny gold motes, covering the shadows. In the shadows lurked ghosts of long-dead people who had lived in the area: Shakespeare, Cromwell's army, Bishop Latimer, who had been burned at the stake as a heretic. Ken had discovered local history in the public library and he sought out the doings of rebels and dissidents, surprised and pleased that he found this information so much like that knowledge passed on by word of mouth through generations, so different from his school teachings. All of it he passed on to David. "Cobbett," he said. "Wrote a book about farm labourers. Said they lived worse than pigs, worse than the Negro slaves in America. He came here once."

"What for?" asked David.

"He was going to Coventry, candidate for the election. They were very bad times then for farm labourers, especially in the south, don't think we were so servile here, having other work—"

Ann said, sharply, "What's the use of telling him all that? All the bad things."

"But it's true."

"Yes, but what's the use of starting him off like this?"

"Like what? I don't know what you mean."

"Like you. Like all the Websters. David's going to have a different life, isn't he?"

"So?"

"So he'll be different. He should be brought up to think different. Like my mother brought up Sybil."

"Bloody hell. Sybil! You do talk daft, Ann."

"If he's going to be a boss, then he's got to think like a boss."

"Rubbish."

"I know." Ann's voice had an edge to it. "It won't matter what I say, will it?"

"Now what do you mean?"

"About David. I can't have any say in his upbringing. And don't tell me he's not mine. I know that."

"I wasn't going to. But he's a boy, he needs a father. Anyway, this is a good place to stop. Come on, David." And he steered the boat alongside the towpath.

Ann was submissive about the annual holiday on the boat. Pressed, she would have said she preferred a boarding-house, where she didn't have to prepare meals, but Ken and David loved the boat so much she would not have dreamed of protesting. But today she was troubled.

She dropped a pebble in the water, the gold disappeared in the shadows, her thoughts swirled with the disturbed water. *I envy Sybil her daughter, I'd have loved a little girl.*

And Carolyn's a nice child, likes to visit us. I suggested we bring her on the boat, was amazed at the vehemence of Ken's refusal. I know he dislikes Sybil, but the child's not to blame.

It would have been better for Ken to have had more children, better for David. To concentrate on one child, depend on one child, was dangerous. But Ken's like that with everything, into it heart and soul. Then if anything goes wrong, he really goes off the deep end, he really suffers. Why can't he take things calmly?

The Websters have such strong personalities they overwhelm me. Why hadn't I noticed it as a child when I wanted so much to belong? Now I'm one of them, but do I belong?

Why can't they be quiet and ordinary, like everyone else? Why do they have to rebel? Take Chris . . .

Chris, like Marta, had a knack of saying something you'd never thought of, yet you realised how right it was. A woman took the status of her husband. I am Mrs Ken Webster of Marley Road. What does your husband do? He's a factory worker. And I'm his wife, no status of my own. I'll never be anything else. The only way for a woman to get on is to be educated or to marry. I'm not clever, so there's nothing else for me. Funny, I'd never thought of all this before. Only of love and belonging.

Ken moored the boat, and together he and David ran into the nearby field. Ann watched thoughtfully. *Funny . . . the first seeds of discontent had been sown.*

She opened her bag and took out the booklet Chris had given her, poring over it as if it might divulge the secrets of the Websters.

She looked up. *I worry too much. David's a normal happy little boy, bringing friends home, running over the yard, dirty faces, muddy caps, Mam can we have some food? Me supplying his wants, worrying when Ken goes into his black moods but contented on the whole even if I do have the feeling sometimes that he holds something back ... He doesn't go with other women, does he? ... He still makes love to me, though it's somehow matter of fact ... maybe it always is ...*

I worry too much. These are the happiest years. David playing on the deck, shouting, "Mam, Mam, I've caught a fish", playing cricket in the fields, laughing, getting into mischief ... this is how it will always be ... won't it? David growing older, going to the grammar school, Ken happy then ... David isn't spoilt, Ken doesn't pander to him in any way. But in any family of three one has to be left out, the remaining two fighting for possession.

I worry too much. Trouble is, I've got too much time to think now. Now I've got the labour-saving house, I'm even thinking about politics. Maybe I should find a job.

There is a lot of talk now about women working, as if it were a new thing. Not that everyone approves, long letters in newspapers about latchkey children ... Doreen's gone back to Hobson's ... it would be nice to have money of my own ...

A shadow fell on the deck and Ken flopped down beside her.

"Dad!" called David. "Another game."

"No more. I'm finished. You play on your own."

David ran round the field. "What are you reading?" Ken asked Ann.

"Chris gave it to me."

"Trying to reform you, eh?"

"I feel sorry for Chris," Ann said in a low voice. "She seems so hurt."

"I tell you what's wrong with our Chris. She needs a man."

"My goodness," cried Ann. "As if she hasn't got enough with the one she's got."

"I mean, a different one."

"Trouble with men," said Ann, "they think that's the answer to everything."

"Well, isn't it?" Ken asked, wickedly.

"Seems to me," said Ann, slowly, "that the happiest women are those like Doreen who put themselves and their jobs first, their husbands second and their children last." And that's true, she thought in the ensuing silence. Not for the first time she wondered how Ken and Marta's passion would have stood up to marriage. But it never would be put to the test, Marta would always remain secure in death.

Ken said, "What's the matter with you today? You seem grumpy."

Ann looked over the field, David was throwing his ball, shouting. "What about Nancy Bell?" she asked.

"Nancy Bell? What's she got to do with anything?"

"There's talk. About you and her. At the club."

Ken was amazed. "I've never . . . oh, yes, I bought her a drink once. Jesus, the way they gossip round here."

"Because you always used to go with women. Like your dad."

Ken felt that was below the belt and his face reddened with anger. "I tell you I've never been out with Nancy Bell."

"Then what have you got to buy her drinks for?" Ann's voice was raised.

"Hush. David's coming back. Hi, David, come and sit down. Now, what's this book say? *If the Industrial Revolution had come centuries earlier it is likely that factories would have been built by some co-operative enterprise.*" His face was still flushed and David stared.

"Co-operative," said Ann, as if it were very important. "Well, that's what you believe in, isn't it? Co-operation?" She was sarcastic.

"Co-operation, co-operation," shouted David.

The air was heavy and still. The three sat immobile as if playing the childish game of statues with only David chanting 'co-operation' in a meaningless way. Years later the word was to reappear in Ann's mind, but she forgot the still afternoon and the figures in the boat.

*

Doreen was born lucky. She accepted life with equanimity, and even her mother did not quite realise that her so-called luck was helped by her favoured position – eldest daughter, father's pet, teacher's delight – and her truly lovely face. She could have taken her pick of a number of swains, but chose a miner, though, once the war was over, had persuaded Jack to move to a factory; she had no intention of being a handmaiden to a shift-worker, getting dinner at half-past three when on days, early and late when on nights. Doreen wanted to work too. She liked the companionship of the factory and the fat pay-packet it gave her. She and Jack had exchanged their steel house for one of the brick semis built between the first prefabs and the People's Houses. She made no secret of the fact that, given the chance, she would buy her house.

On the third Sunday in July, Doreen asked the family round to say goodbye to their two sisters, who were emigrating, and to celebrate her youngest son Alan passing the eleven-plus. It was a sunny day, with a hint of thunder in the air, when the sisters and brothers, their wives and children, Meg and Tom, gathered in Doreen's living-room.

Ann loved all the family gatherings; this, she assumed, was something more than a casual dropping in, something less than a party. They talked, admired the cleverness of the scholarship winner, and sat down to a meal, with cold meat and pies, and a plate of cream cakes. "When I was a kid," Doreen explained, "we never had cake, or at best a bit of home-made. I used to long for 'bought cake', and as soon as I started work I got a couple of cream cakes every Friday—"

"Greedy pig, we never saw them," interposed Ken.

"Now I buy them every day," finished Doreen.

"No wonder you're so fat," and Doreen slapped her brother's ear, playfully.

After tea they went into the front room and the reminiscences started. "Do you remember, Doreen, when you took us all on the top of a bus – they were open double-deckers then – and you hadn't got enough to pay the fares so we all hid under the seats? And when we got off Marta fell down the stairs and the conductor chased us all down the street?"

"Do you remember when Mam and Dad used to go out Saturday nights and Marta came round once when we'd let the fire go out? She started drawing it up with newspaper and nearly set the house on fire?" asked Johnny, and Ann was annoyed at the continual references to Marta, she had been there too that night. She reflected that in all these years the family had never told their parents that Doreen used to go out and leave them with Marta and Ken, and then realised that this, in fact, was what Johnny was saying now. *Do you remember when you went gadding off, Doreen, and left us?* A double meaning, one for them, another for outsiders. Now, depressed, she felt that she too was one of the outsiders, that she would never penetrate the deepest cave. She was not one of them.

She saw Ken move restlessly, yet was surprised when he said: "How about if us chaps go for a drink?"

"Nobody goes for a drink without me," said Doreen.

"Just a little celebration," wheedled Johnny, but Doreen gave a quick glance towards Joe O'Brien, and he was silent. If Joe went he'd get drunk and there'd be trouble for Chris and trouble in this house, which Doreen didn't intend to have. Chris sat silent, passive.

Ken said, "Well, I'm going," and again Ann was surprised, and wondered if their recent quarrel had upset him. Johnny rose to go too, but Ken pushed him aside. "I'll bring a bottle or two back, that won't make much difference to anybody."

Outside Ken drew a breath. Why did they have to keep talking about her? He could think about her, but he couldn't talk, not ever. And the pain never lessened. He could forget for a time, and then it was back, and with it the bitterness and the blackness . . . He thought of Ann's accusations about Nancy Bell. Well, it was true he'd always had plenty of women, he liked women. But then Marta came to him, with her wilful loveliness, her abandon, and he hadn't wanted anyone else, she satisfied him, body and soul. Now she was gone, but the ache remained, and more dangerous, the thoughts of a waste of a life, when he wanted revenge, to hurt, even to kill. He wondered if any other men had these thoughts, kept tightly under control . . .

A car pulled up beside him. "Hallo, Ken," said a voice.

He stopped. "Sybil."

"The very same. Want to come for a drink?"

He stared at her glassily. "Why not?" he asked, and she drove to a nearby pub where he bought drinks and they sat in a corner.

"What are you doing here, slumming?" he asked.

She laughed. "Why have you been avoiding me, Ken?"

"I haven't."

"Oh yes you have. I've seen you slipping out when I call. And I know why."

"Do you?"

"Yes. You are attracted to me."

He didn't deny it.

"And there is Carolyn. Your daughter."

"Don't talk rubbish."

"She is yours, Ken, I swear."

"Oh, come on. Just five minutes when Chris was married—"

"Which you enjoyed."

"I was drunk."

"Not as drunk as all that." She was smiling, and he noticed how well dressed she was, a warm loose coat over a dark wine dress, her black hair swinging round her face. But his gaze lingered on her shapely legs.

"How do you know it isn't your husband's?" he asked.

"He's useless," she said, and he thought, Like Nancy Bell's. No one knew for sure who her several kids belonged to. Nobody bothered. But Jesus, Ann's sister. This was playing with fire.

"We can go to my house," she said.

"But your husband – the child—"

"They are with Peter's parents for the weekend; I don't go, can't stand them."

Little hammers were banging inside his head. "Come on, then," he said. "But you'll have to drive me back to Doreen's."

They left the pub together.

*

Sybil had no thought for any code of manners, formidable or otherwise, apart from her own. She barged into Ann's whenever she felt like it, never waiting to be asked, taking no account that Ken might be eating his dinner, which was very bad form. Nothing was ever said, but Ann thought that was why Ken went out when she arrived. Now, as a knock came at the front door and he stayed put, Ann was more surprised than ever.

Sybil came into the living-room with her daughter, a pale, silent child. "Hallo, all," she said, beaming.

"Sit down," Ann bade her. "I wasn't expecting you today."

"I thought I'd bring Carolyn to see her uncle and aunt. And David, of course, he is her – cousin." Sybil hesitated, as if working out the relationship.

Ken said: "Go and say hello to your cousin, David."

David stood up. "Why do you wear those funny clothes?" he asked.

"That is her uniform," said Sybil. "Carolyn goes to Miss Glimp's Academy for Young Ladies."

Ken gave a yelp of laughter. "Miss Glimp's what?"

"I decided to send her there for I found she was picking up the local accent," said Sybil, much as if she were picking up fleas.

"Oh, quite," mimicked Ken. Sybil's ladylike airs did not infuriate him, as they did Ann; he tried to goad her on to further efforts. So Ann hastened to intervene.

"How do you like my house now?" she put in, quickly, thinking they were about to quarrel.

"Yes, I see you've had some alterations done." Sybil didn't move. "Quite nice. We're looking for a new house."

"Another?"

"Well, I've been wanting a chalet bungalow for some time. And we've had to make some decisions recently. The business is going to merge with Slatter's, you know, the big department store chain."

"You mean they're buying you out," said Ken.

"It seems the new trend, big chain stores; they say the American idea of supermarkets is coming here. Peter will be manager of the shop, of course. We'll still have to do a certain amount of entertaining."

"I know where there's something for sale." Ken had a wicked glint in his eye.

"What? Where?"

"My aunt's cottage in Caldwell. Let it go for a hundred pounds, she says."

Sybil blinked, unsure, and Ann said, "He's pulling your leg, Sybil. It's that tumbledown cottage by the chapel."

"No one will ever want an old cottage," said Sybil, with certainty. "And in a village too. Seven miles to Briarford, no, no, Ken, she'll have to have it pulled down. Talking about travel, will you come and have a look at my car? The engine makes an odd noise."

"I don't know much about cars."

"But you understand machinery. Do come. Yes, Carolyn, we must be away. Say goodbye to David. We'll come again soon."

She rose, and Ken followed her unwillingly, David running at the rear. "Wait for me, Dad, wait for me."

Sybil opened the car door and put Carolyn inside. "You too," she said to David. "While I talk to your father."

She slammed the door and raised the bonnet.

"What's all this in aid of?" Ken asked.

"When are you coming to see me again?"

"I can't keep coming to your house—"

"It's been three months, Ken."

He bent over the engine and inspected the spark-plugs.

"I'll tell her, Ken, I swear it. I'll tell her Carolyn is yours."

"You know I don't believe that." He bent over the engine again. "Why should I have to make up for your husband's inadequacy?"

"Why not? Aren't you doing the same thing? Haven't men always done it? Why shouldn't women? My sort of women, I mean. It's the one thing I envy working-class women for, they've always had sex where they found it. All those women who took in lodgers and had children by them . . ."

He said nothing.

"You've always been out with women, Ken. If it wasn't me it would be someone else. Ann won't satisfy you. And I can give you a good time, as they say in films."

He looked at her and she said, "You'll come."

He slammed the bonnet down, lifted David out of the car and watched her drive away. But he didn't go straight in home, he took David across the field to the canal. Bloody Sybil. How had he got himself into this? He, who was going to be such a model father? Of course, he could call her bluff, for if she told Ann her husband would have to know. But he knew that wouldn't matter, in any battle Sybil would come out on top, she had a way of bulldozing her way over every obstacle, which included people.

Anyway, did it matter? There had always been scandals in Marley Road, whispers and noddings at this woman and that man who sought compensation from the eternal grief of things outside marriage. There'd been a good many whispers about his dad.

Bloody Sybil. Then he grinned. The woman tempted me. And he'd go to her again. She intrigued him. In his eyes she acted like a tart, and he treated her like one; in his black moods he avoided Ann, but he could go to Sybil, he used her as she used him. And she could be good fun in an outrageous sort of way, he even enjoyed quarrelling with her and did not sense the lurking danger. What did it matter, he shrugged, as long as David didn't find out.

He took David's hand and led him back to the house.

Chapter Five

William died, as he had lived, peacefully in his sleep, giving no trouble. Ann and Ken discussed the funeral arrangements. "Do you think I should ask Sybil?" Ann said.

"God, no. There'll be all the Websters and the Phillips from Caldwell, including Aunt Nell—"

"Is she still alive?"

"Yes. Still in her cottage, can't get rid of it."

They went through the list of relations carefully, knowing how many family feuds were caused by leaving out some nephew or cousin. "I don't *want* to ask Sybil," Ann said. "But I don't want her to turn up unexpected, either."

Sybil, however, took matters into her own hands. The following afternoon Ann heard a car draw up, peeped through the drawn curtains, to see, to her astonishment, little Carolyn getting out of a taxi and staggering up the path with an enormous wreath.

"Good gracious me," Ann said, opening the door. "Whatever is your mother thinking of, sending you like this?"

"Oh, I don't mind," Carolyn whispered. "I like coming here."

"Have you got time for a cup of tea, or is the taxi waiting?"

"It's waiting, I'd better go."

"Just have a biscuit." Ann studied the child. "Why do you like coming here, haven't you many friends in your area?"

"Oh, yes. But I like you, Aunt Ann. And David."

"Well, now." Ann was touched. "You can come any time, you know that. When you're older—"

"Yes, Aunt, thank you. I'll have to go now. Goodbye."

There was a note with the wreath. 'Sorry cannot get to the funeral. Sybil.'

"I feel sorry for that child," Ann said to Ken in the evening. "Sybil used to frighten me to death when we were children."

"You're not frightened of her now."

"Course not. She just annoys me when she comes bouncing in here like Lady Muck. Still, I suppose it's not her fault altogether, it's the way she was brought up. Always Mother's little angel, couldn't do anything wrong. I can't help worrying about Carolyn."

Ken walked across the room and put his arm around her, kissing her cheek. "You're a nice girl," he said.

"Why, go on." She wriggled away, "Girl, indeed. I'm getting on for forty." But her face flushed with pleasure.

William's body was laid beside his wife and daughter on a rainy day in February. As the mourners stood around the grave Ken studied the words on the marble cross. 'In memory of Martha Rose, beloved daughter of William and Elizabeth Phillips, who died April 20th 1945, aged 24 years. *Until the day break . . .*'

The rain swirled over the grave, into the faces of the mourners, on to the coffin. Ken could feel her body beneath his in Bates's barn, her fingers tugging his hair . . . Ashes to ashes, dust to dust . . .

I am the Rose of Sharon.

He choked, turning away from the grave.

*

Acacia Avenue was definitely on the right side of the tracks. There were no council-houses in the area, no gasworks or industries with smoking chimneys. Ken always thought there seemed more light and air in the Avenue, even the sky seemed bluer.

Sybil took off her robe and let the shoulder straps of her slip fall, and sat, naked to the waist. It was a habit of hers. Her breasts were full and heavy, her legs exciting. Her bold eyes flashed. "Have you come to see your daughter?" she asked.

"Where is she, in bed?"

"Of course. And Peter's out. Nice of you to come, darling."

He watched her moodily.

"And without being asked."

"Without you threatening to tell Ann, you mean."

Sybil laughed.

"If you did tell her, I'd kill you."

"Oh, my, we are in a mood, aren't we? But I don't mind your tempers, sometimes it makes it better."

"I can't help wondering why it's me you want."

"It's your working-class virility, darling. You know, as in Lady Chatterley's lover."

"Is it? Or—? Why not one of your cronies up here?"

"What? And everybody knowing?"

"Oh, I forgot. Your lot come down our way for their pleasures."

She shrugged, "You were saying *Or*—?"

"Or is it because I'm Ann's husband."

Sybil said nothing, but let her slip fall completely to the floor. Now she was naked. She was, Ken thought, the type of woman that other women could not understand what men saw in them, and would have been shocked if he knew how the factory women explained her appeal.

"Since when have you cared about Ann?" she asked. "It

wasn't Ann you wanted when you were young, it wasn't Ann you had a flaming affair with, leaving her with a child—"

"Ann is my wife."

"Don't be so sanctimonious, Ken. You really are conservative."

"What have you got against Ann?" he asked. "You always bullied her—"

"Because I can't stand anyone submissive. All right, I bully them. I have a ruthless streak. So have you. You married Ann to give David a mother. You'd sacrifice anyone for David."

"Don't push it, Sybil," he warned. "I'm very fond of Ann."

"But love, Ken. Do you love her?"

"What do you know about love?" he asked, harshly. "You should have been on the game."

"Do you know, I think sometimes I'd like that."

He turned away and she followed him, putting her arms around him, pressing her body to his. "Maybe I love you," she said.

"You don't. You want to beat me into submission, like Ann. But you never will."

He turned his head, and for a moment they stared at each other, hostility in each pair of eyes. Then her hands found their target and were rubbing gently. "Come on, darling," she said. "Come and forget what's troubling you."

He followed her into the bedroom.

*

"Going out tonight, Dad?"

"Yes, there's a union meeting."

"What are unions?"

"Unions are people, that's all. A community affair."

"What's community?"

"Men working together for good."

"Like the Salvation Army?"

"Like an army of some sort. We had to fight every inch of the way for better conditions. Men were transported, put in jail, shot. Without the unions we'd still be working long hours in unsafe factories, little boys in pits. You must be proud, David, to belong to these people. Your heritage."

"But you don't like the factory, Dad?"

"No. But in a way I feel I can do some good. Both sides now, we've got a chance. I've always worked hard since the war, don't believe in slacking or wasting time. I'm a good worker and like to see things peaceful."

"Can we have a car soon, Dad?"

Ken smiled. "Soon. And I bet you don't know half of what I've been talking about, do you? Bet they don't learn you that at school."

"All we do at school is intelligence tests."

"Let me see." He studied the books in some bewilderment. "What rubbish," he muttered.

"Why don't you leave him alone?" asked Ann.

"What do you mean?"

"You want him to go to the grammar school. To get there he's got to pass the eleven-plus. These are the tests they do, so he's got to practise them."

"You just want him to be a stupid little goody-goody."

"I want him to do as he's told, yes. And if you want him to get on, that's what he'll have to do."

Ken put on his coat. "We're always arguing about David, and we shouldn't. All right, I'll say no more about the silly tests." He grinned, placating. "I think I might get a second-hand car, Ann. You'd like that, wouldn't you?"

Just fancy, he thought, as he walked down the road. The Websters owning cars. The affluent society. Yippee.

*

Ken loved his work as shop-steward, which entailed far more than the actual meetings. There was always some poor devil who felt he hadn't been treated right, who needed someone to speak for him, or just advice. They brought their domestic problems too, making him feel like a social worker. Getting actual pay rises, the only thing noticed by the media, was a small part of the job, but it was there. On March 1st they put in for an increase, the firm said no, the union insisted, again the firm said no. There was talk of strike action, the firm presented a new offer. The union called a meeting after work.

"Look," said Bill Sanders, Chief Convenor, "we've studied the new offer. It looks good on the surface, but it means we change the whole system of payments, and if you work it all out, we'll be worse off, not better."

There were angry shouts.

"We can't do a good job with this new conveyor-belt," one man said. "You can't catch every one that passes you, have to miss some, that's why there's so many faults."

"We'll strike—"

"They can pay clever lawyers to fight for 'em, don't forget, we just have to use our wits—"

"They want to get rid of unions, then they could push us back down again—"

"I agree with all that," said Bill Sanders, soberly. "But this way you're just playing into their hands. There aren't many orders. Having the firm shut down for a few weeks without pay is just what they want."

Ken said, "Don't let's go back to the days of fighting all the time. Let's at least try for some sort of compromise—"

"We've been doing that for weeks—"

"But just one more try—"

Ken was shouted down. The vote was taken, and a strike was called.

*

"I think I'll look for a job," said Ann. "David needs new clothes. I can do it now William's gone."

She went to the Moonlight and came back defeated. "It's all different now," she told Ken. "There's a great new department called Personnel. What's Personnel? We never had that before."

"God knows. The foreman always used to set us on."

"Well, I had to fill in this great form, four pages of it. When I was born, started school, qualifications, experience—"

"You don't have to go to work just because I'm on strike."

"I've been thinking about it for some time. Anyway, we can always do with some extra money, especially if David gets to the grammar school!"

"If? His teacher says he's a cert. Always top of the class, a bright, intelligent boy, he says."

"You're always pestering the teachers."

"What do you mean, pestering? I'm entitled to know, aren't I? Nothing's going to stand in David's way. Have you told him you want to go to work?"

"Not yet. Why?"

"I just don't want to upset him now. He's doing the eleven-plus in a few months."

"I don't see that'll make any difference to him. He'll get home from school before us, but he can go to your mam's when you start again. Anyway, I've not got a job yet."

"Here he is now, with about five hundred kids from school. Looks as though he hasn't got a care in the world."

"Hi, Mam," said David. "Got anything to eat? I'm starving."

Ann, smiling, brought out a cake, and the room was filled with munching boys, dirty knees and rubbed jerseys, grinning comments about teachers, laughter . . .

"Mam, I want to play football in the field, Mam, can I?"

"Change your trousers then first, David."

"Oh, Mam—"

"Come on. I think I'm going to work soon."

"Good. We'll have some more money." And David, followed by friends, ran to the field.

*

The strike dragged on and was reported in the media, but somehow it sounded quite different. The management said the men didn't want to strike but had been forced out by the militant elements in the union. One or two of the men were interviewed and said they wanted to go back to work. "Where the hell did they find *them*?" asked Ken. No mention was made of the full reasons for the strike.

The shop-stewards met the management again, but were told there would be no further offer. A meeting was called, Ken reported to the men. "I told you it was no use at the start," he said. They voted to return at the old rate, and went back.

The next week the six union stewards, Ken among them, were given notice, but this was not reported in the media.

Another meeting was called. Ken went with mixed feelings, proud that the men he'd fought for were showing solidarity, warmth at their support, and worry that they'd be out again. The men shuffled in, less than a quarter of the number who had been at the previous meetings.

A red-haired Irishman rose to his feet. "It's victimisation," he shouted. "We ought to strike again."

There was half-hearted agreement.

"It's not right," another man said. "But bloody hell, we're short of money now."

The men shuffled, coughed, looked away.

Ken rose to his feet. "It *is* victimisation," he said. "But there's no need for you to suffer. Don't strike for us."

"Save your breath," Bill Sanders muttered, as he sat down. "They don't intend to."

*

"What's the matter, Dad? Are you worrying cos you've lost your job?"

"Am I hell? They can stuff their job."

"But you'll get another one?"

"Course I shall. Only next time'll be different. I worked hard for this firm, was loyal, tried to help . . . people . . . Shows you what it's worth. Come on, loose the rope, let's get going."

Ken nosed the boat out to the middle of the canal, blinking, for the sun was in his eyes. Shoals of tiny tiddlers darted away at their approach, and a great green frog watched them from the side. It was late spring, and the May-blossoms dropped petals into the water. Larks rose from the fields surrounding the canal; the scene was pastoral. He reached a stopping place beside the trees and moored the boat. Friday, they were here for the weekend.

"She needs painting," he said, critically.

"I was reading a book about canal boats, Dad, they say this rudder-post – how tall it is—"

"The ram's head."

"Some say they were patterned on the old Viking ships."

"Could be. The Vikings were all around here, over most of Britain, except perhaps the south. I like the Vikings, I think people talk too much about burning and pillaging; all warriors do that, even today. I should know."

"I like their old gods, Thor and the others."

"And the way they used to die. Put the body on his ship, set it alight, float it out to sea. Yes, I like that," said Ken. "What a way to go."

The sun dropped lower, the water became flame, the sky a mass of red-tipped cloud. Swifts screamed on their last flight, the May petals dropped like snow.

Ken prepared a meal and they ate almost in silence, listening to the occasional plop of the water. Blackbirds gave their last urgent calls and settled to sleep.

David asked, "Are you sad, Dad?"

"Well, I admit I never expected this would happen again. I mean, after the war I thought things were going to be different . . . I kept my side of the bargain." His eyes were bleak. What happened to the truce? To both sides working together? Bosses reverting to type didn't surprise him, but that his mates should let him down . . .

"Couldn't the union have done something?" David asked.

"No."

"Then they're not very powerful, are they?"

Ken didn't answer. Then – "Anyway, David, now you know why I want you to go to the grammar school. Work hard, get out. It's the eleven-plus in a few weeks—" *And I couldn't afford any trouble, to have my name in the papers, not now.* "Go to bed," he said, aloud. "Get some sleep. Goodnight."

David slept, but Ken lay awake. Great owls hooted, the trees swished like small seas in the rising wind. He dozed fitfully and woke just before dawn, dressed and went to the side of the boat, lifting his head to the carols from the trees. A shaft of light pierced the sky far away, tremulously, as if in fear, then lengthened, and the world was full of the half light of dawn. It was cold; he shivered as the birds began to fly in their never-ending search for food. Ken went below. "I saw the morning break." *But it always gets dark again.*

Ann stirred in her sleep. I wish Ken could have taken that teacher training course, she thought. We'd be out of it then. Ken didn't tell me how he felt about all this, he never talks to me . . . Now he's on the dole. I must find a job.

David went to sit his eleven-plus without showing much fear. Ken watched him march down the road and had a fleeting memory of himself marching into battle, the moment of truth, when they'd been ordered to advance and there was no way out. He'd known he was alone, quite alone, there might be death ahead but no going back. He wondered if women ever knew that moment of truth; when giving birth perhaps? Had Marta felt that she was being forced to a summit she had to achieve alone, facing pain, maybe death . . .? The moment was forgotten later, if one survived, there were joyous reunions with comrades and pals: "We went there, we were together . . ." shutting out the moment of terror.

And David was going to his moment, this morning, aged eleven. This morning would decide David's future, the whole of his life, maybe his, Ken's future, too, and Ann's . . .

Ken mooched around the house, got in Ann's way until her even temper snapped and she irritably told him to get out from under her feet. He went and sat in the boat for hours, until he saw David returning. With a supreme effort of control he waited ten minutes then casually strolled into the house.

"Hi, David, How did you get on?"

"All right. It was easy. All the tests we practised at school."

"Good. I knew you could do it."

And then the long wait.

*

"I've found a job," Ann told Ken. "At Brett's."

Ken pulled a face. "That's not much of a place. And it'll be a long way to go, other side of Coventry. Still, there's a good little train service."

"I know all that, but I couldn't get anything else. I haven't been working for years, that's what they all say. Then they want to know if I have any children – and when I say yes they find some excuse to turn me down."

"Say you haven't, then," said Ken.

"Oh, I couldn't." Ann was shocked. "Anyway, I'm to start Monday in the typing pool. I don't know what a typing pool is, seems lots of things are different now."

Ann wasn't sure that a typing pool was an improvement on the old system, where one girl had typed for the several men who sat at her table. Now the girls were bunched together, though at separate desks. But she was drawn back into the different life-style she remembered in the Moonlight offices, and felt ashamed of Marley Road. She thought Brett's wasn't run as efficiently as the Moonlight had been, there seemed so many managers, all changed round every month or so; she hardly knew who her boss was at any given time. She wasn't always sure where her office was either, the firm built, rebuilt and pulled down regularly, and the hapless staff were shuttled around like nine-pins. "I think it comes off tax," said Ken.

When he told her he'd been turned down by two firms Ann worried more than ever. "Come to Brett's," she said, but his face was impassive. If only, she pondered, I knew what he was thinking.

*

I was over the moon when I read the letter. 'Dear Mr and Mrs Webster. We are pleased to inform you that your son, David, has gained a place at King Alfred Grammar School . . .' I'd been on thorns for weeks . . .

So I did two things. I rushed out and got a job at Brett's, for I knew they'd take anybody, though I didn't say that to Ann. I'd been wondering about going to this new Technical College they'd built, getting myself some qualifications, City and Guilds, I could have worked up then. But it would have been difficult, at my age, to get time off work. So I couldn't afford it now, not with David going to King Alfred, so got this semi-skilled job at Brett's, dead boring. Then I took Ann and David out to celebrate his success, dinner at the Grand, Briarford's best hotel. Had to laugh at Ann's face when she read the menu. "Chips?" she asked. "Here?" "What do you want, caviare?" I asked. "My mother wouldn't let us eat chips," Ann said. "Said they were common." "Then have potatoes," I told her. "And wine, what wine shall we have, waiter? It's a celebration, let's have champagne." "I've never drunk champagne in my life," said Ann. "Then start," I advised her. "This is the beginning of David's career."

We received another letter inviting us to the school so the Headmaster could meet the parents, and I went, as chuffed as if I were a new boy myself. Seemed a bit pompous, Mr Tripp. Our sons were the cream of Briarford's children, he told us, as if we'd somehow adopted them from some better land. They would have to work hard, no days off, no trips to Blackpool, ha, ha. He talked of endeavour and loyalty and I understood him again. Playing the game, and I wondered irreverently if my bosses had been to schools like this cos if they had we didn't play the same game.

Before we left I asked the Head why David had been put into a B-form. "Because of the lower marks," said he, distantly, and I wanted to ask where the marks were, but Ann pulled me away.

I was puzzled, all the same. Way it's worked now, kids who pass with the highest marks cannot be refused the school of their choice, no interview. David didn't have an interview, so why the B-form? Everybody's fighting for grammar school places now, and folks chuntering that at the interview kids get picked out as before, all Acacia Avenue seem to get to King Alfred while the others go to the new school, or the comprehensive. So I shouldn't grumble, David's there, don't suppose the B-form makes much difference. But I'd have liked to see the marks.

We bought the new uniform, cost us a packet, good job I'm in work now, even though Brett's don't pay much. Never seen such a dump in my life, I could run the place better with my eyes shut. David'll start at King Alfred in September, so we must have a holiday first on the boat . . .

*

"And this year," Ken said, "we're going to Oxford."

"Why?" asked David.

"Because you'll remember it someday. In another few years you'll look back on this holiday as a foretaste of the future. You'll see."

*

They sailed along the Coventry canal, past the grimy backs of factories which had once had coal delivered by boat.

Into the more pastoral Oxford canal, Ken pointing out the old inns where the boaties used to stable their horses overnight. They worked their way through many locks and Ken was happy.

It was the quiet he loved, listening at night to faint cheeps from water-birds and the hooting of owls. Dawn and the fields, not full of wild-flowers as in his childhood, but still blessedly green. He loved England then.

They moored, and went into Oxford. "I've always wanted to come here," Ken said. "I've read so much about it. City of dreaming spires, they call it. Maybe you'll be here one day, David."

"I can't see any spires," said David. "There's just a lot of traffic, worse than Briarford."

"Yes, well, they must be somewhere around. I wonder where the colleges are? What's this . . .? All Souls." He peered through the opening at the green square. "What's this notice say? 'The Quad and Chapel are open to visitors, the rest is private.'"

"Is this the Quad?"

"I suppose so."

"What are the little buildings round it?"

"I – suppose people live there." Ken walked around, puzzled.

"Come on, Dad. Let's go."

They walked into a quieter road. "What's that place with the dome?" Ken asked.

"Where all the people are sitting on the grass? Perhaps it's a restaurant. I'm hungry, Dad."

"We can get through here, look. The Bodleian Library. Look, David, all these old manuscripts." He studied each one, shuffling around with the crowd, full of wonder. It would be nice to study in a place like this, alone with the classical past. A man could get lost in here, lost to the real world.

They came out, blinking, into the sunshine. "All these Latin inscriptions," said Ken, awed.

"Why are they in Latin?"

"Because that was, well, the language of learning."

"But nobody speaks Latin now."

"Well, it's tradition."

"Seems silly to me," said David. "Why don't they speak English?"

Ken looked at his son uneasily as they went back to the boat.

The Sixties

The Swinging Sixties arrived, the decade of Harold Macmillan and Harold Wilson, the Beatles, the Rolling Stones, student protests and Fanny Hill. *There were Mods and Rockers, long hair and drugs, pornography and Vietnam. To Marley Road there was just more work or less work. Experts talked of the decline of Britain and said it was all the fault of the working classes. Mrs Pandit's High Commissioner in London said that Britain had a caste system far more rigid than India's. Colleges of education were expanded, universities were built. The number in sixth forms remained virtually unchanged, only one-third of the children being drawn from manual workers' homes.*

The Sixties for the Websters was the time when they moved into the places on the chessboard from which the final tragedy became inevitable.

Chapter Six

Ann at forty was plumper, her fair hair fading to grey. She had reached the age when women wondered why they'd married their particular man and why they married at all. Girlhood's dreams of romance seemed, in retrospect, to be as remote as fairy tales in childhood, and as silly. Women with children loved them and cared for them and wondered why they'd ever desired them. Ann, never quite satisfied in love or motherhood, still felt some of youth's longings; she looked serene but there was a sadness in her eyes, a Rachel weeping for the children she'd never had. She consoled herself with the thought that Ken was a good husband, her insecurity was bolstered with the belief that he was faithful.

Ken was thinner, still handsome, wearing the look of a man who had received a number of body blows but was still fighting, because this was what he had always been used to doing, he would always defy the world to do its worst, and the world was always ready to oblige. Within him, two lines of thought ran competitively, like good and evil, each striving for mastery. He talked, but his deepest thoughts were pushed down where he chose not to reach them. He did not consciously deceive, his practice of double-think was pretty much the same as that of any other adult. Once he had come back from Germany to find a nothingness, a pit that he filled with David and the new world. Now, despising those who compromised, he admitted that with David at college, all would yet be right with the new world. Without that, a dark shadow would rise and thrust him into a deeper emptiness that he vaguely knew would be dangerous.

On blue summer mornings he left the house at 6.30 to take the country road to work, driving slowly past the big pool where the waterlilies drowsed, through the old red sandstone rocks into the belt of trees, a dark-green temple with the sun designing mottled patchworks on the grass. On to the factory, through the big gates and the vigilant eyes of the works police, the notices saying you could be searched; past the smart front glassy offices and the managers' car park, on to the long grey road to the back car park. Then the walk back, past the long flat grey buildings where the grey lorries stood waiting besides the piles of grey metal. Into the machine shop and the grease and the smells and the whirring and the clanging. He clocked on at 7.30, the gates were locked till dinner-time, and the sun was extinguished.

I am no longer a man, I am a robot in Brett's Panels and Components. I work for money, cos I've got to have money to live, but I've got no interest. You don't get on any better these days if you work hard, don't know why, never seen such a way to run factories in my life. Could run it better myself, as all the chaps say . . . I'd do this and that, and I'd know when the others were working hard cos I've done the same job myself, like the managers used to, instead of this dreamy lot from God knows where . . . I'd like to use my brain a bit more, but it's not wanted here . . . if I hadn't got my garden and boat I'd go mad. No, I wouldn't, I'd turn into a grey stunted being without a coherent thought in my head. So the materialistic age did something for me, and the better wages. For generations we fought for a living wage, now we've got it and hooray, now I'm a well-paid robot.

I'm not a man, but I have a son. Fifteen now, David,

nearly as tall as me. Be bringing his report home tonight, then breaking up for nearly two months, lucky young devil. Well, I've got a fortnight with pay, that's something.

I'm worried about David.

Went to the school's Open Day, Ann and me, a bit of a disappointment, for though parents were invited to chat with masters, we found we had to rush from form-room to form-room, wait outside in a little queue, dash inside, have a five-minute interview, then rush off to the next form-room along miles of corridors. My old council school organised things better.

Half-past eleven and the machines ground to a halt. Ken went to the workers' canteen, ate his subsidised meal of mashed potatoes, soggy peas and a slice of beef. Apple pie. Talked to his mates about football, then talked about how Brett's had been amalgamated with Car Components.

"It didn't amalgamate, it was taken over," Bill Jones contradicted.

Takeover, thought Ken, where have I heard that before? Oh, yes, Sybil's shop. All those little shops are going, wonder if the same thing will happen with factories? He returned to his newspaper.

Twelve o'clock. Back to the daily stint. I hate this place, wish I could have done that Tech course. But I couldn't, couldn't be out of work for long, I try to help Mam now Dad's not well. And David, couldn't afford all the things he has to have if I wasn't working, there's the sports kit, the pocket-money, the record-player like the other kids have, outings with the school . . . Didn't tell him this, of course . . .

I'm worried about David.

David's first report had been good. He'd have liked to study languages, but he couldn't do Latin in a B-form, and there was no Spanish master, he'd have to go to another school for periods. He wasn't sure about German as to do one thing you had to be sure it was part of your curriculum or something; he was interested in history but couldn't do it as he was doing biology. I asked him why he was doing biology when he didn't like it, but he shrugged and said that's how it was. I thought you could study anything you wanted . . .

Tea break coming up that seems to upset everybody so much. Christ, we don't ask for china cups and saucers like the bosses have, made by their secretaries and all on the firm. All we want is a thick mug of bad tea, fourpence a cup – at least that's all we get.

David's second report hadn't been so good. He seemed to be losing interest, and I told him he'd jolly well have to study. Then the Headmaster sent us a little note. Would Mr and Mrs Webster call to see him?

We went and were told that David didn't work hard enough, he was a slacker in short, and mixed with, and was influenced by, some of the worst elements in the school, and moreover – the Head's voice was hushed now, I wondered what was coming – he was untidy and came to school in shirts that were not always impeccable. We were silent, me from sheer surprise, Ann from shock. We went home and became articulate.

Ann was hurt. "I've never been so upset in my life," she said, and I reflected that the biggest insult you can offer a working-class woman is to tell her she's not clean. Especially when it is not true. "He has a clean shirt every day," Ann wept. I tried to calm her down but I was bewildered myself. Was this the shining tower of learning I'd dreamed about all these years? These petty little doings, talking about clean shirts? When you came from a line of working men who had educated themselves against fearful odds the thought of clean shirts was so irrelevant as to be farcical. Bloody hilarious.

There was a real uproar at home, David saying: "You don't want to take any notice of old Tripp, Mother." Me: "These people get so used to bossing kids around, they just *keep on . . ." Ann said she'd never go to the school again, and she never does. Sybil says that's the wrong approach. Join the Parent–Teachers' Association, visit the school, give donations . . . though if she did that it didn't get young Carolyn through her eleven-plus. Carolyn can't be mine . . .*

Ken wondered, as the hooter went for knocking-off time, half-past three, what David's latest report would say. He braced himself to join the flood of men rushing away from the factory to home and hobby and life. David would be all right. The school had a good record for university passes. No need to worry.

*

Though Ann and Ken worked at the same firm, they were kept as separate as husbands and wives in the old Victorian workhouses. Ken worked from half-past seven to half-past three, Ann from half-past eight to half-past four, so that Ken could not take her in the car, which meant extra fares. Ken had half an hour dinner, from half-past eleven to twelve, Ann an hour's lunch, from twelve to one in their separate canteens. Ken's fortnight's holiday had to be the last two weeks in July when the factory closed down, though the staff still worked, and had staggered holidays, but, as most women wanted the same weeks as their boyfriends or husbands, this meant that Ann usually had to take another fortnight. She was on holiday now, in June, and was spending the time catching up on housework and shopping, for shops did not deliver now as they used to, and Saturdays meant trailing round supermarkets and standing in queues. Today was fine, but blowy, just right for washing blankets, so Ann popped them into her washing machine, marvelling, even after so many years, at the ease of it. She hung them on the line, picked a few roses, and saw Carolyn walking round the yard.

"Like a cup of tea?" Ann asked, as Carolyn slid easily into a chair.

"Love it, Aunt."

"No uniform today?" Ann asked, putting the roses in water.

"We've broken up for the holidays."

"Oh, of course."

"I don't wear it anyway, I hate it. It's silly."

"Do you? I should have thought your mother would want you to wear it."

"She does. But I refused."

Ann studied the girl in surprise. At eleven Carolyn was still pale and quiet, but not, it seemed, submissive.

"I didn't pass the eleven-plus," the girl said.

"No. But you don't have to worry, do you? You'll be able to stay at Miss Glimp's."

"Oh, yes. Only now Mother's got to carry on paying fees." Carolyn grinned as if this pleased her. "The clever ones will have gone, of course, and the professional people's kids are off to boarding-schools, Miss Glimp's Seniors is just for the thickos."

"What will you do when you leave school? I don't suppose you've decided."

"Mother has. She wants me to go into the business. Only I don't want to. I'd hate it."

Ann busied herself with the tea and brought out cakes. "Are you happy at home?" she asked, carefully.

"No, not really. I don't like my mother very much."

"I didn't like mine," said Ann, reflectively.

"But David likes you, Aunt."

"Yes. Boys often do, you know."

"Where is David?" asked Carolyn.

"He's not home from school yet."

"He's late, isn't he? I mean, he breaks up today, and they usually let them out early."

"Yes." David had his year's report today, and being late probably meant it was so bad he didn't want to bring it home, Ken would go on so. A frown furrowed Ann's brow. She too worried about David. He had changed in the last few years, was offhand, at least with his father. He never, even to Ann, talked about school or his thoughts or feelings. Ann supposed it was his age; teenagers, as they called them, were expected to be difficult now. Ann wondered guiltily if her going to work had affected him after all, as the papers said it would. But Ann, although she did not particularly like her job, had no intention of leaving, the extra money came in useful, and it was nice having something of her own, not that Ken ever kept her short. Far from it, and Ann carefully put away a few pounds every week into her Post Office savings account. She hadn't forgotten Ken losing his job ... one good thing, you didn't have to worry about doctor's bills now, and that was a relief. And did not pray, or she would have invoked a nightly blessing on the National Health Service which, she firmly believed, had kept David safe from any inherited tendencies to TB.

Ken entered, frowning at the sight of Carolyn. "David not in yet?" he asked.

"No."

"He's late."

"Don't fuss, Ken."

"I'm not fussing."

Ann poured a cup of tea and changed the subject. "Your mam's been round, she wants to see you."

"What for? Not my dad?"

"Something about Chris."

Ken swallowed the rest of his tea and went round the next yard, to his mother's. The family were all married now, all away, yet rarely a night passed but one or more of them would be round to see 'our mam'. Meg's old rocking-chair was gone, her children had bought her a new three-piece suite, and she sat enthroned in uncut moquette. Her shining hair was grey now, her face wrinkled and lined, but she was always ready to give comfort to her children and grandchildren. This evening she turned a worried face to her elder son.

"You know Chris is having trouble with that Joe." It was a statement and as Ken nodded, "He's been knocking her about again. I wondered, Ken, if you'd go up and see him."

"If you like. Doesn't my dad want to go?"

"He couldn't. Not now. And – she can come here."

"Yes." At the door he stopped. "If she comes – why don't you think about making a will, leaving the house to her? She'll have nothing and – well, she will be helping you too, with me dad." He paused. "It is the custom."

"Yes. I'll talk to your dad."

Doreen was his favourite, Ken thought. *But it's Chris who does most to help, even now.*

He drove up to the estate of People's Houses, more dreary and drab than ever, and knocked on Chris's door.

Joe answered, bleary-eyed. Now what the hell, Ken wondered, made our Chris marry him?

"Chris in?" he asked.

"None of your business."

"Is she in?"

Chris came to the door. Both her eyes were black.

"Did you do that?" Ken asked, dangerously.

"None of your business."

Ken caught him a punch on the jaw, and followed it up with one in the chest which knocked him back into the kitchen where he sprawled among a crash of pots and pans. The little lame boy came out, crying, and Ken's fury was redoubled. He pulled Joe to his feet and smashed his fists into him over and over till he lay, a crumpled heap.

"Get your things," he said to Chris.

"But where—?"

"Come to Mam's. Get your things, and Tommy's. Come on."

"Will she have me?"

"That's why she sent me up. Come on."

What a waste, he thought, as he shepherded his sister and the boy out to the car. Chris, the brightest star of them all in some ways . . . sometimes people made you sick.

Ken returned home. Carolyn had gone, but David was in, and the report lay on the table.

"Not *too* bad," Ken said, judicially. "Though some of the masters say you could do better."

David shrugged.

"I wish you'd try harder. You'll be taking your O-levels next year." He glanced through the exercise books. "Your spelling's bad, and you get low marks in maths. I don't reckon you know your tables."

"Oh, leave it, Dad."

Ken was baffled. David *was* clever, he knew that, he wasn't just being a fond father. So why didn't he do better, as the masters said? What was he thinking?

Why didn't he talk to him as he used to, explain what was wrong? . . . Ken felt as if he stood before a door which had slammed in his face. "Are you coming on the boat tonight?" he asked. "You haven't got any homework now."

"No thanks, Dad, I want to play my records. I'll take the record-player in the front."

"I don't see why you have to shut yourself away to play records."

"I just prefer it."

David took the record-player into the front room. Ken ate his meal in silence, then wandered into the garden. The roses were a blaze of colour, and he moved among them carefully, picking off the dead heads, weeding. Their scent mingled with that of the sweetpeas and honeysuckle. In the borders little pansies stood before snapdragons and marigolds. Cries of children and the whir of a lawn-mower echoed around him, the sounds and scents of summer blotted out David's music.

Chapter Seven

"Four O-levels," said Ken. "Oh, David."

David said nothing, and Ken walked to the front room window where he could see the boat moored on the canal. The westering sun caught the water, turning it to flame; faint shouts of boys playing cricket echoed in the room. "You don't seem very worried," he said, nettled.

"No." David was indifferent.

"It won't make any difference to your going to university, will it?"

"The places go to those with the highest passes, naturally."

"But you have to apply now, you said."

"Yes. Then, subject to A-level passes, we get in."

"So that really means you're accepted on your O-levels?"

"More or less."

"But – what about Oxford?"

"Dad, no B-formers ever get to Oxford."

Rage swirled in Ken, covering the sharp sense of shock, of disappointment, that he hadn't known, that David hadn't ever told him . . . "If you knew," he said, "then why the hell didn't you try harder, get into an A-form?"

Silence.

Ken tried to control his anger. He'd think about it later, when he was alone. "What do you want to be, David?" he asked.

"I don't know."

The anger flared again. "Then you should know. When I was your age—"

"You were going to work. You have told me."

"Would you like to be a teacher?"

"I should hate it."

"Sometimes," Ken said, edgy now, "we have to do things we don't like."

"But there's not much point, is there? Why go to school for years to end up doing something you hate – like you?"

"If you remembered the old days when you couldn't get education unless you had money . . . we fought for this."

"But I don't remember the old days. You can't put the burden of the old days on to me. And doesn't this system make for a new élite of brains?"

"Yes . . . But isn't that good for the country, to have the best brains at the top?"

"But what about those who fail the eleven-plus? The failures?"

"I don't feel a failure."

"Because you passed the scholarship; they just wouldn't take you. But it made you bitter. Today, if a child is sent to a secondary modern he feels a failure. Why, even young Carrie was upset and her at a private school. Imagine how the others feel."

Ken said: "It shouldn't be like that. People should be respected for the job they do, whatever it is."

"But they're not, are they? Remember last year when I did a dustman's job in the holidays? It nearly killed me. And yet, when I went to houses, people would treat me like the dirt I was collecting. Yet we couldn't survive without dustmen."

"I know all that—"

"But you don't want it in practice."

"I don't know what good it will do to dustmen if you fail your exams."

"The system isn't even fair. Some parts have more grammar schools than others, so they can take more, but the kids who are left know, in a way you didn't, that there's nothing for them but the lowest jobs, because you can't get anywhere today without O-levels. What we need is comprehensive education, abolishing grammar schools."

"Oh, no." Ken couldn't imagine life without the tradition of grammar schools. They had been there as long as he could remember.

David said, "You laugh at Aunt Sybil's snobby ideas, but you're no different," and Ken winced at what seemed to be his son's cruelty.

He went into the kitchen and immediately the strains of the latest pop song flooded the house. He picked up David's discarded blazer, lying on the floor, and held it for a moment before hanging it on the door.

"What's the matter?" asked Ann, entering.

"I was just thinking. That interview we had with the Head, when he said David didn't work hard enough, it must have been true." So Ken hid his pain.

"Why? What happened?"

"He won't get to Oxford, he just told me. Why?" Ken asked, rage and pain in his voice. "Why did he change? He was so brilliant at junior school. I've done all I could, insisted he do his homework, told him of the rewards . . ."

"It won't be the end of the world if he doesn't go," said Ann, and wondered at her relief. "He can get a good job round here?"

"Ann. Don't interfere."

"Why not? I brought him up too. You worry too much about him."

"You don't understand," Ken said. How could she?

Marta would have understood. Tired and angry, he went to see his mother and sister. His father was ill, it was feared he wouldn't live much longer. Tom had what he vaguely termed stomach trouble for some time, it was reckoned to be an ulcer, and he'd waited two years for a hospital bed and an operation. Unfortunately, the trouble wouldn't wait, there'd been pain, Meg suspected cancer; he'd had an emergency operation, now was home again, a pale, bedridden shadow.

Meg looked weary and Tommy sat reading. Chris had taken him from his former school and sent him to Marley Road, then applied for a separation from Joe. She went to the magistrate's court, but Joe didn't turn up. His solicitor said he was ill, and unable to work, and therefore would not be able to pay maintenance. Joe then disappeared.

"I can't work," Chris said. "Mam can't manage everything. Anyway, I don't want to work."

"Why not?" asked Ken.

"Because I'm too old to train for anything, and too good for the jobs I should get. I've applied for National Assistance but I don't know if I shall get any."

Ken slipped her five pounds.

*

David went into the Arts Sixth and they had to buy a different, expensive blazer, which he refused to wear if he could possibly avoid it. He was tall now, with Marta's tawny hair, handsome, and a Webster through and through, said the family. He studied English, Geography, Social History and Economics. Ken read the latter and stared in surprise. "Damn me," he said. "I never knew they published books like this."

"They don't do this at secondary moderns, or below the sixth forms. Can't let you ignorant plebs know too much."

"We used to get some good books though when I was a kid," Ken said. "And the papers were more intelligent."

"You're always saying things are better today. Now it's back to the good old days."

"Most things are better, it's just that . . . well, some things are different. Where's the Aneurin Bevans, the Ernie Bevins? They're all Stafford Crippses now."

"But you can't educate people and keep them cloth cap, can you? What do you think I shall be if I go to college?"

"Well, at least you'd have lived it first hand."

"Course I wouldn't. All I'd know is my father's life."

"Why do you always have to contradict me?" Ken asked.

"Because I don't know what was so marvellous about those giants of yours. They nationalised the industries that weren't any good, and left the prosperous ones in private hands."

"They gave you your education."

"And kept private schools."

"The National Health."

"As long as doctors could keep on with private practice."

"Why?" shouted Ken, his anger rising, "Are you always getting at me? Are you like these youngsters we read about, always wanting to smash everything?"

"If I smash your ideals it's because you're fooling yourself."

"I thought you'd feel the same way as I do about things."

"I've got no interest in politics, Dad, none at all."

*

Autumn was dry, with ragged clouds blown by the wind, and dull gold moons. There was the smell of smoke, as bonfires in the gardens burned the last of summer. Frosts came early, the moon became clear and sharp, children hurried home from school, arms swinging, wrapped in woollen scarves and gloves. Winter was cold, snow flurried, then settled down to fall in earnest, the canal ran black between the white fields. Ann put out bread for the birds, and they came eagerly, blackbirds, thrushes and greedy starlings. A robin perched on the mock-orange branch and waited his chance.

David settled down to work for his A-levels, and Ken felt his hopes rise again. He longed for his son's confidence, but was wise enough to leave him alone, for David these days was sullen, argumentative, at least with his father. Ken felt he could endure this as long as David was on the right track. "He's seen sense at last," he said to Ann.

"I don't know why you worry so much. If he didn't get to college it wouldn't be the end of the world."

"That's a damn silly thing to say. Anybody'd think you didn't want him to go."

"Well, I don't particularly. I'll miss him. I mean, will he ever come back? Back here to live."

"He could. Get a job in the Midlands."

Ann shook her head. "They don't, Ken. They move away. It's only working-class jobs that stay near home. That's why—"

"Why what? You don't want him living in the next yard?"

"It would have been nice," said Ann, wistfully.

"The way he is now it might be a relief to have him away. He's always arguing."

"He's all right with me," said Ann, and Ken felt a resentment, almost anger, as he wondered what they talked about when he wasn't there. He felt, obscurely, that Ann was against him, and he needed her support now, he needed everyone's support. Things looked good, but Ken knew that it is just when life looks rosy and calm that it turns and kicks you viciously in the teeth.

*

Tom was ill for a year, nursed by Chris, who had finally been allowed a payment of National Assistance because she had a child of school age at home. Ken, shuddering, watched his father sink into a pain-racked shadow, gave money to Chris, herself white and worn with the burden. There was still no indoor lavatory or bathroom in the Websters' house, and as Tom grew too weak to get out of bed, Chris sent for Ken when he was home from work, to lift him on the chamber. Often he was sent for in the night. Daytimes Chris had to manage with Meg, till in the end Tom lost all control over his functions and, eyes staring in weak apology, became completely incontinent. Every day Chris and Ann washed the sheets, every night one or more of them would sit with him, giving the tablets to stop the pain.

When he died they were all relieved, and as the funeral ended the family sat talking in the living-room. Ken said to Chris: "Why don't you go out more? You've had it rough."

"Where would I go?"

"Dunno. What about your Labour Party meetings?"

"I don't go now. The dream's over." She shrugged. "I don't want to go anywhere." Ken stared, and she went on. "Living on Assistance – you don't want to meet people, especially when they all talk about scroungers. You feel ashamed somehow."

Ken was dismayed. He remembered Chris as a child, the shame of wearing cast-off clothes. "Why did you marry Joe O'Brien?" he asked, angrily.

"God knows." Had she thought Joe could give her love, tenderness?

"And he won't split." Ken snorted. "Go and find yourself another bloke."

"I can't go with men on the Assistance. They watch you day and night. And I might get reported. There's always somebody among our friendly neighbours who'd like to do it."

"I suppose so. Though I wouldn't like to catch 'em. Go on, be a devil, go and play bingo or something. It's not like you to be so – so defeated."

"I suppose I'm just tired."

"You look like death warmed up," he said with brotherly candour. "You need a holiday."

The mocking glance she gave him held something of the old Chris. "I'll pay for it," he said, recklessly. "Have a week at the sea."

"What about Mam?"

"We'll look after her. Go on. Take one of those package tours abroad, they don't cost any more than a holiday in England."

"Oh, Ken, I'd love that." Chris's eyes lost some of their hopelessness.

So it was decided. Ann wished she were going too, wished again that Ken had taken the teacher training course and moved to a better area, and was immediately ashamed of her disloyalty, puzzled at her feelings. She had wanted to belong with the Websters, hadn't she? It was she who wanted David to stay near her ... Well, because she loved him, she was his mother ... And she needed his love, there was still a silent battle raging between her and Ken, if the battle should ever be resolved ... But she rejoiced for Chris, and marvelled at the way they'd become friends in adult life when in childhood she'd been scared of her sharp tongue. She promised to look after Meg and Tommy.

'Dear Ann & Ken,
   This really is fantastic. We've seen Florence, Assisi, now Rome. St Peter's, the Sistine Chapel . . . three days in Capri, blue seas and sky, bougainvillea tumbling over white buildings – the beauty of it all does something. It's like walking out of a tunnel into light. I love it all. The way the waiters burst into 'Santa Lucia'. I'd love to get right away from England, Joe used to say he hated England, thinking it would upset me. Perhaps it did. But England never wanted me. I'll have to work my way round the world or something. But thanks, dear brother, for giving me this.
   Love,
      Chris.'

Ann sighed, and wondered why those like the Websters, so brilliant in childhood, were so easily defeated. It was the dull, the plodding, who took up courses and went on to higher things. Ann suspected that Chris knew all this, and the knowledge only added to her burden.

                                                    Venice
'Dear Ann,
   For your eyes alone. We've been here three days now, and it's heaven. I must have a romantic streak, all these gondolas and the Bridge of Sighs appeal to me. More songs, a moonlit trip on a gondola . . . I had a little affair with him, Ann, the gondolier who sang in the moonlight. I wouldn't have told you but it was something special. Michelangelo has soft melting eyes and a voice to match, he's younger than me. And don't tell me he's just another male after what he can get, I know that type, should do. When you're separated or divorced men are always wanting to take you to bed, and all they want is a quick roll to satisfy themselves.

So I tell 'em to push off, cos for that I might charge 'em for it. One thing about Joe, he did know how to make love, so many don't . . . but Michelangelo knows how to make a woman feel *loved*. I know that sounds corny, but no one has ever made me feel that before, you see. Poor little underprivileged me.

   See you soon,

     Chris.'

Ann welcomed her home. In the fading light her face seemed softer, more like Doreen's. This is how she should have been, Ann thought, if life hadn't taken it away from her.

But an Italian gondolier! "Are you going to see him again?" Ann asked.

"Who knows?" Chris said, vaguely.

"Are you in love with him?"

Chris shrugged. "Does it matter?"

"But he was younger than you."

"Not as young as all that. Hell, I don't want a learner. And you can keep all your women's fiction strong beefy heroes, give me a man with melting eyes." Chris slid a sideways glance at Ann. "Am I shocking you? Actually I don't think sexual attraction has anything to do with age, it's only convention tells us we have to be the same age, and for marriage no doubt it's best. Though, as women live longer than men now, I think they should be older, otherwise they're likely to spend half their lives as widows."

"You won't see him again, then?" Ann pressed.

"Who knows?" Chris repeated. "They do say if you go to a place you leave something of yourself there. The same applies to people. Michelangelo has left something of himself with me."

Ann hoped he hadn't left too much with Chris. Marley Road talked now about her and Joe, her violent marriage and her separation. The Websters seemed to attract scandal, they shocked people right and left. Ann hated scandal.

"Don't tell our Ken," Chris said. And then, grinning: "I'd hate the devil to know he was right."

*

Ken said to David: "Ready for the boat, then?"

There was a pause. David said: "I don't think I'll come this year, Dad."

"But – why not? We always go."

"I thought I'd get a job, then I can buy myself a new record-player."

"You don't have to."

"I know, but most of the fellows do, you know."

David took the record-player into the front room, and soon came the sound of the new modern music Ken didn't pretend to understand. As the blast became louder he opened the door. "Can you turn it down a bit, for God's sake? I don't know what you see in this rubbish."

"It makes us feel, Dad. Your generation's plastic world has no feeling to offer, no rebellion."

"My God, I've rebelled enough."

"I mean, what's put out for us. Blandness, cotton-wool effects."

Ken slammed the door and walked slowly to the bottom of the entry. So many years he'd gone with David on the boat, and now he didn't want to come. Well... David was growing up... But... He used to be such an outgoing kid, friendly, talkative. Now if he said anything at all it was to argue. Funny though, he'd never thought there'd come a time when David wouldn't want to come out with him... Share his success... For without David, what would he have...? He saw young Tommy limp up the street, and his heart twisted with pity as it always did when he saw his nephew. Poor kid, there'd been no grammar school for him, it was secondary modern for Tommy. *So why am I complaining? I got all I wanted, didn't I?*

"Hey-up, Tommy," he called. "Want to come with us on the boat for a holiday?"

The boy's thin face lightened. "Oh, yes, Uncle Ken, I'd love to."

They walked in home together.

*

Ann and Ken were invited to Sybil's Christmas party. Ken would have refused, he never understood why Ann wanted to go to these, admittedly rare occasions. Ann said she loved to see how the other half lived, and this was true, she enjoyed sitting in the spacious lounge of the chalet-bungalow, gazing through the French windows at the lawns and trees; Acacia Avenue was little different from the way it had been in the Thirties, it was still the haunt of Briarford's élite, professional and business men, teachers and master builders. To Ann, a visit was like a holiday. And, dislike Sybil as she might, she was pleased that her sister hadn't dropped her. Ken, knowing the real reason for Sybil's invitations, was uncomfortable, and hid his discomfort under a cloak of banter, about Sybil's visitors who, he said, they met like foreigners in a railway station waiting-room, passing the time of day uneasily before their respective trains whirled them in different directions.

"I wonder what the top brass of our factory are like," he mused.

"What do you think they're like?"

"Foxes. Cunning old foxes who speak with forked tongues."

"Maybe you'll meet them here."

"I wouldn't even know 'em. It's as easy to meet the man

in the moon as for a shop-floor worker to get an interview with one of the directors."

"Well, we shall know if a lot of foxes walk in."

"I don't think they live round here. I can't imagine 'em living at all. Never thought of 'em having a home and family, being kind to children, going to bed with their wives . . ."

"At least these people don't go around pinching batteries out of cars as somebody did to you in Marley Road. And the people who live next door to us now are dead common."

"You sound like your mother." Ken sounded nettled.

"I don't see what's wrong with wanting to live in a nice area."

"You'd like to live up here?"

"Of course I would."

"Well, I can't afford it"

"There are other areas, nicer than ours. If we sold our house, then put it down as a deposit—"

"And then I lost my job—"

"I'm working."

"I don't," Ken said flatly, "want to live in another area."

There was a silence. "But David will, won't he?" Ann asked. "If he gets a good job as you want he'll live in one of these houses, mix with these people."

"Oh, well, that's different."

"It isn't. Though I suppose anything David does will be all right."

"What do you mean by that?"

"You have pushed him a bit, haven't you?"

"Pushed him? Just because I want him to get on in life?"

"Yes, you have."

"The trouble is," Ken said, angry now, "you, for some

reason, don't want him to go away, either to university or whatever. And yet you're the one who talks about people being common."

"I suppose I don't want to lose him," Ann said in a small voice. *He's all I have.*

The car drew up in Sybil's drive. "It's not the foxes' night," said Ken. "I can tell by the cars."

In fact they seemed a pleasant group, he thought as they entered the hall, and he tried to avoid Sybil. But she came to him as Ann went to the bathroom. "You didn't answer my letter," she accused.

"I told you before I'm not coming at your bidding," he said.

"It's been so long. And I didn't write for ages—"

"I thought you'd found someone else." He glanced at her, knowing as always the strange attraction that repelled at the same time.

"I want to see you, Ken."

"Then you'll have to want," he said, and moved away.

At dinner he sat next to a school-teacher who told him she made wine, and he, delighted, talked about Aunt Liz and the wines she made in the days of his childhood. He saw Sybil's eyes flashing and thought: I don't want to see her again, I've finished, reformed. It's to do with David, really, almost a superstition. If I'm a model father everything will be all right.

Later he found himself talking to Peter, Sybil's husband. Formerly he had avoided him, through a mixture of derision and shame. Derision for a man who was too dandified to work with his hands and too ineffectual to satisfy his wife; shame that he, Ken, took advantage of the fact. Peter asked about David, and Ken said with pride that he was in the Sixth, studying for his A-levels.

"Jolly good," said Peter, absently. "I wish Carolyn was getting on better."

"She isn't?" Ken asked, carefully. He didn't want to discuss Carolyn with Peter.

"No. Not that it matters too much, but Miss Glimp's isn't much good . . . Sybil talked about sending her to boarding-school, but Carolyn won't go."

"Oh?"

"I don't blame her in a way. I hated boarding-school myself. Always wanted to get home," and again Ken was surprised, thinking that with Peter's old man he'd have been glad to get away. He thought the same would apply to Carolyn. Kids were funny.

"But I stayed, and got used to that way of life and then didn't want to come back to – the business." Peter smiled thinly. "I had been taught at my school that trade was somehow infra dig, you know."

"Yes," agreed Ken, who thought the same thing about Peter's dad's business.

"So I was glad to sell it really. Of course, Sybil—" Peter hesitated, and Ken looked up alertly. "Sybil thought it wrong. I believe she would have run it herself, given the chance."

Again he smiled, and Ken mused. Yes, and she could have, *given the chance*. She had the necessary drive. Ken, who agreed with the magazine aunties that what an unruly woman needed was a home and babies, now wondered. Suppose Sybil's energy, her ruthlessness, had been channelled into running a business . . . *it might have kept her off my back* . . . And while she was running the business what would Peter have been doing? Sitting in home? Working for Sybil? Peter, not too masculine, sold out.

"She still dabbles in stocks and shares," said Peter.

Ken wondered why she couldn't start up on her own. He supposed you couldn't do it without pots of money, not today, the days of the little shop in the front room were over. He was vague about how much could be made on the Stock Exchange. Gambling, wasn't it?

"She's branching into engineering now," Peter was saying. "Has quite a sizeable percentage in Bronze Metals."

"Yes?" Ken wondered if Peter was trying to tell him something.

"They're taking over a lot of firms," Peter went on. "It's worth remembering. Sybil can be dangerous when crossed."

"Yes." What could he mean? It was as though he were trying to warn him of something. Surely he didn't *know* . . .? Again Ken felt shamed, Peter seemed a nice bloke after all, pity he'd never really got to know him . . .

He tried to avoid Sybil, but she managed to have a word with him before he left. "I'm not going to let you go, you know." The hostility was there again.

"That's for me to decide."

"Don't you believe it." She laughed sharply. "You'll be back."

Oh, no, I won't, he thought, confidently. Not now. When David's at college I'll settle down to a peaceful life.

He turned to go, looking for Ann. She was talking to a man about their own age, whose face seemed vaguely familiar. As they went home she asked: "Do you know who that was?"

"No."

"You remember those Naylors in one of the council-houses?"

"Yes, I know. Rose Naylor."

"That was her brother Ted. A bit older than her. He's a widower now. And guess what he does?"

"Something posh, to be at Sybil's."

"He's a teacher. Fancy. Ted Naylor. He did one of those educational courses when he came out of the army like you wanted to do, remember?"

Ken remembered.

He couldn't see Ann's face, nor read her thoughts. "I always fancied you," Ted had said, smiling. "But when I came home you'd married Ken, so I married a girl I met on the course. She died last year."

And Ann glowed with the knowledge that she had been loved, she, who thought no one had wanted her. But Ken missed the glow.

*

Summer was the busy time for Marley Road men. Gardens were tended, sheds built, houses painted and decorated, the pre-war browns and greens changed to a proliferation of individual colours, red, yellow, blue, each proclaiming bravely its owner's protest against uniformity. From all sides came the merry sound of hammer and saw; new windows were installed, glass doors, little walls built. Ken worked with the rest, he cleared out the old coal-house, making a storeroom, bought a greenhouse and lavished much care on tomatoes. Painted his boat lovingly.

He had accepted the fact that David no longer wanted to work with him, to go out with him. David was a *student*, with the offer of a place at a provincial college, subject to his obtaining two A-levels. The first anger and pain at knowing he would not get to Oxford had subsided, but he felt that somehow something in him had been destroyed, and mentally shrugged off this fancy. I'm getting old, he thought, my hair's not bad, the Websters don't go bald early, and we never run to fat. But he felt obscurely that he needed rejuvenation; as old men needed the titillation of a young girl to restore their flagging virility, so he needed the success David could bring him to strengthen his failing powers.

David wouldn't talk to him, wouldn't share his plans and

dreams for the future – were these young 'uns a different breed, taking everything as a right . . .? But Ken was still proud of his son, loved to watch him swing along in his Sixth form blazer, the only boy in Marley Road at King Alfred. There were a few children at the new grammar, the former technical school, the rest were working. David didn't really have any pals now, and for a brief moment Ken thought of Ann's remark about living in a nicer area; in Acacia Avenue education was the norm, not the exception. He did not pursue the thought. He himself would have been proud to be the only boy in the street going to grammar school; David must feel the same way.

*

In August Ken waited for the results of David's A-levels with feverish impatience. Urged by his father, David took a walk down to the school and came back with his results. Two passes.

"Then it will be all right," said Ken.

"What?"

"College, of course."

David took a deep breath. "Dad, you might as well know. I'm not going."

Ken stood, thunderstruck. "But it's all arranged."

"I'm not going."

"Why not?"

"I don't want to."

"But David . . . I don't understand you."

David said nothing.

"What do you want to do, then?"

"Something round here."

Ken groped in the dark. There were still good places even though it wouldn't be the same. "Some office?"

"No."

"Then what?"

"I'm going to work in a factory."

Ken stared, bewildered. "In a factory? You must be out of your mind."

"Why?"

"You know why. Anyway, you could get a better job, in an office. Is that what you mean?"

"No."

"But you're too old to get an apprenticeship."

"I know."

"You don't have to go into industry at all."

"You'd like me to be a professional? Lawyer? Doctor?"

"They're safe jobs and good pay. And closed shops. Or you could go into the civil service and have a good pension."

"For an idealist, Dad, you do harp on about money."

"Because I know what it's like to be without money. You don't. You've had all you wanted all these years, never gone without. Besides, to throw all this education away, it's plain daft."

Ann said: "You *could* get an office job, David."

"I haven't got maths. Not even O-level."

"Then you should have," Ken said, angrily. "You were too damn lazy . . ." He controlled himself with difficulty. "Think it over, David. Don't do anything you'll regret."

"I've been thinking it over for years."

"But you never told me."

"It's my life."

"But just explain why. Is it just temporary? Get a better job later on?"

"I want to work in a factory, it's as simple as that."

Ken lost his temper completely. "Then I tell you you won't. You'll go to college. I've had a bellyful of your silly ideas. You'll go and that's it."

"I won't."

"What?"

"I won't. You can't force me. I'm eighteen."

Ann said, "If he doesn't want to go, he doesn't."

"Now don't you encourage him—"

"I don't know why you're making such a fuss—"

"You keep out of it," said Ken, angrily.

David said, "Don't talk to my mother like that."

"What?" Ken opened his mouth in amazement, that young David should be giving him orders. He found he had to look up to his son, and David stood firm. Ken walked out of the house.

Hands in pockets, shoulders hunched, he walked along the canal. *Leave my mother alone.* As if he treated Ann badly ... He stopped as a memory from the past came to him.

Home on leave from the army. His dad, still hot tempered, and Meg saying something, he forgot what, and Tom lurching forward in anger. And he, Ken, had stood up and said: "Don't you touch her."

He remembered to this day the look of surprise on his dad's face. But he hadn't touched his mother. There had been a strange look on his mam's face too, and they all knew their roles had changed. He was the man of the house now, his dad had been deposed. Ken remembered the moment of elation, the 'we are masters now' feeling. Funny, he never thought to wonder how the old man felt, just wanted to pay him back for his bullying.

Now it was happening to him. His son was taking over. Did this mean he'd have to take a back seat now? All these years, he thought, surprised, somebody gives the orders and doesn't realise the other person has a point of view. Doesn't try to listen till it's too late.

Slowly he walked back to the house, wondering how to face his son. He wanted to talk to him, hear what he had to say, but would David talk? Had he said much to him, ever?

He let himself in the house. David and Ann sat talking normally, and again Ken knew a spurt of anger. Ann had put David up to this. She had never wanted him to go to college. Wanted him to stay round home, a mother's boy.

David didn't speak and Ken eyed his son warily. He knew that any move would have to come from him. The choice was his, either they could go on being friends, or David might be alienated forever. Funny when you come to the stage when you realise you can't go on being the boss. Part of his mind was panicking.

He said: "I don't want to be hard on you, David – I only did things for your own good."

David said, drily, "That's the comment of tyrants all through the ages."

Damn and blast kids when they grow up and use your own arguments against you. Does he have any idea of what this means to me? No, of course he doesn't, how could he? I didn't with my dad. But my dad never bothered much about me, not really. David has had the best of everything. "We hear about kids like you on the television," he said, bitterly. "They just want to get a job for easy money, then later they regret it. I don't know what the world's coming to—"

"I'm not doing it for easy money." David's voice held contempt.

"Then what is it, for God's sake?"

"I just want to." David's face was impassive as ever. "And in case you think I'll change my mind I'll tell you this now. Speech Day is next month, and I think I've got a little prize coming. When I get it I'm going to tell the whole school I'm going to work in a factory."

"What for?"

"Why not? If I'd won an Oxford scholarship the Head would tell them."

"Do you have to make a fool of yourself before everyone?"

"I should have thought you'd be pleased if I talk about the dignity of labour and being taught to despise the man who works with his hands. I thought I'd tell you, then you needn't come."

Ann said: "David, don't—" but Ken cut her short.

"Leave him alone. I know he's just getting at me, I don't need you to interfere." He slammed out of the house, hurt, frustrated. And somewhere there was a terrible resentment against his son. He'd given up so much for David, the teacher training course, chance of a better factory job . . . He went to his mother's.

Meg sat peacefully in her chair, one hand smoothing the arm, pushing away and away, and Ken thought how many times he'd seen his mother sit thus, pushing away as though to resolve cares once and for all . . . "It don't do to worship kids," she said. "You make a rod for your own back. You know what they say: 'Make your arms ache when they're little and your heart ache when they're big'," and he wondered which of his lot had made his mother's heart ache. The two away in Australia seeking a better life; Chris, with her unhappy marriage and her lame boy; himself when he was missing . . .? But he was comforted all the same, he didn't know what he'd do without his mam to talk to. The next morning she was found dead, she'd died in her sleep.

Chapter Eight

When Tommy left school Chris's supplementary benefit was stopped and she was told to go to work. The fact that she had to help the family, including her sick father, didn't count. She would have liked to study for O- and A-levels, and applied for a grant, but was refused. So she signed on, and was allowed assistance.

After Meg's death, Doreen took on the mantle of family hostess, listening to and comforting her sisters and brothers when they dropped in, handing out cups of tea, the new queen bee in the matriarchal society where women grew stronger with the years and the men, so bold and fierce in youth, gradually took a back seat. It was happening in their own home, Ann thought; David now had little to say to his father, it was to Ann he turned. Ann felt Ken's resentment, noted his black silences, found herself in a dilemma. She loved David sincerely, but didn't want to lose Ken's love.

Love? Sometimes, lying beside him in the night, half asleep, the grey figure of her mother would materialise out of the shadows, wagging an admonishing finger. "He only wants to marry you to look after the baby." And when the singing dawn came she would wake sweating from haunting terrors, and she thought she knew why she wanted David to stay near them. If he left, she and Ken would have to face the truth of why they lived together. *She* would have to face the truth.

So they circled round each other like actors in a mystery play. Sometimes Ken would study his son, wondering what went on behind that handsome face so like Marta's. At the Speech Day fiasco when David received his prize and told the assembly that he was going to work in a factory, Ken had been humiliated and angry. All very well for rich men's sons to turn down their way of life, he would applaud that; this was different, though he never asked himself why. This was the son of men who had fought for generations for rights and justice, and education. Yet, seeing David was determined, he offered to speak for him at Brett's; sons always worked with fathers. David refused and found unskilled work at Startin's, a poor place. Whether he liked it or not he never said, he rebuffed all Ken's overtures, was sullen and untidy. He let his hair grow, wore shabby clothes in the evenings, and when in home spent all his time in the front room playing his records. Youth became a cult and ad-men worshipped at its shrine, for youth had money. Disgusted colonels wrote angry letters to newspapers and Ken found himself in agreement, feeling part of a lost generation.

He went out more often now. Sometimes he would say he was going to the Club, or just to have a drink. Ann waited. But when Chris came round innocently asking why she hadn't gone with him to Doreen's her hurt was unbearable. To visit the family without her. That was appalling. She said, quietly, "I didn't know he had gone."

"Oh," Chris said, awkwardly, and then, "What's he playing at, the damn fool?"

"It's David," Ann explained. "He's upset because he wouldn't go to college – and he blames me."

"He's an awkward devil, our Ken, at times," Chris said. "Always was. He grumbled about my dad, but he's just the same. That's why they didn't get on."

"I suppose so."

"I remember that time he and Marta fell out. You know?"

"Yes," said Ann, thinking of the night over the fields, though she'd never known exactly what happened.

"He wouldn't tell me anything, of course," Chris said. "But he wouldn't ever try to make it up, though he wanted to. Used to sit in home, moody and miserable, when he wasn't dancing. Stubborn, that's what he is. You don't mind me mentioning all this, do you?" she asked, anxiously.

"I don't mind," Ann said. "I've often wished people had talked more about it, instead of somehow pretending it was all over. Cos you see it isn't over, he's never forgotten her." She laughed mirthlessly. "And then they say women are romantic."

There was a silence. "What do *you* think about David?" Ann asked.

Chris hesitated. "Working in the factory? I don't know. I can understand Ken's feelings, here we all went mad to get education for our kids, now he's throwing it away. Is David doing it just to get back at Ken, do you think?"

"I don't know. Why should he?"

Chris shrugged. "You know kids and parents."

"David's never told me. He never tells me anything."

"I'm surprised you don't object more, Ann. After all, you're the one who—"

Who objected to being called a member of the proletariat? I'm the one who'd like to live in a nice area. But people don't always act in character, hadn't you noticed? They go off and do some funny thing and the neighbours say, "Just fancy, who'd have thought it of her?" . . . and she can't explain because she doesn't understand herself, perhaps doesn't want to understand . . .

Chris said: "Ken bothers me. He's acting just the same now as when Marta fell out with him. Something's on his mind and – well, I don't want to worry you, but he looks like a man who's on the edge of . . . something . . . I don't know."

Ann was alarmed.

"Why don't you talk to David?" asked Chris.

"I have. But he never tells me anything. Ken thinks he does, but he's wrong. Anyway, he's always off with girls now."

"He's like his dad, all right," said Chris, caustically.

The next evening Ken went out without saying where he was going. Half an hour later David also made for the door. "Cheerio, Ma," he said.

"David." He stopped. "I wish you didn't look so untidy," Ann fretted. "Anyone would think you hadn't any decent clothes. And your hair needs cutting."

"Yes, Ma." David stood, patiently. "You tell me that every day."

Ann sighed. "Well, be careful."

"What do you mean?"

"Well, I suppose you're going to see another girl—"

"You mean you don't want me to get into trouble, Ma."

She smiled faintly. "Oh, I know what they say, you don't have to worry about your lads, it's the girls bring the trouble home. But I still wouldn't like you to – to—" she broke off, confused.

"Don't worry, I know the facts of life."

But that wasn't all she had to say. She drew a breath. "David. I've often wondered. Did it – upset you at all, about your – I mean, about Marta?"

Surprised, he glanced at the photograph. "What? Oh, you mean because she wasn't married and that?"

"I've wondered if ever people said anything."

"No, I don't think so. Not that I remember. It's never worried me in the least. Why should it?"

"I just wondered if that's why—"

"You've been reading all those psychological articles, Ma." He adopted the bantering tone he often used to her now. "No, I don't see there's anything to be upset about. I was never abandoned or neglected or whatever. I knew about it right from the start. As I see it, they would have got married if—"

"Yes. They would. He – loved her."

"But she died, and he was a prisoner. And then I had you. I've never really thought any other but that you two were my parents."

She knew a sudden warmth. "I'm glad, David. I wondered if that's why you were so funny with your Dad."

"Oh, no."

"Then why are you?"

"I dunno. Suppose we rub each other up the wrong way."

"Well, you've got your factory job, and you don't like it much, do you?" Ann asked, shrewdly.

"It's all right."

"Your dad just wants to know what you're going to do with your life."

"Why should I want to do anything with my life? I'm working, paying my way. So don't keep on, Ma."

"Oh, I know you young ones think you know it all," retorted Ann, a little sharply. "But you don't, not always. Lots of kids leave school early and regret it."

Silence.

"Your dad just wanted you to have a safe job."

"There are plenty of jobs around now, Mother."

"They keep telling us the country's going to the dogs."

"And the unions are too powerful and the workers earn too much money. I do read the papers, Ma."

"Oh," she said, frustrated, "I know you won't tell me—"

"One day I'll write my life story. Now I'm off. Cheerio."

She tried to talk to Ken, to take him out of his silences, his resentment. "You know," she began when they were in bed, "David'll be all right. Maybe he'll get a better job later on."

"Did he say that?"

"No."

"Then what the hell's he playing at?" He sat up. "It's funny. Our Doreen's three lads are all doing well, all went to grammar school, the oldest's at college now, the next one is an accountant, the youngest's going to be a teacher. Yet Doreen's the most easy-going of us all, takes life as it comes—"

"Perhaps you worried too much."

"*You* didn't want him to leave home," and she was silent, not having words to explain that she too was searching for something lacking in childhood and had never found it. Perhaps, she thought bleakly, we never do.

And, as the Beatles twisted and shouted and the Rolling Stones got no satisfaction, Ken found a new worry – Carolyn.

He had always done his best to ignore the child, as one ignores unpleasant facts in the hope they'll go away. But Carolyn did not go away, she was fond of Ann, and when she left Miss Glimp's to attend daily what her mother called a finishing school in the prosperous area of the Midlands, she seemed to be a constant visitor. She hung round David like a leech, brought records and together they'd sit in the front room for hours.

Ken studied the girl. She had been a plain child; now her figure was rounded and her skirts far too short. She wasn't pretty, he consoled himself, but she wasn't ugly either, and he searched her face for signs of resemblance to anyone. But Carolyn remained obstinately a common English type, tall, fair, thin. As Peter was, and Chris and Johnny. And there were occasional hints of mockery, as when she spoke of her school. "We do flower arranging, cookery and pottery. Just the attributes required by the successful business woman." It might have been Chris speaking. The stark memory came, the wedding, himself wanting Marta, taking Sybil. Could that little release possibly have resulted in Carolyn? ... Surely there was nothing between her and David, it was natural for them to be friends . . . wasn't it?

"Does she have to come here so often?" he asked Ann.

"Well, why not? She always has."

"I just get a bit sick of her here all the time. My home's not my own."

"You do get bad tempered," Ann flashed back. "Honestly, Ken, I don't know what's the matter with you."

"I don't want her hanging around David."

"Oh, for goodness' sake. Are you going to tell him who he's got to go out with now?"

Ken was silent, wondering what to do. Tell David? He already seemed to hate the sight of his father, what that would do Ken dare not think. He couldn't do it. He'd just have to watch them. He took to walking into the front room when they were there, and David would wait politely for him to go out again. "I only want to look at my boat," Ken would say. "After all, I do live here." But when David said: "I'll have to take the record-player to my bedroom," Ken left them alone. Better the front room than that.

He went to see Sybil.

She had an ultra-modern mock-Georgian-type house now, with antique furniture reminding Ken of the stuff Uncle William had thrown out. It was Tuesday, Peter's golf night, and Ken hoped he wasn't at home.

Sybil came to the door. "Hallo, stranger," she said. "Do come in. I knew you'd be back," and she led him into the kitchen and placed two mugs of coffee on a plain scrubbed table. "It's the new way of living," she explained, and he had a fleeting memory of his home in the Thirties. He sat down.

"I'm sorry about David," Sybil said. "To think he's thrown away all his chances. Really, when you hear about all these wild young people, drugs and hippies and wanting to smash society, I wonder what the world's coming to."

"I haven't come to hear your views on David," he said. "It's Carolyn I want to talk about."

"Really? You acknowledge her at last?"

"If it's true, then I'd rather she saw less of David."

Sybil was silent.

"Frankly, I can't see anything of me in her, and never have. I've never believed you, Sybil."

"You mean you've never wanted to. Ken, I honestly don't know. After it happened, I managed to bring Peter up to scratch for once, so she could be yours or his. But as we've never had another—"

"Perhaps you learned a bit more about birth control since then. Anyway, I'd be grateful if you persuaded Carolyn to come to our house less often."

"I can't do that."

"Why not?"

"Because she wouldn't do it if I did. She never does. If I ordered her not to see David, she'd simply walk out of the house and do as she pleased. She's always been like that. Quiet, but self-willed."

"You seem to have met your match, then, Sybil."

"Young people aren't what they used to be."

"They never were." But he thought of David.

"I used to do everything my mother wanted. She found my job, insisted I marry well – they won't do it today. I mean, we used to have this old-fashioned conception of honour and duty, principles . . . all gone today."

"I wouldn't know. I never saw much in the way of honour and principles myself."

"All I want for Carolyn," said her mother, "is a wedding

at St Margaret's, to a decent young man. The working classes are all very well—"

"But you wouldn't let your daughter marry one."

"I'm thinking of security—"

"And an index-linked pension. So that lets David out."

"I'm afraid so."

"Except, as you say, Carolyn might not ask you. But what about Peter? Does he have any influence with her?"

"She's fond of Peter, and he'd do anything for her. Leave it now, Ken, I'll arrange things."

He wondered if she would. If he could trust her.

She leaned towards him holding out her hand. "Peter's playing golf," she said. "Come on."

He hesitated. It was a struggle for power. And yet – why not? He had nothing at home now. Nothing but a dark shadow that threatened to engulf him.

They went into the bedroom.

"You've missed me," Sybil said, as they lay side by side. "You've missed our love-making."

If you can call it that, he thought. More like mating with a tiger. But yes, he had missed it. Because the black thoughts would always come – he'd always had a devil inside him, only Marta could drive it out. Thoughts of black destruction to be exorcised by lust for Sybil.

Her hands moved over his body and she was murmuring four-letter words, which shocked him momentarily, for he never used such words before women. "Swearing is getting fashionable now, did you know?" she asked. "My mother would turn in her grave. They used to chalk these words up in the girls' toilets when I was at school and I wondered what they meant. Now they're printed in books."

Ken wondered who in hell past school age got a kick out of writing four-letter words. Ann would be shocked too . . . what did it matter now? His home had become a place to be avoided, where the only reality was the photograph of

Marta, and memories of a laughing, wilful girl. He turned to Sybil, and even she was surprised at his force.

"You'll come again," she said when it was over, and he nodded wearily.

"I'll come."

"Don't let me down," Sybil ordered. "For I wouldn't forgive you again."

*

"Whatever's this?" asked Ken from his newspaper. "Is this where you went yesterday?"

"The demonstration, yes." David was cool as always.

"So what's this one about?"

"Vietnam. Don't you care about it?"

"Not much."

"You really are bigoted. Aren't you interested in nuclear war, then?"

"That's just talk."

"Dad, we're making bombs."

"For defence. Did any of your mates from work go?"

"No. They're as blinkered as you."

"No. You went with Carolyn. You wouldn't be a student yourself, but you're acting like one."

"What do you mean, acting like a student?"

"All this protesting, and meditating, and beatnik rubbish—"

"Surely somebody should protest?"

"Aw, it's just a game to them. Another five years and they'll all be in safe little jobs, forgotten it all."

"We're sincere, Dad. We're concerned. And we're trying to help the workers."

"But the workers don't want your help. Not from a lot of kids who don't know their arse from their elbow."

"So why did you want me to be a student?"

Ken said: "Wait till there's a bit of unemployment here, see if your students are so keen on marching then."

"Honestly, Dad. You talk about everybody being friends, yet you don't trust middle-class MPs, and you don't like students—"

"I'd like 'em better if they didn't look so scruffy."

"It's all part of the anti-establishment thing. I'd have thought you'd approve—"

"Well, I don't know why you want to go traipsing around with that silly bit of a kid—"

"Who? Carolyn?"

"Yes."

"She's got the right ideas."

"Huh. Nobody in that family had any good ideas."

"What do you mean?" cried Ann.

"Oh, I didn't mean you." Ken was confused. "I mean Sybil."

"Sybil? We never see her now. She never comes here."

"We visit her sometimes."

"Not for ages. You didn't want to go last time. What's Sybil—?"

David had been studying his father thoughtfully. Now he interrupted. "Mother, I'm hungry. Where are those cakes?" and he put his arm around her waist and pushed her into the kitchen.

*

Looking back, Ann could never pinpoint the exact moment when the Sixties stopped swinging and the mechanism proved to be not some wonderful new space-age structure, but the same old clockwork, running down. There were stray bits of information as the decade entered its final years, little factories closing down, jobs not so easy to get. But outwardly everything looked just the same, property was booming, Farmer Bates was doing well now with his battery hens and cows in sheds. Ann wondered what had happened to the horses which used to graze in the field, long since dead, she supposed, poor old nags, you never saw a horse these days. It gave her a feeling of age, as did the sight of Carolyn swinging round the yard, looking quite grown-up. Ann could never quite pinpoint the moment either when Carolyn had changed, or even if she had, the girl had always been quiet and self-contained. Was it just imagination that some little light had died out of her eyes? Was it something to do with David? Ann too, had thought her niece was 'fond of' her son, but David showed no signs of settling down; was this why the girl seemed more reserved with him? Or did she sense Ken's dislike? Whatever it was, she still came to the house, as a moth drawn to a candle, telling Ann about her school, her friends. Ann did not in the least understand Carolyn, or what she talked about, she had no idea what the finishing school training was for, or what Carolyn intended to be; she sometimes thought Carolyn didn't know either. But she greeted her niece warmly and made a pot of tea.

Carolyn sat down quietly. "Are you alone?" she asked.

"Why yes. David always seems to be out now Sunday afternoons, and your uncle is painting the boat. Is anything wrong?"

Carolyn drank her tea carefully. "I'm going to leave home," she said.

"Oh dear. Why?"

"I've had a talk with my mother. She told me to go."

"Oh, I'm sure she wouldn't. Or at least—" Ann thought

of Sybil, and floundered. "I suppose it was just in a temper, if you'd been rowing."

"The decision was mutual."

"Oh, dear," Ann repeated. "I'd ask you to come here, but I don't know—"

"Thank you, Aunt. I don't want to come here. I want to go right away from Briarford."

"But what about your school?"

"That was just filling in time."

Carolyn stood up and went to the window, looking over the garden with its roses and lilies. When she turned she had a grown-up air, the know-all condescending air which young people seemed to assume these days, and which Ann found irritating. "Is that cottage still for sale, Aunt, you know, the one in Caldwell?"

"Old Aunt Nell's?"

"Yes. Is she still alive?"

"I've never heard she died. She must be about ninety. And she's been wanting to sell the cottage as long as I can remember, to go and live with her daughter."

"You see, I thought I could buy it. Daddy would buy it for me."

Ann stared, amazed. "Whatever for?"

"To live in, of course."

"You want to live in that tumbledown old cottage?"

"I should love it. I could have it modernised."

"I should think you'd have to have it rebuilt. The one next to it fell down."

"I should be able to grow my own vegetables ... It's macrobiotics, you know."

"Macro what?"

"Do you realise, Aunt, how many chemicals are used in the preparing of food today? How many poisonous pesticides?"

"I had heard," said Ann, drily.

"Well, you see, that's why I should grow my own. Fresh garden produce, can't you understand how good it would be?"

"You mean like Uncle William used to grow in his allotment?"

"I suppose so," said Carolyn, uncertainly, the grown-up mask slipping momentarily, revealing the little girl beneath. "I should bake my own bread too."

"Whatever would you want to bake your own bread for when you can buy it in the shops?"

"Because it's better. Women always used to bake their own bread."

"Yes, and women didn't like doing it either," said Ann, tartly. "It's a long job."

"I could have my own career," said Carolyn. "You've heard of Women's Lib, Aunt?"

"Vaguely. I don't see that it's much to do with working-class women. We've always worked."

"You don't approve?"

"Not if it means doing more work. I'm trying to do less."

"But you go to work."

"I need the money. And," said Ann, reflectively, "I like being independent, having my own money."

"There you are, you see."

"But," Ann said, baffled, "if you want a career, why not go into the business? I thought that's what your mother wanted."

"She did. But I should hate that." The mask had slipped completely now, Carolyn's eyes were wide, frightened. "So this will be a chance to get away . . ."

"Carolyn, what is it?" Ann stepped forward, wanting to hold her, to comfort her, but the girl stood rigid, refusing to confide. When she spoke her eyes were cool again, she was a little girl, coaxing. "Tell me all about Uncle William's work as a potter."

"In the *brickyard*? He hated it, it was a rotten job."

"I'm interested in pottery. I thought, you see, I could live in the cottage, make pots and sell them, perhaps have a little antique shop."

"In *Caldwell*?"

"Yes, Aunt."

"But you'll be like a common labourer, the people'll think you're daft—" Ann broke off, reflecting that her expensive niece would hardly look like a common labourer. And if that's what the girl wanted . . . something had upset her . . . Sybil? . . . Whatever it was she wouldn't tell. Ann had another thought. Ken would be glad to see Carolyn out of the way; he disliked the girl for some reason, probably because she was Sybil's daughter. Ann wondered, with sudden perspicuity, if Ken's intolerance of students was due to the fact that Carolyn happened to be one, and David did not. Ann saw little of Ken these days, he was out most evenings, and when he was in he was either in a black mood or quarrelling with David. Ann had never expected Ken to be a home bird, yet sometimes, seeing Doreen and Jack together, she would wonder why her marriage couldn't have been at least a little like theirs.

Yet Doreen's happiness was in one sense Ann's gain, for, with her three sons away, she and Jack went out practically every evening, leaving her no time to be at home to her sisters and brothers when they called – a revolutionary change in working-class lives, for women to be *out*. So, as Doreen abdicated her role, Ann found to her surprise and joy that she became the family hostess, for Chris was somehow regarded as an outsider even by her own family, and Ann wasn't sure why. Perhaps her views were too unorthodox; the men might want better conditions but only in the framework of the present set-up, and they didn't take kindly to being prompted by a woman, even if she was their sister.

Tommy had managed to get a job with the Council, sweeping the streets and picking up litter from the parks, for the local authority often provided work for those whose disabilities made them unacceptable to private enterprise. Newspapers were full of talk of scroungers on the dole, and more than one kind soul had mentioned this fact to Tommy, to his shame and sorrow. So he patiently picked up litter, overjoyed to be working.

Chris, who enjoyed sparring with the National Assistance officials, was found work by them, and forced into being a home help, the only thing suitable for a woman of her status and lack of education and experience. She came round to Ann's most evenings, Johnny and Doris dropped in more often, even Doreen condescended to call occasionally. And if Johnny came early, as he usually did, this meant that Ken would stay in home. Without Carolyn, Ann thought, things would be happier all round. She was still sorry for the girl, sensing bravado beneath the irritating grown-up manner, but reasoned that if David didn't want her, she'd be better away.

So Ann put the case to Ken as persuasively as possible and Ken, eager to get rid of Carolyn, went to Caldwell. Old Aunt Nell, more aware of current trends than Ann, with peasant shrewdness sold the cottage for £2,000. "Bloody old capitalist," said Ken.

*

As winter approached, the efficient little train service was cut as part of the Beeching axe, and Ann had to take two buses, which meant queueing and waiting in the cold and wet. Workers who owned cars and charged for transport were prosecuted. And the following week David was sacked. His firm had merged with another; there were two hundred redundancies.

"Best thing that could have happened," Ken said to Ann. "He can get a better job now."

"Maybe he will."

"He'll have to. Nobody will want an unskilled worker from Startin's. Anyway he's still got his qualifications. A-levels."

"Well, don't push him," Ann warned. But David appeared unconcerned. For a year he was in and out of jobs, any jobs, it seemed to Ken. Filing clerk at the Ministry of Social Security, sorting office at the Post Office, milk roundsman. Ken's last hopes were dashed.

*

Snow ushered in the Seventies in Marley Road. Man had reached the moon, but back on earth the thinkers and talkers were gloomy. Carolyn came to visit the Websters, and Ann noticed the girl's look of hopelessness. Yet she said she was happy in the cottage and that everything was fine.

February brought more snow, and Ken drove home from work to find David already there, looking perky. "I've mashed the tea, want a cup?" he asked.

"Please. You look happy."

Expansive for once David said. "I'm going to the Star."

"The motor-bike place? In the factory? Well, they say it's a decent place to work for."

"Yes." Talk lapsed.

"There's something else, Dad. I've got a girl."

"Another?"

"And I'm leaving home. We're going to live together, Jeanie and me."

"Who's Jeanie?"

"I met her at that student demo I went to. We lost touch, then I met her again recently."

"But – can't you get married?"

"She doesn't want to."

"Well, if that's how you do it these days." Ken was relieved that Carolyn was out of it. "I don't know what your mother will say."

"You're not getting married?" asked Ann. "Why not?"

"Jeanie doesn't believe in marriage."

"Well, I read about these things in the paper, didn't know they'd come to Briarford."

David raised his eyebrows and Ann flushed. "Anyway, we've decided. I wondered if you wanted to meet her."

"Of course we want to meet her. Does she have a job?"

"She did sociology at college. Worked in London in an ordinary office job, says it's high pay for less work than they do in the rest of the country."

"Where will you live?"

"There's a room going in Stansgate Street."

"Where the Asians are," said Ken.

"An Asian owns this house. Any objections?"

"Don't start arguing," put in Ann. "At least we'll have a bit of peace if you go, David. Though you could come to live here."

"It wouldn't work, Mother."

"No, I suppose not. Well, bring her to see us."

Jeanie had been born in a Glasgow slum, eldest of six children whose father had deserted them, leaving them to the tender mercies of National Assistance. Her mother had let her go to college for if she had stayed and worked the assistance payments would have been reduced ... might as well get out ...

She had a round, almost childish face, and a candid innocence that was in no way ignorance. Remarkably intelligent, she could speak at length on any given subject. A fervent Women's Libber, she said she would live with a man, as equal partners, but not marry him. Ann found she could not dislike the girl, and Ken took her into the garden where she followed him around in wonder, asking the name of each plant, and how they grew. "Why?" asked Ken, touched. "Don't you have gardens where you come from, then?" trying to imagine that hell on earth, life without a garden.

"No," said Jeanie. "Your house is much grander than where I lived. Glasgow has the worst housing in Europe."

Ken looked at the girl in concern, and Ann said, "Why don't you live with Chris? She's working now, and Tommy, but they don't earn much. They'd be glad of the money."

They thought it over, went to see Chris, and decided to move in. The neighbours were a little shocked at their living openly together but then, they said knowingly, them Websters were a rum lot all right.

"Well," Ken said to Ann, "he's living in the next yard. Just like you wanted."

*

With David and Jeanie settled in, and Tommy courting a local factory girl, another Webster scandal rocked Marley Road. Chris disappeared. She left a note to Tommy. *I'm sorry, but I must have a bit of life before I die.* "It's bound to be a man," the neighbours said, knowingly, nodding their heads. "We all put on Chris," said Ken, remorsefully. "Always taking from her." Ann remembered the one man who had replenished Chris and wondered if she'd gone to Italy. Was that why she'd been working, saving money? Had it been planned, arranged? No one knew. They never heard from Chris again.

The Seventies

The Seventies were years of promises. Joining the Common Market would give us new friends, more employment by opening up an enormous free trade market for manufactured goods. Marley Road grumbled at losing pounds, shillings and pence, but Marley Road always grumbled. In addition to the Common Market we were to have our own oil, and would be self-sufficient in oil by 1980. How could a nation built on coal, surrounded by fish, with oil and North Sea gas, fail? asked the experts.

Equal pay for women was brought in, and Ann, a skilled typist, found that she was equal to the lowest male clerk. Maternal and infant mortality dropped dramatically during the years of the National Health Service, helping to push up the life expectancy rates for women by five years, men four years.

The Seventies were years of bewilderment; economic crises, oil crises, balance of payments crises. Numerous strikes, although, contrary to popular belief, Britain's record was better than the US and other countries. In 1979 Margaret Thatcher won the election and promised to bring harmony where there was discord. While the new monetarist policies would cut taxes, unemployment and be the answer to all our problems.

A male stripper came to Marley Road Working Men's Club on a Ladies Only night.

Chapter Nine

Ken left the union meeting held outside the factory, and wondered if the fog was in the streets or in his head, he knew no more now than when he went in. No one knew what was happening or what the future would be. He was depressed. There could be a future for engineering if we got back to the old ideas of quality we had in the beginning. The old bosses were hard men, but dammit, they knew what they were doing. *But who am I working for now? Some financier in the City? I don't know. Don't know where I'm going, or why, just flung around like flotsam on the sea of factory takeovers. Helpless.*

He turned into Marley Road, wondering how many of the family would be in. Would Ann be home? Johnny might be in now the miners were on strike. He opened the door and heard Johnny's voice.

"This time," he was saying, "we're really in earnest."

"Do you think you'll win?" Ann asked, doubtfully.

"We earn damn-all now. And we got good money after the war."

"And how many used to take a day off cos he was paying too much tax?" asked Ken.

"Oh, hark at him. Hark at Mr Righteous. You don't work on the face for fun, mate."

"Funny," Ken mused. "We all thought nationalisation was the answer to the bad old days."

"Ah," Johnny said, "all we've done is change one set of

bosses for another. *We* don't own the pits any more than we used to."

Ann put Ken's dinner on the table. "You're late," she said.

"No use getting home before you do," he replied moodily.

"We're organising pickets outside the power stations," said Johnny. "Want to join us, Ken?"

"I don't know."

"Always the good little boy," Johnny mocked. "Where's all this working-class solidarity, then?"

"I went on strike once, and I didn't notice you come out for me," Ken told him. "I lost my job." He stood up, suddenly angry. "And I might lose this one. They're talking of closing the place down." And without another word he walked out of the house.

The family stared in amazement. "What's the matter with him?" Johnny asked.

"I don't know," Ann replied, troubled, wishing for the first time that Johnny wasn't here, that Ken could come home to peace and quiet. "Maybe you were too nasty to him."

"Me?" asked Johnny. "I always am. I'm his brother."

Ken walked through the town. So many new buildings replacing the funny little places that used to be there, the cobbled alleyways, the theatre, the Penny Bazaar, all gone now, all submerged in a mass of glass and concrete. Trouble was they took all your memories away, so now you felt like displaced persons struggling in a world you didn't understand.

He stopped outside the Weavers' Arms. This was where the riots took place a hundred and fifty years ago. *Riotous tumults, windows broken, a factory set on fire in Coventry by a riotous mob, violence, weavers striking for a regulation wage* ... The beginning of the Industrial Age.

He looked round vaguely. Why had he come here? A pang of hunger shot through him; he hadn't had his dinner. The smell of frying fish hung on the still air and he saw the shop, dirty chip wrappings flung on the pavement outside. He went in, ordered fish and chips, sat down to eat. An Indian brought the food, saying nothing. Ken wondered if he ought to talk to him, introduce him to the old community spirit folks talked about. What bloody community spirit? We had to have it to survive then, necessity not love. But was there something else that had gone now? Now it's every man for himself . . . Should I have moved out as Ann wanted, looked out for myself and devil take the hindmost? He left the shop, utterly depressed.

Home again, there was more noise than ever, and someone was asking David what the matter was. It could have been himself.

"He's upset about Carolyn," said Ann.

"What about Carolyn?"

"She's just been here. Going into her father's business. And Sybil's invited us to a celebration party."

"A *party*?" Ken looked with dismay at David, who turned away.

"I'd like to go," said Ann, stubbornly. "Carolyn seemed to want it. I feel sorry for that girl somehow, though I don't know why. Will you come, Ken?"

"What happened to the cottage and the good life?"

"It didn't pay," said Ann. "And Sybil won't allow her any more money."

What had Sybil said? "I'll arrange things." Let her go off to the cottage when it suited her purpose, knowing all along she'd get her into the business sooner or later. When David was safely out of the way. He too thought of Carolyn, the girl he'd been too afraid to like up to now, and, seeing her dispassionately for the first time, felt sympathy, and guilt that he'd made her suffer. "I'll come," he said.

*

"Dad. Are you alone?"

"Yes. Your mother's out. Did you want her?"

"No. I want you."

David eased himself into the room and sat down. "Dad. Why are you always going to Aunt Sybil's? I mean, visiting her on the quiet."

"Who told you that?"

"Carolyn."

"She knows?"

"Of course she knows. Do you think she's a fool? In the same house year after year . . . there were always men . . . you're not the only one. Seems it was like a brothel. Mind you, she never told me till now."

"Why now?"

"I think Aunt Sybil's got the purse-strings in her hands now. I don't know how, but she seems in control. One thing I know, you won't catch me going to her house again."

"But you promised your mother to go to the party."

"I can change my mind."

"She'll want to know why."

David frowned and Ken said, a little maliciously, "It isn't so easy, is it, to do the right thing all the time?"

*

Sybil's visitors were not the pleasant dilettantes of their previous visits, they were mostly local businessmen; brought in, doubtless, to initiate Carolyn into her new world, Ken thought, glancing round the table. David was there, seething with suppressed rage, Jeanie, stiff, Ann, a little bewildered, Carolyn, her face white and set, and somehow, empty. Ken knew a feeling of wretchedness, that he should have a part in this. David would never forgive him. How bright and shining the world looked when you were young, one touch and you could turn it all to silver. How tarnished it all became as you grew older. How many mistakes you made. But did Carolyn have to give in so easily? Didn't she care any more now she'd lost David? She'd always defied Sybil in a quiet sort of way. If only she didn't look so hopeless. Couldn't she get a job and still live in the cottage? No, Sybil wouldn't let her. Damn Sybil to hell . . .

Ken's neighbour, a plump woman named Mrs Beverley, said querulously that she couldn't understand why people were so different today. Ken agreed, wondering what she'd said, and she turned to David on her other side. "Read any good books lately?" she asked archly.

"Peter Pan and Wendy," said David.

"Really?" Mrs Beverley was impervious to sarcasm. "So much better than those grim bitter kitchen-sink stories." Mrs Beverley's face creased with pain. "I can't stand those tales full of hatred and envy, they make me really ill. I just refuse to read them, and if everyone did the same, they'd have to stop publishing them."

"And the *plays on television*," said David. "All that sex and violence. Censorship is what we need."

Mrs Beverley bent nearer. "We need beauty and refinement, not ugliness around us. I believe . . ." she paused impressively. "I believe I am doing my own little bit if I go all out for beauty and ignore the ugliness."

"I understand Marie Antoinette felt the same way," said David beaming.

Mr Branston, opposite, was talking about the miners' strike. "Disgraceful," he boomed.

"They're hooligans."

"Picketing should be made illegal."

"You've forgotten the Communist infiltration," said David, sweetly.

"True. The majority of miners don't want this strike, they're led by a few extremists, wanting to start a revolution—"

"You've had word?" asked David. "From Russia?"

"David," said Ken, warningly.

"People want too much today," said Mr Branston. "That's the trouble. Too much materialism."

"All those washing machines," said David dreamily. "Thinking of selling your Aston-Martin, Mr Branston?"

The man flushed a dull red. "There's no need to be offensive."

"Why not? You are. My uncle's a miner."

"*David.*" Sybil spoke, majestically. "We all know you are a Red, but don't bring your militant talk into my house, if you please. We are civilised here."

"Oh, don't worry. I'm going—"

He went out, followed by Jeanie.

Ken caught up with them in the hall, hearing a dull rumble behind. "Do some of 'em good to be in the army—"

"Leave me alone, Dad. I'm off."

"Off where?"

"To join the pickets. Come on, Jeanie."

*

The three-day week was at its height. Lamps were out in the streets and shop-windows, reminding those old enough to remember, of the war. Ann sent for David.

He entered the living-room and she stood up. "Look, David. I've had enough of this."

"What?"

"You needn't look round, we're alone, that's why I wanted you. So listen to me for once. You and your father, it's got to stop."

"What do you mean?"

"You know damn well what I mean. I've put up with it for years, and it's been hard for me too. What have you got against him?"

"Nothing."

"Then why can't you be civil? You seemed better after you met Jeanie, now it's all started again. He thinks the world of you."

"So I'm always being told."

"And you don't like it?"

"All he did for me was really for himself. Giving me what he couldn't have."

"And what's wrong with that? Would you have preferred to have been neglected?"

"Oh—"

"Never mind 'Oh'. So you're doing what you wanted, but couldn't you ever talk to him, just try to explain how you feel?"

"He wouldn't understand. We don't see eye to eye on anything."

"I know you're awkward."

"I suppose you're annoyed about that rumpus at Aunt Sybil's?"

"It didn't exactly please me."

"But you don't like that crew?"

"No, but I've got more manners than to say so."

David paused. "You really love my father, don't you?"

"Yes. I always have. And – I'm worried about him."

"He's not ill?"

"No, but he doesn't seem himself somehow."

"Well, what do you want me to do?"

"Just be friends. You've got Jeanie now, she seems a nice girl. Let's have an end to this bickering."

"Or—?"

"Or," said Ann, "I'll give you a clout on the ear, big as you are."

He grinned. "All right, Ma. I'll have a go."

*

The miners were still holding out. The Prime Minister went to the country, asking the moderates to speak against the militants. The government fell, and the country went back to work with Labour.

*

"You're having trouble at your place then, Dad?"

"Same old rumours about closing it down. Lots of chaps leaving."

"How would you like to come to the Star?"

Ken's eyes were dull. "Do you know how old I am?"

"Over fifty. But I can ask for you. Course, if you'd rather wait till you're made redundant, you'd get redundancy pay then."

"Yes, but if all the blokes are out there'll be more wanting work."

"True, you could wait too long."

Ken studied his son. Was he holding out a hand of friendship at last? Or was Ann behind it? Did it matter?

"We should be all right," David went on. "We're the only motor-bike firm left. Metal Bronze has bought out the other."

Something stirred in Ken's mind, some half-forgotten memory about a warning, but he couldn't remember what it was.

"All right, see what you can do," he said. "I've always hated Brett's."

So Ken went to the Star.

*

The British motor-cycle industry was a shambles in the early Seventies, practically wiped out by the Japanese, whose success was based on investing in up-to-date technology and low-cost production, with high wages for its employees. Facing such competition the British simply retreated, refusing to reinvest and modernise. Ken, with the rest of the workers, sensed all this, and industrial relations were bad. But he shrugged philosophically. He was used to it. He'd be all right here for the rest of his working life. He'd put things right at home too, settle down with Ann. Perhaps he could even do something about Carolyn.

*

He went to see Sybil.
"Well – Ken. It's been quite a time."
"I'm not stopping, Sybil."
"Oh?"
"That's what I came to tell you. I've finished."
"Why?"
"I'm over fifty, getting past it."
"Not till you're nailed in your coffin."
"It's true."
"You just want to go home to your little wife, put your feet up."
"Something like that."
"Now you've had your fun."
"Was it fun?"
"I can still tell Ann."
"I'm going to tell her myself."
"How touching. Listen, Ken, don't come the holy act

over me. I'm a bit sick of your family too. That scene David made, insulting all my friends."

"He knows about us."

Sybil drew in a breath and said nothing.

"And Carolyn. What the hell are you doing to her? Forcing her into the business when you know she doesn't like it."

"Do you know," Sybil said, "sometimes I get tired, really tired. Who was it asked me to do something about Carolyn?"

"That was years ago."

"True. And I let her have her silly cottage to get her away, and who had to pay? We did. I didn't mean it to last. Why do I have to do everything, arrange everything and then get blamed for it? I used to run the business before Peter sold out because he couldn't. I've always had to push him—"

"You wanted a well-off husband, didn't you? He was the only one you could get. Now you despise him. What is it you want?"

"I wanted you."

"Only after I married Ann."

"That's how it started." He was silent, and she went on rapidly. "You don't know what my life was like. My mother didn't allow me to do anything. Never go anywhere, nor mix with the girls at school, not Doreen, not anyone. Can you understand how that made me feel?"

Ten years ago he would have been interested in unravelling the riddle that was Sybil. Now he no longer cared.

"And I didn't know a thing about sex," she went on.

"Oh, come on. You said yourself there were four-letter words chalked up in the girls' lavatories."

"But I didn't know what they meant, I didn't listen to the other girls' whispers. When I was sixteen I was bursting and didn't know what with."

"You soon found out."

"Peter – was pathetic, he hadn't a clue."

"What about all those rumours of you and Peter's dad?"

"Oh, Ken, you know Marley Road. Hotbed of gossip."

He didn't believe her. "And all the other men you've had over the years?"

"Well, you didn't come very often, did you?"

"And you couldn't live without it?"

"Well, could you? Why is it different for men? It was you I wanted. It was you I loved."

"Love." He laughed, harshly. "You don't know the meaning of the word. Take Carolyn. What are you doing to her? Don't you love your own child? If you did, you'd let her do what she wanted, not what you want for her."

"As you did with David—"

"Leave David out of it!" he shouted. "You want to beat Carolyn into submission, then you'll despise her. That's what you want to do to me. And it's something you'll never do, I told you that years ago."

"I can't help the way I am," she said. "I can't help being strong. That's why I always wanted you, you're the only person I can't bully."

"You didn't bully Peter into giving you the business."

"That was the typical action of a weak, fearful man. But he's suffered for it over the years, I've seen to that."

"You talk about the business as if you still own it. What's it matter if Carolyn works there or not?"

"I nearly do," she said. "I've been getting control of our money over the years, bit by bit. I've bought back into the business, other businesses too." She smiled. "I can always win, and I know it. Carolyn used to defy me in a quiet way, but she's given in now."

"You're a selfish bitch."

"Why? Because I want to win? Like men do?"

"I know one man who's stronger than me by far," said Ken, half to himself. "David. My son." He saw clearly that

that had been the trouble between him and David, a battle of wills. A manoeuvring for power. Just as between him and Sybil. Was that all that life was about, then? Power? Winners and losers? Well, he'd known that, hadn't he? He'd been born a loser, he'd just wanted David to win. How would it help the losers to put David among them? But wasn't that what they all said?

Hastily he switched his thoughts back to Sybil. The winner before him, the one he could fight. The epitome of all the winners he'd ever known, her father-in-law who'd won by crooked dealing, her mother who won by spite and push, the bosses who held all the cards. "You'll never get the better of me," he said, and it was a challenge.

They faced each other, hostile again. Ken said: "If you want to fight like a man then don't come the bits about love, right? You can't have it both ways."

Sybil's face was flushed, her eyes glittered. "You're right," she said. "I do hate you."

"And don't start about telling Ann. You've had more than she. You've had your fun, you've had a child. You're running businesses – or something. You're just spiteful about Ann, you always were."

"Because I envied her. She had the freedom I was denied."

"You really have got your knickers in a twist," he said, brutally. "Just leave her alone now, right? Cos I think it's time Ann and me settled down together."

*

David said to Ken, "I don't like all this, Dad."

"All what?"

"The firm setting men on. We aren't doing as well as all that."

"What do you mean?"

"I think there's something going on."

"What?"

"I don't know . . . but I was talking to the union bloke, he gets to know about these things . . . he isn't too happy."

"But surely if there was something wrong they wouldn't be setting on?"

"How do we know how their minds work? Could be a smokescreen. Reg thinks there's something."

"But wouldn't they tell us?"

"Oh, come on, Dad, a boss is a boss, even at the Star."

The news broke quite suddenly. The Star had been taken over by Bronze Metals. The new company didn't think the Star was viable as it was, they were closing the factory down. Everyone would be made redundant.

Chapter Ten

Ken put the last tool down by his machine and left the factory. He got into his little car and drove away.

He ignored the country road, drove through the streets, cold and shabby in the early darkness of winter. The factories were still lit, they worked all night, as did the pits, and always, summer or winter, there was the faint throb of the industrial night, a machine that held you so tight in its maw that you were afraid when it spewed you out. You hate the slavery and you fear freedom. And freedom was the worst, for inside the maw you were warm, so you cuddled closer and closer, shutting your eyes, shrinking year by year.

Getting on for sixty and I've nothing to look forward to ever again. I saw a vision, it so nearly came off. But it's over now. Like me, finished. Won't get another job now, there's nothing. Nothing but the old-age pension and the downward slope leading to the grave. Dear Christ, how little you thought about age till it crept up on you.

What happened to my dreams? I didn't think it'd end like this when I fought my war. I'd been recognised in the war, given self-respect. I was one of the brave boys who saved the country. And when the war ended I thought it would keep on like that. And it could have . . . You could have welded a nation of wonder, we were ready, waiting. Where is the Dunkirk spirit? Well, you tell me.

Everything I believed in thrown back in my face . . .

everybody in Europe earning more than I do, Ken Webster, Private 544671, who won the war.

But I'd love to do something to the bastards before the night closes in, make one grand protest . . . *Riotous tumults, a factory set on fire in Coventry by a riotous mob* . . . The black shadow was rising, blotting out the barracks of the People's Houses . . . They shouldn't live here . . . Surely if you worked all day in a dreary factory or dirty mine you should come home to something bright and lovely and light . . . spacious houses in singing streets . . . A fleeting memory intruded of Marta in 1944 . . . How the years flew by; it seems only yesterday I was dancing with Marta, at least they can't take that away from me . . . wish I believed there was an afterlife, it might lift me out of this frightening void, this emptiness . . .

The vision that died. Did they con me or did I con myself? . . . Why didn't it work? . . . *And did those feet in ancient times walk upon England's mountains green?* . . . No, if they did they'd have crucified him, they'd do the same today, call him a Marxist.

Wish I'd got my mam to talk to, she always understood. I feel so alone, no one thinks the way I do. David . . . I used to talk to David when he was a kid. Wonder if he ever listened? Really, we've never been on the same wavelength, funny that, you hope and dream for your son and expect him to feel the same way as you . . . I should have gone lefty-militant, fought to hell and back for my beliefs, but I didn't because of David . . . What beliefs? That we are all equal, except David . . .? Forget it now, don't let the black shadow rise any higher, some things can't ever be worked out, can they . . .?

How my head pains. I must get home. Home to Ann. I'd forgotten Ann yet she's always there. Maybe, if I'm careful, if I stop thinking, it'll be all right. I'm sorry, Ann, if I took you for granted in the past, men do, you know

... you've been a good wife, a good mother ... I suppose I was jealous that David preferred her to me, he shouldn't have, he isn't hers. *Don't think about David or the things that can't ever be put right.*

Go back to Ann, and safety.

He turned his car round, heading for home.

Ann was in when he returned. And David.

"Well, David," Ann said, and her voice was unnaturally sharp. "Your dad was right, after all. You would have been better in a good job." She turned to Ken. "What are you going to do?"

"I don't know."

She stood by the table. "Do you think you'll find another job?"

"Everybody's cutting down now."

"So what shall we live on? You'll have benefit and earnings related that last – what? Six months? You haven't been at the Star long enough for redundancy pay and you left Brett's of your own accord. And it'll affect your pension if you don't get work."

"Don't keep on—"

"You're not at retiring age yet." Her voice went inexorably on. "Not on your job. Some people might retire at fifty-five and have a good pension. Not you."

He was bewildered. "Look, Ann, let's talk this over."

"We are talking it over. I'm not going back to poverty."

"I can't help the place closing down."

"You're in the union, aren't you? The unions are powerful, they tell us. So do something."

"What do you want me to do?"

"Well, you're always saying you know how to run things better than them. So go on and run something."

"You mean take over the factory?"

"I don't care what you do. All I know is that I'm not going back to poverty. You take over the factory; you couldn't make a worse job of it."

"But—"

"All these years," Ann said, "I've listened to your talk. That's all you do, men, talk. You love it. Politicians, trade union leaders, just talk."

Ken stood, startled at her outburst.

"It's a free country," said Ann. "So we can talk. Trouble is, nobody takes any notice. So you have your big meetings and pass your resolutions and nobody takes a blind bit of notice."

"But, Ma—" began David.

"You can keep quiet as well. I'm not living with a man who's out of work. That's what they've been telling us to do, isn't it, when our husbands were on strike, get 'em back to work?"

"Yes, Ma, but I don't think they meant it in quite this way."

"Work's work," said Ann. "It's all the same to me why they stop."

"It's just a matter of economics—"

"Economics," said Ann. "I'm sick of the word. Does economics mean thousands thrown out of work, then? If so, give me my own strip of land and I'll grow my own stuff. Better than letting apples rot, and butter mountains they don't know what to do with, while we can't afford to buy ... If that's economics give me the other way."

She left the table and went upstairs abruptly.

"Women," said Ken, wonderingly. "You never know where you are with 'em. Women are all right till you upset 'em, somebody said to me once, and then look out, boys. Look out, politicians, if they ever get going, they'll really put the fear of God into you."

"It's women who have the trouble when there's poverty," said Ann, re-entering. "Not politicians."

"You do keep saying the same thing, Ma," said David.

"There's nothing else to say," said Ann. "And I'll have less of your cheek as well."

"I think I'll go," said David.

He left, and Ann sat down suddenly as though all the breath had been knocked out of her body.

"What's the matter, Ann?" asked Ken.

"Nothing."

"Oh, come on."

"I'm going to leave you," she said.

"Leave me?" He thought she was joking. "Why, because I've lost my job?"

"No." She hesitated. "Sybil."

"Sybil what?" he asked, his heart dropping like a stone.

"She told me. You and her – all these years. And about Carolyn."

Oh, God, he thought. Oh, Christ in heaven, that Sybil should come today of all days. As if she knew. No doubt she did. Sybil knew all about putting the boot in. He sat down. "I'm sorry," he said.

"*Sorry*. Much good that'll do."

"It didn't mean anything, Ann. Honestly."

"I can believe that," she said, slowly. "Nobody meant anything to you did they, except Marta?" She looked at the photograph. "All these years I've had to sit and look at that, did you realise? I knew how you felt about her, but I thought, 'Well, she's dead and I'm here . . .' But you never admitted she was dead, did you? You live in the past, always, in your childhood . . . I wanted to leave here, to move to a nice house, we could have, but you never would; I thought it was this working-class sentimentality, yet you went with Sybil . . . Sybil . . ." She drew a shuddering breath that seemed to rack her body. "I could have forgiven anybody but her."

"I suppose it's no use saying anything."

"No. I'm going to leave you."

"Oh, come on, Ann. Don't be silly."

"I'm not being silly. Not now."

"But where will you go?"

"Well, not to Sybil's, that's for sure. I've got some money saved, I shall take a room. I've got a job."

"Ann. Don't leave me."

"You said that to me once before, I remember. When you came home from the war. At the cemetery."

"I can't do without you, Ann."

"That's man's blackmail. You'll manage all right."

She went upstairs again, and Ken left the house, rage mounting in him, driving him on. He jumped into the car, went round the corner on two wheels, through the town, up to Sybil's house. Knocked on the door. She came, hurriedly. "It's all right. Peter's out. Come in."

He entered and said: "Go into the lounge, or whatever you call your front room."

She backed away, fearfully.

"Go on. Or I'll drag you there."

She went slowly, and he followed, shut the door.

"I told you," he said. "I told you what I'd do if you told Ann." He hit her on the face, knocked her to the floor, kneeled above her, hands round her neck. "I told you," he said, over and over. "You waited till today, when the Star closed . . . you knew . . . By God, you had shares in Bronze Metals, you'd have heard . . ." his hands tightened. "Carolyn'd be better without you," he added, conversationally. "Peter would let her live in a cottage if she wanted, sell this house and buy ten cottages . . ."

But Sybil could no longer hear.

He left, drove back to the canal, jumped aboard his boat.

The Rose of Sharon. I am the Rose of Sharon. Marta, her childhood, her dancing, her love . . . but she was dead. The glory and the passion had been dead for thirty years. All these years he'd looked for Marta in David, her high spirits, her recklessness, her laughter. All these years he'd lived for Marta through David and he'd been wrong. Where was she now? Was that the freedom he sought?

He pottered round the boat, jumping down to the storage room, moving along the deck. *If I smash your ideals it's because you're fooling yourself.* Maybe I was and that's what I can't face.

No, face it, Ken. The grand socialist victory of 1945, you talked about equality, but you all went for making money, just as before, and those who couldn't were left behind, just as before, and those who were above us looked down on us, just as before. A man doesn't kill the thing he loves, he kills that thing in others that he can't face in himself.

He went into the cabin and up again on deck. Marta. She's just a picture in a frame. But God, he could almost be dancing at the George tonight with the air thick with smoke in the blackout and the boy singing: 'We'll Meet Again . . .' *Why did you keep away from me so long?*

He jumped ashore and loosed the mooring-rope. So you know what you can do with your jobs, don't you? Stuff 'em. He pulled the rope on board and lifted two fingers to the sky as the boat slid away.

Ann moved around the bedroom, packing her clothes, quietly, automatically. Someday, she guessed, the hurt would affect her, make her cry perhaps, know her loss; now she just felt deeply offended. Offended. Funny, they'd used that word when they were kids, and it meant more than a mere quarrel, it was deadly serious, the finality. Now, in her pain, she reverted to the childish word, finding no other.

She wondered dully where Ken had gone. Not that it

mattered now. She'd go to bed, couldn't sit up all night, couldn't leave till morning. Wearily she went to the window to draw the curtains. And stopped.

The street-lights shone through the gloom of the night. Across the road was the field and the canal. What was that on the canal? A fire?

Shooting flames moving along the water, what was it . . .? A commotion in the street, little black figures running . . . and slowly came the chugging of an engine. The flames grew and spread till their reflection turned the black water to fiery blood, and she could clearly see Ken standing at the tiller. The mass of flames sailed on until there came an explosion, and the whole boat splintered up into shooting stars, beautiful in its ferocity.

David's Book

Chapter One

Why did you do it, Dad? You did it deliberately, I know, for I was running along the towpath towards you. At the inquest Mother wanted to pretend it was an accident, but I wouldn't have it, and the Coroner listened to me. I went in my old school tie which he recognised as if it were a mason's badge, and his indoctrinated mind immediately got the right image. Educated man. Reliable witness. I could hear his brain ticking over. And I said, loud and clear in a posh accent, "My father had just lost his job, been dismissed, he set his boat alight and went out like the old Vikings, making his last protest." A funeral pyre, Dad. What a way to go.

Mind you, I don't think it was just that, was it? It was everything, everybody, even me . . . Mother said it was me. "He thought the world of you and you let him down." She quarrelled with me. Mother. And six months later went off and married Ted Naylor. I shall never understand parents.

I suppose I did let you down, Dad. But I had to live my life, don't you see? I should have tried to explain, yet how could I when I hardly knew myself what I was doing? Not at first. You wanted me to get on, Dad, yet all the time you told me the very things to hold me back. Wrongs, injustice, slavery . . . get out and forget, you said. But that would have meant forgetting you, Dad . . . don't you see? Oh yes, I might possibly have written the story of my father's life, unreal because I wouldn't have lived it; most likely I'd have been caught up in the money-making machine you hated so much. And if I'd tried to explain, in justifying myself I'd have smashed your ideals. I saw how hurt you were when I talked that way, so I had to stop . . . You could have read my book, it's here, Dad, the story of my life, all my thoughts and feelings, because I always had this idea of writing about factory life first-hand. But you can't read it now, can you? Only I can read it . . . David Webster, the educated proletarian.

*

My first memory is of the photograph over the fireplace. Marta, they told me, and I used to sit and look at it because it dominated the room somehow. And my second memory is of Uncle William, dressing up in his best clothes on Sundays and going out with a bunch of gorgeous roses. "Poor old man," Dad said once. "His poor hands, all bent, the finger ends bent right over with rheumatism, yet he will go every week, croffling along, poor old soul." Dad never went with him; sometimes I thought that he never admitted the fact that she was dead.

One Sunday as I stood at the front gate, Uncle William came out with his roses and I shouted, "Can I come with you?" He looked at me and nodded. So I put my hand in his and together we plodded down to the cemetery. After that I went every Sunday.

Uncle William told me about the world he'd known as a child in the village, and the world of his grandfather who'd been a chapel preacher, though he couldn't read or write. "He hated the Church," said Uncle William. "He'd never have any pictures of angels in the house," and I thought that was a bit strong. "He said angels were Roman, and people were very anti-Catholic then, why I can remember folks tarring and feathering each other. Things are a lot quieter now," said Uncle William.

"The Quakers used to come to the village, had a meeting

place there. George Fox was born only five miles away, over the border in Leicestershire. Course, at one time, they persecuted the Quakers somethin' terrible, put 'em in prison, so they had to have secret meeting places, and even when they were free they still used to ride for miles to meet at our village, my grandad'd put 'em up . . . I remember the old mounting stones . . . I went to a Quaker funeral once, nobody said anything, we just stood in silence, till at last one man said: 'As the tree falls so let it lie', and that was it, we all went home . . ."

"Why did they put them in prison?" I asked.

"Oh, well, the Quakers didn't believe in the Church, you see, nor the hierarchy, they assembled for worship as equals, a community of believers, their beliefs led to the start of socialism. Brotherhood of men of all races, and women too, women preachers there were. No authority, no domination of man over man, no wars, no violence. Freedom of conscience; they were . . ." William paused – "incorruptible. And that's why the powers feared them, Cromwell and King Charles alike, they all persecuted them. They didn't believe in bowing to the gentry, you see, or taking oaths in court." And I thought they were real revolutionaries, those good gentle people.

And at the grave he mused aloud. "Honest labour and good works they believed in . . . Allis worked hard all my life . . ." He sighed, puzzled, and on the way home he'd talk about Marta. "Never hurt a living soul," he'd say. "She was a lovely gel."

"What made her die?" I asked when we got home, and Uncle William said: "She had the consumption," and Dad said: "She was overworked, that factory took all her strength." And I knew factories were bad places, like workhouses, because my Dad talked about the one where he worked, all the time he talked about it to me, as though he couldn't get it out of his mind, though he said things were going to change. "We're going to have a new world," he said.

Dad told me Marta was my real mother, and I knew he loved her so much that he couldn't stop thinking about her. She haunted me, although I never admitted it; she was a symbol of the oppressed.

Uncle William died, and I was sorry, for I loved him. They buried him in the grave with Marta and Aunt Liz and I thought he'd be happy there.

I was happy too, at that time. I'd started school, same one as my dad, though it was different now, just a junior school. Lessons were easy and I got on well. The last couple of years we just practised intelligence tests, and I soon picked up the knack of answering. As bull is to cow, fox is to . . . Pen, paper, crayon, which is the odd one out . . .?

I liked my school, I liked my pals, I liked the field opposite and my dad's boat on the canal. I liked going out in the country, we studied wildlife, Dad and me.

I started the grammar school in an idealistic frame of mind. From the age of five I had been taught that passing the eleven-plus was the height of all earthly ambition; my dad spoke reverently of education, and by education he meant King Alfred School for Boys. There was the High for girls, not quite the same, and the new mixed grammar was definitely inferior. King Alfred was old, it had been there since BC, and from here men ruled the world. King Alfred was tradition, superiority, the British Raj, officers and gentlemen, all-male clubs, playing fields, bosses. The establishment starts here.

So my dad and the junior school pushed me through the intelligence tests in order that I might enter the portals of that heaven. I entered heaven under the not surprising misapprehension that the masters were archangels and the Head God himself, a benign deity whose wisdom surpassed that of ordinary men. I suppose no one could have lived up to that ideal, certainly not Mr Tripp.

Mr Tripp was an elderly balding gentleman who always

made a point of writing MA (Oxon) after his name, which for the first year I thought was something to do with cattle. He was an autocrat, ruling boys and masters alike with a rod of iron. He looked back with nostalgia to the days when his school catered for the sons of gentlemen who paid fees. I gathered they were gentlemen *because* they paid fees.

He was against the 1944 Education Act, and once he realised that Other Persons were to be forced upon him, he decided that the Other Persons' way of life must be wiped off the face of the earth. He took his pupils as old William had taken the cold clay and moulded them into as near his own image as he possibly could. He made it clear that he Would Not Tolerate Bad Behaviour – Mr Tripp always spoke in capital letters – he had Made Rules, and Rules Must be Kept. Boys must learn that a School Tie meant something, that Team Spirit and Loyalty to the School had won us an Empire. Tripp didn't seem to realise that we'd lost the Empire.

He was very strict about exams, and from the moment we entered the school it was made clear to us luckless lads that the Team Spirit and Old School Tie meant one thing only – passing GCEs in as many subjects as possible for the Glory of the School. I found that my whole way of life was considered to be wrong, my dress, my voice, my accent – most of all my accent; this had to be whipped out of my body as though it were a demon – and had the effect of making me afraid to speak in school debates for many years. Some of us Other Persons accepted the school teaching, some refused, and these did not seem to stay after they were sixteen. There were three of us Other Persons in my form, Ron and Norman were council-house kids, and our relations with the Head were far from amicable. We were told repeatedly that we were untidy and lazy, which had the result of making us more untidy and definitely lazy. (We hadn't been lazy in the first place, just bewildered at the new language, 'formroom' for 'classroom', 'detention' for 'being kept in', 'yard' for 'playground'.) Ron and Norman refused to be pushed on the middle-class conveyor-belt, but at first I was uncertain. I was, it seemed, being taught a superior way of life, but that logically meant that my dad and his way of life was inferior. My dad had been my greatest pal and I loved him. Up to that time I'd been outgoing, happy, now my confidence was shaken and I began to think.

I was really unhappy in the first year, for the school was run on pseudo-public-school lines, with the full prefect system, and much bullying by older boys of the new kids. Being a day school there was no homosexuality, so I was spared that indignity, but my life was made a misery by orders to run here, run there, and punches to help me along.

In the B-form we had the poorer masters, the best being reserved for the A-form, which pupils were pushed and pummelled through tests and exams till they obtained the final glory – university entrance. And because Briarford was not a residential area it was used as a passing-through place for young masters eager to get on, or who found they couldn't stand Mr Tripp, and we never knew from one term to the next who'd be taking us. And of course, I couldn't do the subjects I wanted, just those available to the little unimportant being that was me.

I drifted through my second year, almost completely losing interest. And it was then, after my poor exam result, that my parents were asked to see God himself. And this was when the balloon really went up in my head.

My parents went for the interview, looking the way I'd felt when I started school, and when they came home they were shocked and upset because they'd been given the idea that I was a scruffy little toad, lazy and careless in dress (like most boys), mixing with the worst elements in the school (the council-house kids) and Not Always Wearing a Clean Shirt.

I saw my parents' distress, my mother hurt, my dad bewildered, and I realised, at the age of twelve, I'd have to take sides. The Head's way of life, or theirs. I'd have to accept my parents, or reject them. I was angry that my parents should be so patronised. I began to sympathise with Lucifer, why should God have a monopoly of pride? I pondered on leaving school but reasoned that would make it all too easy for the Head. Better stay and fight from the inside. But how to fight? How to get my own back? I was sharp enough to realise that being an ordinary rebel would simply put right on the Head's side. Ron and Norman were stupid, they were getting more lazy and didn't care, soon they'd put themselves in a position where they'd be forced to leave. I'd have to find a better way.

I didn't really care at this time whether I stayed or not, or whether I worked or not. I thought the school was potty, and refused to wear my uniform if I could help it. This caused some trouble at home, for both my mother and dad were keen on uniforms and couldn't understand why we weren't. Even young Carrie had made some trouble about her silly pudding-basin hat, and I remember when she was about eleven there was one big row with her. "You should be proud of it," Aunt Sybil told her. Proud she paid fees for a private school, she meant. Showing they were superior. My mother said that when she was young uniforms were a badge of superiority, whereas they reminded us of Victorian orphanages with their white pinnies.

Mind you, there were some daft ideas in Briarford about uniforms. The working classes too were going mad to put their kids into uniform, so in an effort to make everyone equal, the education bods decided that every child should wear the rig, but this still divided schools, so they changed the names of the secondary mods to high schools. It would have been much simpler just to stop wearing uniforms, the rotten things were very expensive, and it seemed to me to be ridiculous to pay a lot for a school cap which I rolled in the mud – or had it rolled for me – at the first opportunity. It seemed to me that both Mother and Dad wanted me to go to grammar school simply to wear a uniform; I told them I might as well go to jail, they get them there – or did – but they didn't like that at all. "Sharp-tongued little devil," said Dad.

When we had the O-levels coming up I didn't care whether I passed or failed. I was bored sick with King Alfred, and his little god headmaster before whom all bowed their heads. My written work was good enough, for it's easy to memorise facts and just write them down, and that's pretty well all education is, to my way of thinking. One of the boys said something of this to Hegrave, one of the more enlightened masters, and Heg said: "Well, as soon as you've got your passes, Jones, you can forget all you've learned." Oh, we had some occasional laughs; King Alfred wasn't one of those public school horrors you read about, for the most part it was just dead boring, with old Tripp posturing round like a cat on hot bricks.

I didn't say much in debates and discussions. This was mainly due to the fear of public speaking old Tripp had instilled into me, but partly because I didn't see much point in endless chat, when the facts were there and presumably had to be accepted. I refused to play games, this seemed unutterably childish. In Marley Road boys still went to work at fifteen, and to be playing rugger at the age of sixteen seemed to be a sort of arrested development. I didn't object to a friendly kick-around with a football, but to Play for the Glory of the School wasn't worth thinking about, especially as we only played other grammar schools. So I got out of it when I could, forging little notes from my parents to say I wasn't well.

We studied for O-levels, and Carney, our form master, young and a little bitter, told us that the number who passed depended on the numbers allowed to pass each year. "A sort of Parkinson's Pass, sir," said Smith. Also, Carney told us, the Cambridge was harder than other boards, although the universities took more from our school than the new grammar, a sort of gentleman's understanding like Oxbridge taking 60 per cent from public schools. "It's all a fiddle," I muttered. "Most things in life are," said Carney. Well, I knew that; you don't live in Marley Road without coming to that conclusion sooner or later, and I wouldn't have minded if only Tripp and his ilk hadn't given us all this fancy talk about decency and honour.

I scraped through four O-levels, one less and I'd have been thrown out. I thought about leaving, and I think Trippy would have been pleased to see the back of me. I wasn't rebellious, but gave him that sort of dumb insolence masters find so hard to bear. I still hated him, and wondered what I could do to upset him most. Then I had my Plan.

Of course. How simple it was. Tripper wanted me to Go On to Do Big Things, to get A-levels for the Glory of the School, to become an Important Man. I would get a place in college, pass as many A-levels as I could, and then do the thing that would upset Tripper most. Go to work in a factory. Revert to the peasant way of life from which he'd been trying to drag me by the hair, from which I'd been saved by my grammar school education. Maybe in a hundred years' time this will seem a ridiculous sort of revenge, let's hope so, but in England, 1961, an educated boy did not do any sort of manual labour, except in vacations and between jobs, and this was a step up; the last generation didn't even do that, my dad says. I must add at this time I wasn't working my Plan out of any high-minded thoughts of equality, merely revenge.

I entered the Arts Sixth, doing Eng. Lit., in which the

dissecting of poems put me off poetry for life, Geography, being easy, and Social History and Economics, for which I was grateful, and which made it worth spending all those years as a grammar-bug, as the proletarian elements in the town called us.

Ron and Norman had three passes. "Tripper says there's no point in our continuing, we're neither use nor ornament," Ron told me. "Thank goodness we can get out. I'm sorry for you, David. Another two years of the Hitler Youth."

I smiled bleakly as carelessly Ron and Norman passed from my life. I felt I was striking a blow for them as well as myself, but they didn't know that, and probably wouldn't have cared if they had. I wished I could talk to my dad about my Plan, but knew he wouldn't understand, or approve. Apart from his strong desire to see his son have the chances he'd been denied, there was some disillusionment with his own grand new world. He'd already lost one job, had been let down by his mates, and I knew this hurt him deeply, so he redoubled his efforts to get me well out of it. So, although his disillusion influenced me, I could no longer talk to him. I pondered the loneliness of the rebel.

I liked the Sixth a little better than former years. A few of the school rules were relaxed for us, but uniform, including cap, was still insisted on. Tripper said that on very hot days Boys Might Remove Their Blazers in School provided they were not wearing Braces. But caps and blazers must be worn outside the school. I still drew my friends from my home area, where I was accepted provided I didn't wear a cap and blazer.

I felt I had entered the Arts Sixth more by luck than judgement, as my studies had been decided in my B-form days. I began seriously to wonder what this imitation public school was preparing us all for. A scholastic world hidden in old cloisters just as five hundred years ago? Hadn't they heard of the Industrial Revolution? Possibly, but industry was *infra dig*. The very fact that to work in a factory was an act of rebellion proved my point. They recognised the professions, of course, greater (A-forms) and lesser (B-forms). And I realised why I felt out of it; my family were in industry. And there was no room for industry at the grammar school.

The Head took the Sixth form for General Studies, in which he endeavoured to inculcate his theories, and it was during one of these sessions, after a talk about Communism, and lack of individual freedom, that he mentioned that he'd seen me without a cap and asked for an explanation. My long-seething anger suddenly exploded and my long fear of speaking in public left me. "I was being an individual and thinking for myself," I said. "Are you being insolent, boy?" Tripper asked in genuine surprise.

"No," I answered. "You did tell us that education is to make us think for ourselves and be individuals. That's what I was doing."

"There is the little matter of the school rules," pointed out the Head.

"I refuse to be regimented," I said in a voice of sweet reason.

The boys grinned, but not too openly. Tripper gave me detention, but I was exulting. I had found another weapon to beat the Head, and by God, I'd use it.

Every General Studies period now became a running battle between the Head and myself. And here, alas, Tripper was caught by his own rules. One did not beat or bully the Sixth, by this time we were presumed to be well and truly moulded, and the clay set firm. In any case, I was taller than he, and although thin, was younger. Physically, the Head could hardly thrash me into submission. I suppose he could have expelled me, as he expelled several boys caught smoking in the bog. But he didn't. I think that in some obscure way Tripper enjoyed these duels as much as I did. They say bullies like to be stood up to, and I reckon he got some sort of kick out of it; after all, the masters dared not say anything to him, poor sods. I seemed to be fighting everyone's battles, and I smiled cruelly every time I forced the Head into a corner. I would show no mercy.

The General Studies period became the talking point of the school, and I found myself a minor celebrity. Little first-formers scattered as I approached, and at first this pleased me until I realised that I was in danger of becoming godlike myself. Absolute power, etc. It was then I really started thinking about democracy.

My dad's idea of democracy had been equal opportunities for all, he hadn't really thought out the bit about an élite of brains; he wanted manual workers to be recognised and respected, yet he was satisfied simply because I was fulfilling his own dreams. I suppose I could never understand deprivation as he knew it, but I couldn't help thinking equality of opportunity wasn't enough. What about my cousin Tommy, fatherless, handicapped, unable to get a job? Where did he fit in the scheme of things? At the bottom of everybody's pile.

When the Head told us in the Sixth that he hoped we would always endeavour to be good middle-of-the-roaders, moderates, I said: "Sir, may I make a comment? I have been pushed, from the age of five, to train for one aim only, to get to university, from where, presumably, I shall go on to get a good job, er, that is, *position*, and make money. So where is the moderation?"

The Head pursed his lips, and I cried, suddenly angry, "Why have we been taught all these years about honour and bravery and courage, now to tell us to descend to the safety, the mediocrity, of the middle of the road?"

The Head burbled something, but I said: "It's the

pretence I object to. All this talk about decent honourable citizens is just so much cr—er, rubbish."

Tripp said heavily: "Leave the room."

I went home.

I didn't, I suppose, fully realise just how odd my ideas were to the staff. My ancestors had been fighting rebels, what did middle of the road mean to me? I was merely bringing my home culture into school.

My form master tried to warn me. "The Head has to write a report for the universities," he said.

I looked at him, and saw a man who dared not speak his mind because he was under another's power. He suffered from ulcers and I pitied him. "I don't care," I said.

"It might not be – er – too wise to – er – state such dogmas on examination papers," said Smithson.

"Might it not?" I asked, but I took the point. You had to write to please the examiners, not your own ideas.

"You do want to pass, I assume?" asked Smithson, and I realised that he knew I was up to something.

The examinations were approaching and the Head changed the General Studies periods for revision. He allowed his face to shine upon me once more for I was working hard.

Again the talk came up that only so many passes were allowed; if you were in the first lot to be marked you were OK, then a line was drawn and you'd had it. But if you failed in June you could sit again in January and were pretty sure to get it the second time round when there weren't so many entrants, that was the chat and it originated from the masters. I didn't tell my dad about these things, I felt a vague desire to protect him, thinking parents couldn't know much about life.

But oh God, where is the courage and honour and bravery?

I wasn't getting on too well with my dad now. He couldn't

understand what I was playing at, and I couldn't tell him. Couldn't tell him that part of it was for him. But it wasn't only that, I was eighteen, and all around me in Marley Road boys were working; they looked on me as a sort of big kid going off in my fancy blazer. I had always got on so well with my dad, but even so I resented the pressure, so many pressures from him, from the school. Get On, David Webster. You've got this marvellous chance such as has never been known before, you should be grateful. And pressure from the country as a whole: We're not giving you anything, David Webster, when you've got all your passes we demand a return for our money. We aren't educating you for your own sake, or for what *you* want to do. I realised then what I objected to. Nobody thought about *me*.

I got two A-levels, Geog. and Soc. Hist. I had been sure I'd get English, for I was pretty good at it, but no one even passed at King Alfred, not even Clough, who was top in English, and really good. We must have been low down on the pass list that year. I didn't worry too much, but I'd have preferred to have gained more glory.

For, at the prize-giving ceremony with its visiting Bigwig, and the Mayor and Mayoress, then I simply told everyone that I wasn't taking up my college place. I turned it down publicly, when I was fetching the little prize that I received for Social History and Economics. I tried to say that in future we needed brains in industry, but everyone looked blank. I said I was going into a factory and everyone looked uncomfortable as if I'd said a dirty word. Perhaps I had.

But I knew then why people in the past had been burned at the stake for their beliefs rather than give in to pretence for the rest of their lives. Because there's nothing, nothing to compare with the glorious feeling of standing against the shoddy world of compromise. Nothing.

I'd told my parents beforehand, and they were horrified.

This was upsetting, though I just sat, stony-faced, pretending I didn't care. It had been a personal battle, an attempt to show Tripp I rejected him and all he stood for; perhaps, I thought, as I saw my dad's face, a childish battle, except that I was beginning to realise that there was more to it than I'd admitted. I was the far-flung outpost of the new Sixties' movement that no longer accepted the old ideas. Students dressed in rags and tried to look like workers. This was the heady air of the Sixties. Hippies. Later, there were the beatniks and the flower people. All you need is love, they sang, and believed it. But in Briarford I was alone.

This was the hardest part. For everyone was against me. After the first row my dad said little, seemed frightened to upset me, as though I'd turned into a monster. Even the neighbours thought I was mad to turn down an easy well-paid secure life. There was no word from the school until one day the careers master, Mr Grant, came to see me.

Grant was a decent bod, and I liked him, but, not knowing the motive of his visit, I stared in some defiance. He asked me why I was going in the factory. I shrugged. He said, "You'll find it boring."

"So do the others, why should I be special?" I asked.

"You're rebelling," returned Mr Grant, equably. "But is it worth cutting off your nose to spite your face, as they say?"

I said, sulkily, "It's the whole set-up I object to. Surely the whole idea of education shouldn't be to push a person into a certain job?"

"That is the ideal, I grant you, and I suppose it looks clearer to you. But if you turn down your opportunities, aren't people going to say it's a waste of time educating children? That it isn't necessary to know higher maths and Greek to work in a press-shop?"

"Ah," I said, suddenly illumined. "But what an ideal.

Educated press-shop workers." I poured out my feelings. "I thought that's what it was all about. I thought education really meant liberation for me and the others. Instead, it's just a rat-race to fit us all into little employment slots. For King Alfred the best employment slots. And at the same time we get this public school ethic, read classics and don't soil our hands. All right for the gentry who didn't have any work to do. It's all a bit schizo."

"But parents want children to get good jobs. Your father wanted you to go to college, didn't he? Is it perhaps your father you're rebelling against?"

Was I? Fighting Dad and transferring to the Head. Or vice versa. Authority. Mixed with the desire to work as Dad did. Oh, definitely schizo.

"Don't you think you have a chip on your shoulder, Webster?"

I considered. "Yes. Odd, isn't it? I, who have the things my dad and his dad fought for, have the biggest chip." I grinned. "Case of pushing grapes into the children's mouth and finding them turning sour."

"Don't misquote scripture to me," said Mr Grant, who was also the senior English master. "How about sociology? Wouldn't your background help you there?"

"Help me enough to leave it alone," I said. "Making surveys of the poor, teaching the workers culture . . . it's wrong, Mr Grant. Why is it only recently that Shakespeare and the classics have come to mean middle-class culture? Why, Arthur Bryant says that humble craftsmen up to the eighteenth century were culturally the equals of those who employed them, and that poor children committed Shakespeare and Milton to memory not because they wanted to better themselves, but because the literature of their native land was a heritage for their sharing. We should have educated press-shop workers, Mr Grant. Other countries do. In Sweden eighty per cent are in full-time education up to the age of eighteen. In Russia, half the working population goes to night-school."

"You're very well informed, Webster."

I grinned. "You taught me."

"But you have a point, even so. It is wrong that the great mass of people should be left without culture."

"But they aren't, Mr Grant, they make their own. All poor peoples do when they're neglected. The Negroes made jazz and the Spaniards flamenco. When they're no longer poor they don't need it so others take it over. That's what's happening now. And until something new comes along for them they'll be—"

"Unhappy?"

"And worse. I was thinking along the lines that Satan finds work for idle hands. Same with idle brains."

"It seems a pity to waste *your* brains."

"I don't think I have any more brains than the people I live among. My dad and others." I walked to the window. "If I could grow as lovely roses as he does, as my uncle did—"

"But growing roses isn't exactly a profession—"

"No, you see what I mean. You teach us not to think too much about money. When I say I don't want to take one of your professions, or even to work at all, which is a logical outcome of that, you don't agree."

Mr Grant rose, and I said, "Look, thanks for trying to help . . . I don't mean to be bloody-minded, but I honestly don't know what I want to do. I only know what I don't want to do."

"And that seems to be practically everything—"

"What I mean is," I mumbled, "If you had been Head things might have been different."

Mr Grant was still. "You know," he said, almost inaudibly, "you make me wonder if I have been too submissive with – the Headmaster. I think he honestly tries to do his best . . . but perhaps we have allowed him too much power. This is strictly confidential, Webster, but some of the masters have been taking the line that we should express to the Headmaster that a little more understanding is called for in certain quarters."

I looked down, almost embarrassed. A strange feeling shot through me. Not power, but the realisation that I could be powerful. And I hadn't known. I had still been thinking of myself as the little first-former, the working-class yobbo, kept down, told I was wrong. *And yet*, part of my mind said, *if I hadn't protested, wouldn't I be just that?*

New lines of thought seemed to be opening up. Exhilarating. Under authority I'd thought of nothing but protest, now my blind rebellion seemed to be leading to something, though I didn't know what.

But first I'd go in the factory.

*

The Personnel Officer who interviewed me was amazed that, with my qualifications, I wanted a job on the shop-floor. He pointed out that on the staff conditions were better, salary was good, there were perks, a car . . . Of course – hopefully – if I wanted to get shop-floor experience before moving to management . . .

"Do you ever move ordinary workers into management?" I asked.

"Well, it isn't that simple—"

No, it would be easier for him to keep everyone in his own little groove. I was impatient. "I reckon that for all our advanced education people are fitted into slots more than they used to be. Funny, isn't it? Years ago there was more chance of getting from log cabin to top house in England than today. Today you have to have a minimum of five O-levels." Now I was angry. "Council-house estates, surburban semis, stock-broker belts . . . and we all go into our slots like sheep—"

The Personnel Officer said coldly. "I'm sorry, Mr Webster, but I don't think I can offer you a job with us."

I left. This was a harsher world than school. At home I told my dad. He laughed. "You don't have to *talk*," he advised. I thought how many years had been spent in teaching me to debate, to discuss . . .

"If you go around spouting things about equality they think you're a left-wing agitator." Dad patted my arm. "I'll speak for you, if you like, at our place, but for God's sake keep your mouth shut. Leave the discussions to the intellectuals, you're inarticulate in public."

But I didn't want to work with my dad, I'd have felt embarrassed. And of course, he didn't understand that either, sons always went to work with fathers. But not me. I was set apart, no longer bona fide working class; I had been disenfranchised. I was a half-caste. I found my own job at Startin's, and my dad was further alienated.

I entered the machine shop on my first day a little doubtfully. I knew my limitations and I am not particularly mechanically minded. For all my fine words about equality I found it irksome to be taught by some young lad who seemed to know so much more than I did. From being high in the grammar school I was now bottom of the factory, not even one of its brightest boys. My qualifications meant nothing to my fellow workers, they looked on me with something approaching pity, a pen-pusher, a nonentity, in the ancient world of skilled crafts. I joined the union, but here too, if I'd thought that my superior judgements were wanted I was wrong. It was made clear to me that the workers were perfectly capable of managing their own affairs, thank you, they'd been managing them for many years. Humbled, I was silent, but I went to the meetings.

From the other side of the fence came a different set of

attitudes. As a young gentleman of the grammar school I had been looked up to by the middle classes with whom I came into contact. Now it was hard to be told curtly to wait till some little official could see me. I became aware, as I hadn't previously, of the full weight of public opinion against me. Sections of the media bashed me right and centre (there was no left), I was lazy and wouldn't work, or I worked too hard and should be made redundant, depending on the financial situation of the country. And always, whether working or on the dole, I had too much money. Morons, us. It's not being crippled that I objected to, what I can't forgive is being mocked for my deformity. Plays of that period struggled to keep the former image of the downtrodden, ignorant and/or criminal poor, with stereotyped trade union officials as unlike the real thing as those in Victorian novels, where no doubt they'd come from. Clever people discussed the problem that was me. I was preached at, preached about, admonished, exhorted, lectured, and above all, surveyed. I felt like a performing monkey or someone living in an occupied country. I wished I could laugh about it all as my shop-steward, Jamie McEwan, did. "Seventy per cent of the middle classes say there is no such thing as class. Sixty per cent of the working class say they are middle class. And fifty per cent of all classes are congenital liars."

It would have been so easy to become apathetic, as I had done long ago in the first form of the grammar school, caught up in a system that was nothing to do with me, that required nothing from me but to work for it, not for me. But the magic of the Sixties upheld me, the glorious future we, the young, were going to bring to the world. I am always grateful that I was young at that time. Bliss was it in that dawn to be alive, but to be young was very heaven.

The Beatles had burst upon the world and gradually

the pop image was changed to working class, the suave smoothies were gone. Songs were no longer about moon and June, but about human rights. More revolutionary songs were put out than workers ever dreamed of; the workers didn't take any notice.

But it was the Stones who caught my fancy, their rebellion was stronger. Even the very noise, which my parents hated, really did something for me. Every night I'd sit in the front room, dressed in my oldest clothes, my hair long, feeling part of the youth who were going to fight for a new world, listening to Dylan, the master. A heady time indeed.

And looking back, I see a fault. We, the young, were the new classless society, but it excluded the old. We were a caste as privileged as any other. And yet – the old didn't, couldn't, understand. My mother moaned about my slap-dash appearance – a joy after the rigours of my school uniform – my dad was lost in a little claustrophobic world of unions and bosses, he cared nothing for Vietnam and outside events.

I looked round for something I could do, and it was then I thought about writing a book about the factory. I even made a start, and it was some time before I realised that I was an outsider in the sense that I had two A-levels so knew I could get a better job, or felt that I could, which is the same thing. *I still didn't know what it really felt like to be at the bottom.* My story would be no different from any other survey.

I mentioned some of this to Dad. "It's the difference between George Borrow writing about gypsies and the gypsies writing about themselves."

"But the gypsies can't write themselves."

"*Can't?* Why can't you write a book?"

"Oh well, you know I'm not educated."

"You mean it's not for you. Writing books is for the élite. But that's all wrong, Dad. Working men used to write.

There's nothing to stop you except the thought that it's not for you. Your point of view is needed, no one knows it. I told Mr Grant I didn't want to write surveys of the poor. If you wrote yourselves there'd be no need for them."

"End of flourishing industry," said Dad with a grin.

"In a hundred years' time people will read about this age and it will be all wrong."

"I see what you mean," Dad said. "But it's too late for me to start." And I was startled to see how much older he looked, how sad his eyes were.

I took my bright ideas to the factory. "Och awa'," said Jamie. "We're not poor enough to be fashionable."

"Or foreign enough? Russian dissidents? South African Blacks?"

"I'm a foreigner," said Jamie. "Please God."

"Get thee to thy Tartan Army," I said, "deportation for Scots."

The foreman was rolling by on his merry way. "When you've finished the Battle of Bannockburn," he said, "you can get some bloody work done."

At dinner-time I put my ideas to the other workers, who stared at me as if I were one of these taking-art-to-the-people bods, carrying a pole round on my shoulders or morris dancing in the streets. "What bloody time have we got?" asked one bloke surlily, who spends all Sundays fishing. It was as though I'd asked them to go to the moon.

Oddly enough it was my cousin Tommy who explained it to me. "You're taught to write at your school," he said. "We're not." I didn't know what he meant.

"I'd love to write something," Tommy went on shyly. "All about being handicapped, and not getting a job you know. But at school we only did little compositions, and I often made mistakes in grammar."

"Grammar can be corrected," I said. "I just want to

know what you really feel about life." I was puzzled by his attitude, yet when I saw his first efforts I understood. It was mostly an imitation of every well-worn theme of the day, how he'd been taught to write and to think, interspersed here and there with one or two sentences of his own, bare, bald. 'I wish I was normal. I wish I could run. I wish I had a good job, but nobody wants a cripple.' I set to work with Tommy, unlearning most of what he'd been taught, putting him on the right lines. It made him happy.

I had never believed in segregating the bright pupils from the others; now I could see the harm. I began to realise that others felt dissatisfaction with the current regime. Briarford began talking about comprehensive education and Mr Tripp died, probably from shock. Mr Grant was made Head, pending reorganisation, and I thought I should make an effort to see him, congratulate him. After all, he had been decent to me. I called on him.

"I was pleased to see you got the headship," I said, sincerely.

Mr Grant was enthusiastic, and I wondered if he'd always been so, with feelings hidden in the long subservience to Mr Tripp? Or had he been suddenly converted, like St Paul? Did my own little rebellion have anything to do with his changed attitudes, after all, what's the point of a rebellion if nobody takes any notice? I remembered the talk at the school, the criticism of the exam system put out by the masters. Were they, then, having their own little rebellion?

Mr Grant asked me about my life. I decided to be frank. "You were right," I said. "I don't like the work, but don't know what else to do. I mean, the basic problem's the same as when I was at school."

"Things have been changing, hadn't you noticed?" Mr Grant asked. "The youngsters we're getting now just won't go along with the old ideas. As for accents and dialects, they're becoming quite fashionable in some quarters. You were just a little ahead of your time. And much as you object to grammar schools, David, don't you think this change is in part due to working-class pupils going there and presenting plays and documentaries on television and so on?"

"I suppose you think I should have done something like that?" And maybe I should. They had been constructive, after all.

"Are you still bitter, David?" Mr Grant evaded my question.

"Yes. I was really unhappy at school."

"Most children are, for one reason or another, you know."

I sighed. "Yes. And I suppose, now we have so many immigrants here with different ways of life, there will have to be more understanding."

"You must try to understand," said Mr Grant, "that what was done in the past was out of fear – and insecurity."

"Mr Tripp – insecure?"

"Of course. He saw his position threatened."

I was silent, thinking.

"You must not be too hard on him," Mr Grant went on. "You were a child, and children tend to see things in black and white, as do adolescents. You were insolent, David – one of your failings – and why do you think he didn't expel you? Because you were working hard in the Sixth and had a college place? Yes, but mainly for your own sake. I agree he went about things the wrong way, he was heavy-handed and insensitive, but he had the scholar's respect for learning. He did what he thought to be right, but no one is perfect, David; as we get older this is something we all learn."

I saw Mr Tripp standing before me, a huge figure on a pedestal, brandishing a cane. The pedestal began to move, to rock, and slowly Mr Tripp dwindled, shrank, till he became a pathetic little man trying to keep his balance, an ordinary little man brandishing a paper cane.

Chapter Two

I love Jeanie. That sounds like something scrawled on the bus station where we used to congregate when we came home from school. It was reserved almost exclusively for sixth-formers, King Alfred and the High School girls – the real High, not the sec. mods, not even the new grammar, for a form of apartheid existed, and we were only allowed to mix with the girls of the High. I don't suppose Tripper would have given us detention if he'd caught us with inferior girls, though I wouldn't have put it past him. As it was, dances were held for us, we were encouraged to mix. I didn't object to this at the time for I hadn't time to go chasing other girls, I had to take what I could. So they stood in the bus station in their short skirts and with hats under their arms, blouses unbuttoned, rousing us to a frenzy, and then we had to leave them, go home and study Eng. Lit. I was doing Gerard Manley Hopkins, never a favourite of mine, and I grew to hate him those summer evenings because he kept me away from the girls.

Once I left school there were girls in plenty. Girls at work, in factory and office, girls at the discos, girls in pubs – for even young kids went in pubs these days, instead of the quaint custom of walking the streets Dad told me about. As my work got more boring I found more girls. And they all said the same thing: "Why, whatever are you doing working in a factory when you've been to the grammar school?" We all knew our places even in the wonderful new society, and I didn't fit in. But it didn't matter too much, I didn't want to talk to these one-night stands.

I could talk to Jeanie. I could, for the first time in my life, really discuss my problems with someone who understood.

She talked of the streets where she'd been born, where living conditions encouraged drinking and violence and prostitution, and I thought romantically she was like a lovely flower growing on a dung-hill. There was plenty of fight in her, she was a Scottish Nationalist. "I hate the English," she said, tweaking my ear.

"When we were at school we were taught to be proud of being Scottish," she went on, "proud of our Scottish accent," and I envied her then, because I hadn't been taught to be proud of what I was, only of what I was not.

She came to me readily, and we made love at our second meeting. She wasn't immoral, she might have been amoral, for I wasn't the first. Conventional morality meant nothing to her, she wasn't trying to flout conventions, to her the only immorality was poverty. I wanted to marry her, but she wouldn't hear of it. She wanted to be an equal, sharing. She insisted I did my share of washing up and even housework, which I did, to my mother's astonishment, and to mine.

She taught me about women. Up till then I hadn't thought of women as *people*. They were either mother and family or – dare I say it? – sex objects, to be giggled over when we left our all-male enclave. We learned to rule the world there, but we didn't know anything about women. Jeanie said there was more to a woman's life than cosseting the men as my mother did, and I saw she had a point. My mother had a job, though it could in no way be called a career, for the rest she devoted her life to her family – and the family disappointed her. As I grew older I saw I took Dad's place in her affections and wondered why. I admit I was on her side against Dad, and had been for a long time, there just isn't room for two adult males in one family, ask any animal.

"But Jeanie," I said, "a lot of men are treated as inferiors, and some women are bossy, take Aunt Sybil."

Jeanie sighed. "We have a long way to go," she said.

We met at a demo against the Vietnam War. We are both against war. All the money spent on bombs could be used to build hospitals, fight poverty . . . Nuclear war? I can't see that blowing up the whole planet is going to benefit anyone. So we talk, Jeanie and me, and wonder. Why aren't there enough houses for everyone? Why so many unemployed? So many old people dying of hypothermia? Questions without answers. David and Jeanie, seekers after truth, unable to find it.

*

I was dead bored at the factory, and I honestly thought it was because I was intelligent. Some of the teaching about me being one of the élite rubbed off after all. I first realised my mistakes when I was talking to Stan Jakes, lives up the road, works in a foundry. No brains, Stan, thick as two short planks, he seems quite happy doing the heavy laborious work that would kill me in a week. Then he told me he used to work in a car factory. "I was bored," he told me. "Standing there, twiddling little knobs, waiting for the next piece to come down. Bored." Christ, I thought, if he feels bored, what price all the others? "We were always on strike," he finished. "Reckon we got so fed up we were ready to go out any time. But I got fed up with that as well, losing money. So I went to the foundry."

After that I began to study people, trying to find out what made them tick. Pete Jennings, belonged to a family of fourteen, dad on the dole, been in trouble with the police. If he couldn't understand anything he hit out with his fists.

He worked in a car battery factory, in lead and acid, bad for his health, wanted to get out.

He had a girl, worked in a shop. And one day he told me how he spent his spare time. Helping in the shop. Doing electricity – for nothing. Because he liked it.

Illuminating. The working-class idea of work. Something you can't possibly *like*. Have I inherited some of it, is that why I'm in the factory?

I started looking round. My dad, works in a factory, hobby, boating, country. Uncle William, worked in brickyard, hobby, rose-growing. Jim Foster, railway porter, hobby, making models out of bulls' horns. He showed me his collection. "You want to sell them, Jim," I said, watching. He was affronted. "Never," he told me. "I'd give them away, but I'd never sell them." He sounded as though I'd insulted him.

Once I'd started looking I saw it all around me. Working for money in a job they hated, working at home for pleasure, but seldom for money. They refused money like old-time aristocrats refusing to go in trade. But they'd screw the last penny out of their bosses . . . to make up for something . . .? Making somebody pay?

I suppose we all need a creative outlet. But can't work ever be enjoyable? If not, why blame people for being bloody-minded? Well, we've got to do as we're told, I suppose, or we'd all be layabouts, all happy little craftsmen making our little ships and growing roses just as we were supposed to do generations ago. Trouble with England is that half the people are dreaming of a world to come and the other half of a world that's gone, or never was, happy little peasants dancing round maypoles. Most of the peasants I know would have been more likely to go in for bear-baiting and cock-fighting. So what to do? We can't go on living on dreams of past glories and dreaming spires. My dad did that and he lost.

I was pretty unbearable about this time I know, for I couldn't find a solution either. When we went to Aunt Sybil's so-called party I was really insulting. But I'd just learned about Sybil and my dad – my *dad* – and Carolyn ... the party was to celebrate Sybil forcing her into the business and we were all upset for her. Then those people annoyed me with their smug talk. I could understand it coming from the stock-broker belt, who wouldn't know a pit-shaft from a capstan lathe, but from people in a mining district ... Sybil accused me of being a Militant Red, well, I'd learned a bit about psychology at school. Tell a boy he's lazy and he'll become so. The same applied to me. There wasn't much to join in Briarford so I went to join the miners' pickets. When I realised what a stir I was making I decided to keep on stirring.

My dad accused me of wanting to smash society, but I didn't. It's just that sometimes I'd dream of a different way of life, a sort of international society of friends, a *sharing*. Dimly I felt I could see what was wrong, the inability of both sides to see the other's point of view. I fought on the side of the workers, but I pondered the waste of all this in-fighting. That's where I felt my dad was wrong, but I didn't know what to do about it – except hit out. That's all I ever wanted to smash, hypocrisy, the hypocrisy of a permissive society that flaunted sex to hide – what? Answer that, O Freud. Perhaps that's where the guilt comes from, not what was done, but the cover-up. Pretence, the English disease.

Mind you, I had left Startin's when I went to Sybil's; I had been made redundant, which is the modern word for sacking. I still wasn't too worried, I still had my qualifications to fall back on. Though the Sixties were over now, the love-ins and the love-everyone, the world was changing. I should have changed too. Maybe I'm stuck in a permanent Sixties groove, Peter Pan David ... So I took several jobs until Jamie, bless his heart, told me he was at the Star and would get me in there.

The Star was a revelation. Most firms used to be like this, my dad said, before they were taken over by huge conglomerates and run from another planet. The people were friendly and men took a pride in their work. I mean, you can be proud of a motor-bike, even if you don't do every little job; in a small place you're near enough to the beginnings to know what goes on. And there at the end is the shining symbol of generations of work – a bike. For men said proudly their fathers had brought them there, and they would bring their sons, it was almost a family concern. My dad said there had been a lot of this pride in the old days, pride in a famous name, but it had all been eroded away, with takeovers and even little things like changing the name. You couldn't go in for years being proud to work for Rolls-Royce, and in a day find its name had been changed to Big Banger. You'd feel different. Something would have gone. And that's when you stopped working for pride and worked for money, and lost interest.

So I was glad I went to the Star, it made me understand such a lot more . . . Man does not live by bread alone. I joined the union, went to all the meetings. And when Dad thought he'd be out again I got him in too.

I'd known, of course, that my dad wasn't exactly deeply in love with my mother. I suppose I'd always known. It didn't worry me unduly, although the experts told me it should, they'd suddenly discovered that broken and unhappy homes are the cause of all our woes. But the experts think of the nuclear family, and this mine was not, not with the myriads of relations in the next yard, and Uncle William who was really my grandfather. My parents were only part of my family, so I wouldn't have worried about my dad having a fancy woman, not till I found out who it was. I'd always treated Carrie as a sister, but as we grew older I sensed she fancied me. Always ready to oblige, I tried to kiss her once, but she didn't tell me all until the night of Aunt Sybil's party. I thought it was rotten of Dad to hurt Mother. I couldn't understand him, all his fancy talk about ideals and so on. I supposed, until then, I'd never really thought of him as another man. I had sympathised with his love for Marta, but *Sybil* . . . And the odd thing is she died the same night as he did, was murdered, in fact. Uncle Peter found her, gave evidence, said that the house had been broken into and burgled, that he caught a glimpse of two young thugs making off with the loot. The papers made much of it, of course, but we were more upset about Dad. Frankly, I wasn't concerned about the loss of Sybil, Uncle Peter took Carolyn away after the inquest, sold up, went down south, so dropped out of our lives. My mother seemed extraordinarily upset about it, turned on me when I mentioned it, went off and married Ted Naylor, a teacher in Sussex. She transferred the house to me and I've never seen or heard from her since, though I keep writing. I'll admit I was upset, and I wonder if she found out about Dad and Sybil, but why quarrel with me . . .? Is it all part of shock or something? I often ponder on going to see her, but if she doesn't want me . . .? Why, Mother, when I loved you? . . . Jeanie says she'll come round, so I keep writing, but she never replies.

But to get back to the Star. I'd begun to feel uneasy, and I knew I wasn't the only one. None of us had anything to go on, the bosses were just the same, things ran like clockwork, it was just a feeling. Funny how people get these feelings, they know when something is wrong, even when it's government and top secret. I have noticed that the working classes seem to be better than others both at seeing through people and of knowing when something's going wrong. I suppose it's partly due to being born suspicious, and partly that, feeling unable to put their real aspirations before the world, their senses are the more alert, like wild animals. It's a joke that when we go to the zoos we know all about the animals except what they think of us, and that's more or less our position. We let out an occasional roar, we're caged, but we're very alert to danger.

The union man said when he asked the bosses about future plans they were evasive. That alarmed us.

Why didn't they tell us? It happens over and over again, the boss comes in and says: "That's it, the factory closes tomorrow. Goodbye." It couldn't happen in Europe, where some form of industrial democracy has been introduced in law, or in fact almost everywhere. Workers participate in the management of affairs at all levels, especially in Germany. Management decisions are accountable to the workers. But ... would the unions want that here?

So when it happened we weren't even surprised, just shocked. We all had our redundancy notices, and went home on the Friday. For my dad it was the last chip. He'd been having little bits chipped off his ideals for years and years, this stripped him to the heart. And that night he killed himself.

*

You were a fool, Dad, to let 'em get you down. You were a fool to let anybody get you down. You've got to fight and fight and keep on fighting right to the end. You don't *really* have to believe in anybody or trust anybody all the way. You shouldn't have given up, Dad, thinking you were finished. You were never finished, because there's me. And I'm going on fighting and it'll be for you as well as myself. And for Marta.

I went to work on Monday, though I knew folks would think I was callous. But I wanted to know what was happening. You can't live with the dead. All my mates were shocked by the closure, shocked to the marrow, we walked around like zombies, silent for the most part, occasionally muttering, "They can't do a thing like that." Utter disbelief. As though putting our blood and bones and brains to work for them for generations would make them give a generous gesture.

You can't live with the dead. They didn't bury Dad's body, they didn't find a body . . . all I saw was his hands, and they'll haunt me till the day I die . . . the hands that worked for you . . . I shouldn't have taken him to the Star, he trusted you . . . and you used him as a pair of hands to mind the machinery and when the machinery went you cut off his hands, dispensable man. Was he not a human being too? No, just hands, in times of boom bring 'em in from anywhere, in the slump, goodbye. That's why you didn't ever mix with him, isn't it, why you keep your separate houses and golf clubs and schools. Because you couldn't bear to watch what you do to him when you cut off his hands. As long as you can pretend he's subhuman, as the Victorians did, or inarticulate or a layabout or militant thug, then you can stand at your door and mock when the unemployed vans come through. Once admit he's an equal and you couldn't bear to know you'd murdered him, could you? You would suffer. I'm suffering; those hands used to pick me up when I was a child, comfort me, they painted his boat and tended his roses. I didn't comfort him, I taunted him, mocked his beliefs. I'm still doing it, trying to justify myself.

I went to the funeral on Tuesday, and a cold wind blew round the cemetery. I remembered Uncle William saying: "It's allis cold in the cemetery." Now you're cold, Dad, forever, and you shouldn't have done it. Nobody's worth that much sacrifice. Mother was crying, and the aunts, only I was stony-faced. I am the Resurrection and the Life . . . Fine words meaning nothing. A sacrifice for all mankind ... making a joy of sacrifice ... to enable the unscrupulous to take and take and take ... What good did Jesus Christ do anybody hanging on the cross? We'd all have been better if he'd stayed alive and taught us a bit more about the rich selling all they have and giving to the poor, because it's never been done. Wars have been fought in the name of Christianity, but Christ's teachings are never kept. So shut up, parson. As the tree falls, so let it lie.

I went to work on the Wednesday and there was a change. The chaps were getting over the shock, but there was still surprise. That we, who had been so happy, and so trusting, should have been sold down the river ... as if it had never been done before.

It was on the fifth day that somebody said it. "There are still orders, and the work is still here. Why can't we carry on?"

And someone else, "If the bosses aren't willing to run it, we ought to do it ourselves."

Then we all looked incredulous at this blasphemy, that the workers knew as much as the bosses. And then we realised that we did.

"We'll sit in," someone said. "Keep the bikes here."

"Yes, but what about money?"

"If the government can give to capitalist concerns they can give to us, can't they?"

"They won't want to."

"Let's have a meeting. Keep it quiet for now. Not a word to a soul."

We did all that. We had our meeting. We announced that we wanted to carry on working, and intended to carry on working. To this end, we would stay in the factory and keep the bikes with us. All those in favour say aye. All with us, stay, but we can't promise anything but blood, sweat, toil, and probably tears. Those not in favour, go home and goodbye. Some went, we stayed, and the gates were locked.

We arranged pickets outside the gates, and we stood, summer and winter. People came and talked to us, argued with us; we were adamant. We wanted to work, and not go on the dole, we don't believe all this defeatist talk about England being finished. God Almighty, if we didn't give in when we stood alone in the war, why the hell should we give in now? If *you* won't work with us, then give us the tools and we'll carry on with the job. We want to work, and work at what we loved doing, we were craftsmen, we produced a shining work of art, our children wanted to follow us, just as people had gone before us, my dad, and Marta, and Uncle William and their ancestors, way back, sometimes I thought I saw them on winter nights when we stood outside with a little flame burning in the brazier. The flame of life. It was cold on those winter nights, and eerie too, with the big sky overhead, and the lights of the city in the distance, and a handful of us standing guard patiently. Courage and honour and bravery, I found it there but no one took any notice.

And sometimes in the dark nights I wondered. Why do I do this? I could have taken a good job, conformed, gone the way of the world, made money, I don't even know why I do it, I have no good reason. I don't believe in God, much less love him. I have no particular love for my fellow men, I don't feel sentimental about the workers or think they are better than anyone else. I have no political belief, no cause, no desire for fame. So why? Causes are ephemeral things, men will come after me with different beliefs, society will be changed and changed again. Why do I even care . . .?

And then the little flame burns, and I know what I am fighting for, the man who works in lead and acid but loves the clear whiteness of electricity, the man on the shop-floor who builds fireplaces for the love of God, the porter who makes ships out of horns and loves all things lovely, Uncle William who grew roses. Marta . . . And a little flame was lit inside me, and all of us, we wanted to work at something we believed in, work together in trust. It's difficult to explain what this meant to us; before, it had been Us dependent on Them, for jobs, for a living; the little flame set us free. And we had the free people's determination and exhilaration and energy.

Jeanie was with me all the way. She was a source of strength. Funny this strength women have, it is in my mother. And while men shout and fight, women wait with their strength and silence. And some men never see this, never understand. But when they do, how beautiful is love between men and women.

No one took much notice of us. One MP was on our side. One or two odd television cameras came to have a look at us, and a visiting journalist from a Tory paper. "Are you Communists?" he asked us, being original.

"No, we just want to keep on working."

"Are you Trotskyists?"

"What the hell are Trotskyists? We just want to keep working".

"Who is behind you?"

"The bogey man."

"You're all union men, aren't you? Militants?"

"Oh, get stuffed. Fuck off, mate, you get on our wick." And he drove away in his big car, expenses paid.

*

The weeks and months went by and spring came again. Some of our band, with family commitments, tried to find other jobs, and we didn't blame them, it's hard living on the breadline. When we felt down, first Pete would keep up our courage, and then me, for I knew now I had to win, I owed it to my dad, and to Marta, his love. They'd never know, but I'd know, and be satisfied. So we kept up our courage and our honour and our bravery.

It wasn't easy. Oh, God, it wasn't easy. It's easy to go and fight when everybody cheers you on, and bands are playing and flags waving, but to stand against the world on a cold night when all the world ignores you, that's when you need courage. We put our case to the government. Look, we can carry on, we can work and export for England. I know the country is hard up, but you'd have to pay out in unemployment benefit. You pay big firms subsidies to keep people in work, and to schemes to train young people for jobs that aren't there. We'd be willing to work for £50 a week flat rate, all of us, and that's more than you can say. We had a Labour government now, and the Minister of Industry who was slated by the press as the bogey man of all time. He was on our side.

The troubles and the struggles are best forgotten. For in the end we won. Shining victory. The siege was over. No one took much notice. A little bit on television (Midlands only) and a few lines in a daily paper. If we'd have done a train robbery our wives could have sold their stories for a fortune. If we'd been muggers or rapists we'd have been in the news every day. We were allowed to go on working with a loan from the government, which means all the tax-payers. Tax-payers' money. To keep men's hopes alive.

But we won.

We didn't celebrate when we heard the news, we took it quietly, thinking over our new duties. It was up to us now. We sent out to our depleted army and called the roll. Some who had left wanted to return, but Pete said not yet. Some of the staff had been with us all along, and the cleaning women, plus a senior executive who became our MP. I salute men like him, and it's here I differ from my dad, he couldn't see how valuable they are. Another executive was a woman, and I salute her too.

A committee was formed. We held a meeting. What to do? How to start? Suggestions, please. No shouting, no rowdiness. In quietness and confidence shall be our strength.

I felt happy. We were blazing a trail. Or were we? There's nothing new in co-operation, it's as old as time. Early communities before people got greedy.

My high hopes for a new world sank a little when I told my mother. She'd been really peculiar since my dad died, but I suppose I was edgy too. "What are you planning to do?" she asked.

I told her about the co-operative. "We own the factory now, it's ours. We may employ a few professional managers, and they may earn more, but they won't share any of the profits and have no voting rights. The board will be elected from the shop-floor and will make policy decisions. We shall all start work at the same time, eight o'clock, there'll be no foremen, no union rule books—"

"That doesn't sound like your usual union talk."

"We're working for ourselves now, Mother, not fighting bosses. We don't want any fighting, we shall share the work. I shall do my bit on the shop-floor when my office work is finished—"

"That's a laugh, after all the demarcation that went on before."

"We had to do it before, Mother, because if an engineer was put cleaning windows then the window cleaner was sacked. Now we just work together in trust."

I didn't remind her that she herself had suggested a sit-in because I thought it might make her think of the night Dad died. But she remembered anyway, for she said: "He trusted you, your dad. He loved you, and you killed him."

"I didn't. I couldn't help him losing his job—"

"You refused to get a good job, you messed about for years. After all he'd done for you, all he'd sacrificed."

She had never talked this way before, and I knew she

was upset, but I was angry too. "He did a lot for me, Mother, but it was of his own choosing."

That's true, isn't it, Dad? You gave me whatever you say, and you wanted me to become what you planned for me. But I'm not what you wanted me to be, Dad, I'm what *I* want to be. That's the problem that arises when you help anybody get on, whether it's your own children or the Negroes in Africa. You want us to take what you offer and still be your dear children, going the way you want us to go. We want to be independent. If we go wrong and hurt ourselves, we're only finding our feet, but you can't keep control. You should be proud of us, Dad, really, all the dissident peoples in the world who are turning and hitting you between the eyes. You should be proud, because giving independence on a leading rein means nothing. You gave me freedom and I have taken it. My way.

But the credit is yours, Dad. You made me possible.

*

Only it didn't last.

The Eighties had come in, cold and harsh. Now there was no more generosity from governments to co-operatives, now it was every man for himself and devil take the hindmost. Car factories closed down all over Coventry and we went with them. Now the winds blew chill, freezing the marrow of goodness in men's bones. Love became a dirty word. Profit was in.

I was shocked.

Now I had to find a job, for though Jeanie was working we wanted to start a family; after all, we were both getting on in years.

I wasn't too worried at first, I had some experience plus my qualifications. And it came as a shock to learn that there were no jobs for me, not now. Unemployment had crept up on me. My piddling little A-levels weren't wanted any longer, even degrees did not ensure you found employment. All these years I had been feeling secure with my qualifications, now I was a reject too. Now I knew how the others felt.

I wrote hundreds of letters, and in the rare cases when I got an interview I no longer enjoyed myself telling the managers about my homespun philosophies. Now I humbled myself for they had the whip-hand. I went to the Department of Employment, the new name for the Labour Exchange, and after standing in a queue for half an hour was told I was in the wrong building for first claims. So I wandered off to find the other place and waited another half-hour. Then, surprise, surprise, I found I knew the girl there from my schooldays and she said that with my education and qualifications I should sign with the Professional and Executive Register upstairs.

"Hell's bells," I said. "I've been walking round all morning."

So I went upstairs to a more comfortable room with no crying babies with runny noses. But for God's sake, is there any other country in the world has two classes of unemployed? It didn't make any difference, they didn't have any jobs either.

No work. Shoes wearing thin, yet how can I look for jobs without new shoes? Brother, can you spare a dime?

For the first time I was glad my dad was out of it, that he couldn't see his brave new world had collapsed.

Dad . . .

And then I knew what I had to do.

Epilogue

The Survivors

1981

Ann had forgotten it was the carnival. Now, as she and Ted struggled through the crowded market-place, she saw that they wouldn't be able to drive the car out till the procession had passed. They stood silently, between children waving streamers and eating ice-creams. On the corner a man was selling the local paper and his posters fluttered in the breeze.
NEARLY THREE MILLION UNEMPLOYED. SDP FORM NEW PARTY.

The procession approached, led by a band of Gurkhas, and Ann felt like someone from another planet, distanced from those who could enjoy themselves while her own feelings were in such a turmoil. Pleasure there was at the thought of seeing David again, horror at what she'd had to learn before she could do so.

"Are you all right?" Ted asked, anxiously, and she nodded, dumbly. Ted was a good husband, kind and considerate, she really enjoyed being a teacher's wife; no need to defend her way of life, she belonged now with the norm, the correct class. She tried to concentrate her thoughts. Seen through Sussex eyes Briarford was remarkably commonplace with its glass and concrete buildings, its High Street shops, many with closing down sales. She'd been shocked at the sight of Coventry where they called first. The once shining city was drabber, the smart girls had changed into dreary women in cardigans, groups of young Blacks stood silently at street corners. Something had gone, some exhilaration that had been there even after the bombing, a strange air over everything, the smell of defeat. David's letters said that the dole-queues were long. "Factories closed – all those big names . . . Cuts in expenditure. Tommy's had to go, though his wife still has a job. Doreen's retired, and her husband took early redundancy some years ago, with payment . . ." *Trust Doreen, Ken would have said.* "Uncle John's a widower now, they say he's courting again. His pit might close . . . Too many old people, they tell us, too many young people all on the dole . . . is that what's wrong? We fit people into the economy instead of the economy into people?" David wrote regularly, though she had never replied until he'd invited her and Ted to his wedding, and then she knew she had to face her problem.

The procession went on, people were shouting and laughing in lorries, holding out little nets on sticks to catch coins. Not many people walked round now, and certainly no children . . . *I think I went a little mad when Ken died . . . I wrote to Ted – knew his school . . . I had to get away . . . I didn't tell him everything. Not till a month ago . . .*

"I knew there was something on your mind," Ted had said. "All along there's been something . . . at first I thought it was losing Ken." She flinched. "Can you tell me now?"

"Sybil," she said, carefully. "Did Ken kill Sybil?"

"But the inquest . . . Peter saw the intruders . . ."

"I know. That's what I can't understand."

Oh, yes, Ted had been very kind. He'd drawn it all out of her, her fears, her worry. "It's too much of a coincidence," she'd said. "We had this row – about Sybil. He went off, but it was later that the boat set on fire."

"You didn't say all that at the inquest."

"No." *And that worried me too, I'd never told lies. I said nothing about the row, said that Ken had gone out to his boat* . . . "No one else knew."

"David?"

"David had gone home."

"But," Ted had asked, puzzled, "why won't you see David when you love him so much?"

And she gasped out the truth that she'd never dared face before. "I blamed him for Ken's death . . . because if I hadn't I'd have had to blame myself." She'd wept then, and Ted had talked soothingly for a long time.

"You must see Peter," he'd said. "Find out the truth."

"But if he told me that he was lying . . ." She was afraid.

"Then we'll face it together."

The colours of the procession jigged up and down before her eyes. Lorries and tableaux, hardly anyone walking. Lorries and tableaux, the Amateur Dramatic society. Spare a penny for the carnival . . . Peter and Carolyn, this morning . . .

It was nice to see Carolyn again. I thought, when Sybil told me that she was Ken's, that I'd never want to see her again, but I clasped her in my arms, crying . . . Carolyn and Peter living in a pleasant little cottage bought with the remains of the business money, looking somehow alike so that Ann wondered anew . . . Carolyn making her little pots, Peter pottering in the garden, a retreat, healing the wounds inflicted by her, Ann's family . . . And they talked, and then Carolyn had left them alone, and she turned frightened eyes to Peter.

"Do you really want to know the truth?" he'd asked, and her eyes grew big with dread, but Ted said, steadily, "We do."

Peter said: "I was in the house, Sybil didn't know. I would do that sometimes, wait and watch, knowing I couldn't do anything, knowing I would someday . . ." His lips closed tightly. "I heard Ken come in, crept down, heard every word. 'I told you what I'd do if you told Ann . . .'"

Ann was jerked out of her fear. "And you let him . . . let him?"

"I let him," Peter said, calmly. "I had been wanting to do it for years. You must know what sort of life I had with Sybil, you of all people. I couldn't divorce her when Carolyn was young because it would have meant losing the child, and she was all I had."

"And yet you condoned—" Even now Ann shrank from the word 'murder'.

"It was what I wanted," Peter said. "I had thought I'd leave Sybil when Carolyn was older, take her with me. But then I found out Sybil had been manipulating the money, it had been in our joint names. She'd taken it, saying she was buying stocks and shares; I didn't realise at the time she was putting it all in her own name . . . that's why I couldn't buy the cottage for Carolyn when Sybil insisted we withdrew, that's when I found out I had hardly anything left. I'd wanted to get rid of Sybil, I sat for hours wondering how to do it . . . That's why I let Ken go. Of course, I didn't know he'd commit suicide."

Ann was appalled to hear Peter say he harboured thoughts of murder too. And yet it somehow made it easier to bear, it was as if all men were in a league to kill, and Ken was not an isolated case, but part of a weird brotherhood. She said: "But as he did, you needn't have covered up for him."

"Call it a sort of loyalty, if you like. More than that. I felt I was to blame for doing nothing all those years; he acted for me, so I owed him something . . . It wasn't difficult. Tampering with the locks, hiding a few pieces of jewellery, saying money was missing, oh, I'd seen it on television hundreds of times. The police wouldn't suspect me, why should they? Respectable Peter Bailey, a pillar of the establishment, timid Peter Bailey, oh, no, Ann. I'm not the type of person to be suspected of crime. Carolyn was so unhappy, you see . . . Ken said that. 'Carolyn will be better without you . . .' She's safe now." And Ann thought, suddenly startled, *Doesn't he know about Carolyn?* What did it matter? He was her father, whoever had planted the original seed. "Of course," Peter was going on, "it's easier that she thinks an intruder, a stranger, killed Sybil rather than a relative, the scandal would have been terrible. That's what used to worry me when I thought of killing Sybil. How could I do it without hurting Carolyn?" His voice had been cool, almost clinical in its detachment.

A Scottish pipe band swung by, then the carnival queen, again on a lorry . . . a pretty girl . . . Briarford Silver Band marched in the rear. And it was over.

The crowd dispersed, Ann and Ted stood together among the castaway streamers, ice-cream wrappings. He said, again, "Are you all right, Ann?"

They returned to the car and she said: "I'm all right. You see, I knew . . ."

And I'll have to live with it. It would be a relief never to see any of the turbulent Websters again, to live in quiet Sussex with nice quiet Ted, in peace, ignoring the pain of the outer world . . . But there's David . . .

"David mustn't know," Ted said, and she knew a moment's anger that he should thus be spared, while she had to suffer.

Marley Road was shabby after her own modern cottage. She entered the house where she had known so much joy and pain, and it meant nothing to her, it was a small terraced house in a small industrial town. David and Jeanie were waiting, and as she stared at her son, so like his father, she felt a searing pain, knowing that, however kind and considerate Ted was, she could never love him as she had loved Ken, that the loss would be with her forever, and the pain. She stood a moment, and then ran to David, holding him in her arms. "Oh, David," she cried. "David."

"Don't cry, Mother," he said, gently. "It's all right."

"Oh, David, I should have come. I should have written."

"It's all right," he repeated. "We'll talk later. First I have to get married and make an honest woman of Jeanie."

And Ann smiled through her tears, and they drove to the register office.

The service was short and, to Ann, meaningless, though perhaps her own turmoil had something to do with her lack of interest. She wondered vaguely why Jeanie had agreed to marry after so many years, more than ten surely, and David well over thirty. Was it possible? How could she herself be sixty when she felt exactly the same as when she was sixteen?

The family were crowded into the Marley Road house when they returned, Doreen, plumper than ever, Jack, and two of their sons, Alan and Robert, tall prosperous men with houses in Acacia Avenue. No word from Chris, but Tommy and his wife; Ann was pleased that the boy who asked for so little should have found happiness. Johnny, thin and craggy, a little shrunken, his face that peculiar grey-white that comes to men who spend most of their lives underground, a bronchial cough.

The Websters were cool with Ann, the one who'd gone away from them. David opened wine and beer, Doreen put on an old Beatles record, there were the usual marriage jokes, then, as always, the talk turned to work.

"They'll be closing all the pits down next," Johnny said.

The Beatles sang, 'All You Need Is Love', their voices sounding disembodied, far away.

"They're making it difficult to pay the levy to the Labour Party—"

"The Labour Party's finished—"
The Beatles slithered to a grinding halt.
"Come on now," said Doreen, authoritatively, still the eldest sister. "It's time to go."
Johnny stood up and Ann looked at him, wondering vaguely which were his children, she'd never known them very well. One girl was in a library in the north, didn't come home much. Bit of a snob, wanted to forget the Coronation estate and her mining father. Ann sighed. Had it all been worth it? It was my generation who fought for their rights, who sacrificed . . . and in the end they went away and didn't fight for their parents, left them to the old age pension . . . But I didn't fight, she thought sadly. I wanted to hold David, yet in the end I left him . . . because it was all tangled up with Ken and I couldn't bear to think of Ken and that night when I had to face the fact that he didn't love me . . . so I blamed David in my panic and turned away. Or was there something else . . .?
But she didn't want to listen to the Websters' endless talk. Being away for so long she had forgotten just how they went on. No one talked like this in her village. There might be some unease now about teachers' jobs and pay, but Ted was safe, he'd retire next year. They'd stay in Sussex, she didn't want to get entangled with the Websters again. She'd see David, of course, but he could visit her in future. She looked at the old clock on the wall, still there; it had been a wedding present to William and Liz, how much it had seen through the years, births, marriages, funerals, joy and tragedy . . . and still it ticked away. She felt a wry fondness for the old clock, it was like William himself, an old man, plodding away, doing his duty, even when Marta died, his pearl without price.
They were straggling out now, in twos and threes, throwing last-minute jokes at David, still cool with Ann.

She sat silent, with Ted, till they were alone with David and Jeanie, the radio playing softly in the background.

"You'll stay the night, won't you, Mother?" David asked, and she said, uncertainly, "I don't know . . ."

"Come on," he urged. "Let's sit round the fire like we used to," and it was easier than she had imagined to talk about Ken.

"I'm sorry, David," she said. "It wasn't your fault, I only blamed you for his – death – because if I hadn't I'd have had to blame myself."

Ted shot her a warning glance, but she went on calmly, "We had a row, you see, that night. Sybil had been to see me, told me that she and your father . . . I don't know if you know . . ."

"Oh, yes, I know. I had it out with Dad. But, Mother, he told me that it happened once, years ago when he was drunk, and then Sybil swore that Carolyn was the result. Dad never believed her, but she held it over him all those years – said she'd tell you if he didn't go to her. He was protecting you, really."

And Ann felt balm.

"But I don't think he killed himself because he'd rowed with you," David went on. "I still think it was because he lost his job. I suppose I had a part in it too, his disillusion, I never became what he wanted."

Jeanie said, robustly, "Why blame yourselves? Ken did it of his own free will."

"It is a normal thing when a person dies to blame oneself," Ted put in. "Thinking of all the things one could have done. Remorse."

"He told me once when I was a kid," David mused, "That he thought the old Viking funeral pyre was a marvellous way to go. It was what he wanted, Mother."

Maybe that's true. Maybe he intended suicide and thought he might as well take Sybil with him.

Ann was consoled, knowing that she had always obtained love and solace from Ken's son, if not from Ken himself.
Jeanie eased the strain. "We didn't tell you why we are getting married." A smile spread over her face. "I'm pregnant."

"Jeanie! Oh, how lovely! I'll love to be a grandma." Though even in her pleasure Ann knew disquiet. Would it mean coming back, being involved with the Websters again?

She took a good look at the photographs on the mantelpiece. There were three now: Marta in the middle, below it, on either side, herself and Ken. Marta smiled down, Ken faced sideways towards her, while Ann stared at the two.

That's how it always was. But I have their son. And grandson.

"So," she said, "You'll be settling down now, with a family."

There was a moment's silence, then Jeanie said. "You don't know, do you? We might have to go away." Ann stared, wanting to cry out. *Oh no. You haven't given up. Not you.* She was dismayed that the shining beliefs might have disappeared, even though she didn't agree with them. We need people like Jeanie, she thought, with a sudden flash of insight. And Ken. And we don't realise it until they've gone.

She turned, half-fearfully, to David. "What about your co-operative?" she asked.

Again Jeanie answered. "It finished," she said. "After all their effort. You don't know," she turned, almost accusingly to Ann. "You didn't see them, standing there, night and day in the cold and wet, standing with a little fire with nothing but hope for the future . . ."

Ann stared, shocked. What would they do, and with a baby coming? Irrationally, she was angry with Jeanie for making her think of stark facts, when now she was so happy and comfortable. Jeanie had changed. Once she wouldn't have married, pregnant or no. Ann, who had been pleased at the wedding, now felt disturbed. She said, "I'm sorry, David, I didn't know. Why didn't you let me know?"

David didn't speak, he was looking at Ken's photograph. Ann, alarmed, cried, "I shouldn't have told you. I'm sorry—" She glanced over at Ted, wishing he would help her, but he said nothing, and she knew he didn't want to intrude on a family matter.

David said, "It wasn't easy what I did—" and there was a faraway look in his eyes. "It cut me in two. I was alone. But it made me strong."

David, the unknown quantity, Ann thought. But he's been hurt. Underneath all the know-all talk he was hurt. So do men fight from pain? She heard echoes . . . Ken's bravado. "They can stuff their jobs." . . . She hadn't understood Ken. She knew nothing about him, and she groped in a world where everyone was alone, running for comfort to strangers, a man, a woman, a god . . . taking from each what they desired . . . but still alone.

I'm alone. I've tried all my life to find someone to belong to. Ken, then David . . . I wanted to keep David with me. To belong . . . Was that all? Memories of the boat on a sunny afternoon. I'm Mrs Ken Webster of Marley Road . . . If I'm forced to stay in Marley Road, then you must too . . . calling it motherhood . . . Was that it? Why else did I run away at the first opportunity?

Thoughts swirled like ripples in a whirlpool, round and round. *Co-operation.* The still afternoon when she'd deliberately turned her love away from Ken to David . . . *Peter: I was to blame, I did nothing.* We're to blame, the nice quiet ones who let others take the action and the punishment. Now we're all suffering guilt because of Ken. David too. He has to make up.

But where did it all start? Who threw the first stone into the whirlpool?

"Dad influenced me, you know," David said. "He used to talk to me all the time, about his childhood, Marta, and his bitterness; he passed it all on to me."

Ann stared at the photograph. Ken was right. She isn't dead. *She never will be.*

In the silence the echoes grew stronger. Ann knew she could never leave him now, not to live safely in her own little world. She said, "If I can help, David—?"

Still silence. Why was Jeanie smiling? Ann said, "How long have you been on the dole?"

"Months and months," David told her. "But I haven't been idle, I've been working—"

"David!" Alarmed. Was this what Jeanie meant, working on the side? Would he be going to prison?

"I've been writing a book," said David.

A *book*?

"And I sent it to a publisher," put in Jeanie. "It's been accepted."

Ann gasped. "But you never told me— Did the others know?"

"The family? Yes." David grinned. "They didn't take much notice."

"Tell me about it," Ann commanded.

"Well, it was what I always wanted to do. I wanted Dad to write his story, but he wouldn't. I wanted the fellows at work to do it, they wouldn't. And I thought I couldn't write their stories because I didn't know how they really felt. But now I do. Now I know what it's like to be on the dole, to apply for hundreds of jobs of all sorts and never get one. To have to rely on my girl's wages, to be thankful we have a roof over our heads, but know we can never afford a holiday or a car. Now I know." He grinned. "And I even wondered if this is why – subconsciously –

I did it all, to write about it." He paused. "All along I was looking for answers. But now I guess I can't find the answers, all I could do was write about my experiences, hoping others may learn from the mistakes that have been made. So I wrote about Dad, and Marta – the lot."

Again Ann glanced fleetingly at the photographs. No, she isn't dead now, she never will be, nor will Ken.

Then she ran to David and threw her arms around him. "Oh," she cried in a muffled voice, "your dad would be so proud of you."

David held her tightly, muttering. "I missed you, Mother."

And Ann thought gladly, Why, I really do belong. This is my family.

"There, there. It's over now, all the heart ache." Gently David wiped her eyes as she stood back. "Come on now, Mother, let's go in the garden and look at the roses."